Dustin's Novel

By

June Kramin

Dustin's Novel
(Dustin Time III)
By June Kramin

Published by Pau Hana Books through Createspace,
April 2016

ISBN: 978-1530577125

Published in the United States of America
Cover Art by Valerie Kramin
Stock images: Shutterstock
Edited by Julie Fletcher

Dedication

*They say, "It takes a village to raise a child." The same is true for a novel. Thanks to the fans who encouraged more, *cough*even though I thought this was a 2-book series*cough,* and to all the extra eyeballs that helped beat this baby into shape! BIG ((HUGS)) to Julie, Rhea, Ann, & Lola!*

*And to the lunatics of Big Daddy's.
You know who you are! I told you to behave or you'd end up in my novel! ;)*

Chapter One

Captain Victor Skinnard stared out the porthole of his living quarters, deep in thought. Mostly he thought that as captain he should have a bigger window. Space is what he loved, what consumed his every waking moment, and invaded his every dream. How could he settle for a twelve inch circle to view it from over a good Terian ale? Okay, the ale wasn't that good, but one made do with what one had. It would be a long time before the ship would dock to take on any restocking of supplies. Hopping over a few galaxies to get a good beer was hardly a priority. Victor reached into his small cooling unit for another bottle, and then headed toward the ship's bridge.

He held the bottle up to Jodessa Opex, as if in a toast, as she passed him in the hall. She was the ship's communications officer, the best he'd ever seen. Her keen ear was like no other.

"Late stroll, Captain?" she asked as she stormed by.

Vick smiled when her arm harshly lowered. She'd almost saluted him. It had taken him months to get her to quit doing that. Formality was the only aspect he hated about the Navy. He demanded respect, but not ritual. Going out on his own was the best thing he'd ever done, but a ship still had a captain and a crew with all their titles. The best of the best usually came from military training. They were tough to break of habits instilled on them over years, especially when there were usually severe penalties for not following the smallest detail.

"Need a better view is all, Jody. Are you done for the night?"

She indicated his bottle. "I'm looking for something stronger than that."

He changed direction and started to walk with her. "You having problems?"

"Just the usual. My asshole captain is being impossible. Again."

He grinned. He'd gone from almost saluted to being called an asshole in record time. Being Terian, Jody wasn't usually one for nicknames, insults, sarcasm, or euphemisms. She'd come a long way in their time together.

"Still pissed, huh?" he said with a grin.

She turned to him, planted her feet, and crossed her arms over her chest. The tight one-piece jumpsuit was a poor design for a uniform in his opinion. Her perfect figure left very little to the imagination and was a distraction, if he was being honest. He took in her stance and downed another long draw, figuring he needed it for whatever she was going to yell at him about this time.

"Gee, do you think? Getting as close as we'd planned to this nebula wasn't enough for you. You had to push the limit. Now we're sitting here practically…damn your terms." She snapped when the phrase finally came to her. "Dead in the water! That's how you say it. And what do you want to do?" Her eyes lowered to his bottle. "Get drunk and stare at it." Jody spun on her heel. She tried to turn away, but he caught her arm.

"Don't." He leaned into her, his face just inches from hers. "Just don't. Dead in the water means we're broken down, and we're not."

"Might as well be."

"It's a minor blanket of debris. Our shields are more than capable of handling it. I needed the view from here for reasons I can't put into words. We're several weeks away but it looks like I can reach out and touch it. I'd just like to savor this for a little longer, if you don't mind terribly."

She let out a loud huff. "Like I have a choice."

"That's right. I'm the Captain. I have a say in what goes on around here. There's another matter that I don't have a choice in, however."

Her arms crossed again. "And what's that?"

Captain Victor Skinnard took Jody by the hand and pulled her toward his cabin. He keyed in his code and yanked her through the door. Once it closed, he pressed her hard against the wall and planted his lips firmly on hers. She only struggled for a few seconds before she ran her fingers through his short brown hair, keeping him there.

When he finally broke the kiss, he said, "Who you love. We have no choice in who the hell we love, Jody." His hands stroked the sides of her uniform…

Kaitlyn put the manuscript down and called for her husband. "Dusty!" When he didn't answer, she headed down the stairs.

The living room was empty. She glanced at the clock. It was already past five.

"Shit. I've been reading for two hours?" Wandering to the kitchen she called out again. "Dusty?" She found a note on the counter.

Took the kids and ran to the store. It's a great night to grill, cupcake.

Be back soon

Love you!

D~

P.S. Hope the part with Jody makes you want to jump my bones when I get back!

She laughed and crumbled up the note. "Your daughter is going to start reading soon, jackass." After tossing the note in the trash, she went to the fridge and reached for a beer. "It's no Terian ale, but it'll do." She walked outside to sit on the porch swing.

More than almost anything, Kaitlyn loved reading Dusty's work. As she swung, she thought about when she'd sent works of his to the local newspaper without his permission. It turned out okay and actually led to his career now. He was finally doing what he wanted: writing. He'd become editor of the newspaper where he'd started out only a few years ago after he submitted short stories. Now, he was on the third book in his Captain Skinnard series. Proud did not come close to how she felt about her husband.

Some days when she reflected on her life with him, she still thought she was dreaming. After having dated for almost a year, she'd tried to break up with him, certain he was too young and just not "father material." She could not have been proven more wrong if she tried to confirm the world was flat. She was grateful that Frank made her travel through time and discover differently. Well, technically Dusty. Somehow he came back to her when he was well into his seventies and fixed whatever had gone horribly wrong in her life. She couldn't even imagine a time when she wasn't with Dusty, let alone some alternate universe where she'd lived a lifetime without him.

"I'm sure that's not it, my sweet," Dusty had said to her. "I don't believe there are all these different alternate universes and such. What we're living is what's happening and that's all."

"But how can you be sure after what we've been through?"

"I refuse to believe there's a time when I'm not with you."

"You're such a sap."

"If I came back to you when I was older, that was just because I was so happy, I needed to do it all again, not to mention a little sooner."

"But it drove me crazy time hopping like that."

"And I did it to myself to make us even."

This was true. After she'd tried to break up with him, she'd been sent back to their college days so he could win her over sooner and prove he was who she truly was meant to be with. Years later when her best friend Courtney was in danger, he went back to make things right for her. He'd gone through everything she had, and more.

She took a long sip then wrapped her arms around her legs. If she tried really hard, she could pretend they were normal people. Nothing had happened in over a year. Their time traveling made it very hard to have the normal, married people arguments over remembering small details. Usually, they were both right. Everything had happened, they just had different orders and memories of a lot of things.

Katie's memories consisted of their best friends living next door since almost immediately after they'd moved to this neighborhood. Dusty told her this wasn't always the case. She had no recollection of Courtney moving to Seattle and Dean being one of those lawyers other lawyers love to hate. He's one of the highest paid in Minnesota and Courtney makes more than her share as a surgeon, but the couple is fun and down to earth. They couldn't ask for better neighbors, best friends, or godparents for their kids.

A car door slammed, which snapped her out of her daydream. The unmistakable pattering of feet quickly approached. Katie put her beer down to pick up her son as he barreled toward her.

"Mommy! Did you finish Daddy's book?"

"Not yet, sweetie. I have quite a way to go."

Alyson wrapped herself around her leg. "It was boring without you today."

Dusty dropped two canvas bags on the counter. "Boring? We were at the park for an hour, then at Mrs. Nelsons for another hour."

"Yeah…but…we didn't have Mommy."

Dusty crossed his arms and curled his lip, pretending to pout. It was a maneuver he'd learned from his daughter, like using the phrase: "We're in a pickle." The first time Katie had heard that was from Frank…Dusty. He claimed to have gotten it from their daughter, Alyson. If she thought about it too hard, her head would explode.

Alyson laughed and ran to her father. "I love playing with you, too, Daddy."

He picked her up and threw her as high as he could in the kitchen. "I know, mini-cupcake. You want a burger or a hot dog?"

"Hot dog!"

"Alex?"

He said, "Both," as Katie put him down.

"Both? You sure, buddy?"

"Uh-huh." He ran away, with his sister following.

"You'd better measure him before he goes to bed, puddin'."

Shaking her head was Katie's only defense. She'd decided long ago that it was easier to ignore Dusty when he used those names than to fuss. It had been so many years of nagging him with no results; she truly believed he had no control over it.

"He's gonna grow another foot if we stop and blink," Dusty continued.

"You made them sleep together too soon, Dusty."

"What? They've had separate room since they were babies. What are you talking about?"

"Jody and Captain Skinnard. You have them sleeping together already?"

He grinned. "Oh." He closed the gap between them, grasped her hips, and pulled her to him. "So does this mean I'm not getting my bones jumped tonight?"

She gently shoved him away. "Yeah, right."

"You slept with me on our first date."

"I was drunk."

"Baby, you weren't drunk. You were warm for my form," he said, drawing out the words and waggling his eyebrows.

"Good lord. Sometimes I can't believe you're my talented writer husband."

He grasped her hips. "You really think I put them together too fast? I had all that tension with them through the last few chapters of the second book. I don't think it's too fast. Crazy chick had to admit she loved him sooner or later."

A mild shrug was her response. "I guess with all the tension, I knew it was coming. But I would have liked to see it dragged out a bit more. She's not going to get all lovesick and ga-ga now is she?"

Dusty pelted out a laugh. "Hell, no. She still keeps his balls in a vise. Hello." He waived a hand over himself. "Who's your husband?"

"Let me read it a little more tonight. I'll let you know."

"You were afraid to read the sex scene without me, weren't you?"

She grinned. "I knew you were already at Mrs. Nelson's. I wasn't going to abuse her again today."

"There's always Courtney and Dean. What good is having your best friends next door if they can't watch your kids so you steal afternoon sex?"

Katie gave him another not-so-gentle, but playful, shove. "Start the coals and feed your children, oh love of my life."

He dug into the bag and said, "Nag," with a wink. "You want to invite them over?"

"I'll call Courtney. She wasn't feeling so hot earlier. She's really pissed about getting so huge this time around."

"Most women get bigger with their second child."

"But I didn't."

"You women worry too much."

The back gate opened with a thud against the fence, startling them both. Courtney stomped over with Dean at her heels.

"Hey!" Dusty shouted. "Were your ears burning?"

"More like my uterus," Courtney said as she slammed her purse on the counter.

Confused, Katie's attention went to Dean, who was grinning like the Cheshire cat. He placed his son down and said, "Go find Alex, Champ."

"What's up?" Dusty asked him. "Something wrong?"

His grin got wider. "It's twins."

"Twins?" Katie squealed and hurried to Courtney's side, placing her hand on her belly. "You just found this out now? You had an ultrasound early on."

"Apparently, one is Houdini." She still sounded mad.

"This is great news! Are you really upset?"

She let out a heavy sigh. "No, just pissed to discover this now. I'm a freaking doctor. You'd think if anyone, I'd get decent prenatal care."

Wrapping an arm around her, Katie said, "Come on, hon. Breathe. You're going to have twins!"

Courtney finally allowed a smile to show, and then a tear ran down her cheek. "Yeah, I am." She wrapped her arms around her best friend. "It's twins."

"So," Dusty said. "This lady was getting married for the fourth time and she was still a virgin. Her soon-to-be husband asked her how she could still be a virgin after being married three times. She proceeded to explain that her first husband was a therapist so all he wanted to do was talk about it. Her second husband was a gynecologist so all he wanted to do was look at it. Her third husband was a stamp collector so all he wanted to do was lick it. And so she told him that since he was a lawyer, she figured that she would be screwed for sure."

Courtney laughed, then walked over and hugged him. "Does that well of lawyer jokes ever dry up?"

"Not any time soon."

Dean said, "Great," as he headed to the fridge for a beer.

Chapter Two

Jody cupped Vick's face, then planted a gentle kiss on his lips. "I hate you with all of my being."

"Yeah, I could tell that somewhere after your second orgasm."

"That's not fair. Do you have any idea how long it's been for me? This is wrong on so many levels. We should *not* be doing this."

"Why not? Because I'm your boss?"

"That's a very good reason why not. You know how hard I fought to get to the position I'm in."

"You are quite limber."

She slapped at his chest. "You know what I mean. I'm a woman with one of the top five positions on this ship, not to mention a *Terian* woman. You know many of my people don't ever leave our planet. How will it look? I can't have it known that I've slept with you. The entire crew will treat me differently. Any time you agree with me, they'll think it's because we've been together. Not to mention the fact it's forbidden."

"One, stop saying it like it's in the past. You're still here and naked in my bed and I'm not quite done with you."

Her eyes slightly scrunched together. "And two?"

"I'd never agree with you. Don't think just because you're an animal in the sack, that it gives you any leeway on my plans."

She sat up, bringing the sheet with her. He liked it when she got angry. She had no control over the dark pink hue her skin took when he pushed her buttons. Terian women were beautiful in any shade. Although because of the ways of their world, he hadn't met many. Of the handful he'd met, Captain Skinnard preferred them to earth women. You could never tell when humans were lying, pissed, or…faking it. He gently stroked between her breasts. Other than the dark pink hue, you'd never know Jody wasn't human. His gentle touches calmed her down slightly.

"Damnit, Captain. I won't have all those years at the academy sucked into the waste hole."

He couldn't help his chuckle.

"You think this is funny?"

"No, my sweet." He took her hand in his and kissed her palm. "It's just that on earth we say, 'flushed down the shitter.'"

She tilted her head. "Shitter?"

"Never mind. It's just an expression." He kissed her hand again. "I have no intention of ruining what you've worked for. I'm sorry if I couldn't control myself. We can keep our relationship a secret, but I'm not letting you deny me more of this," he said as his hand slid to her behind and pulled her to him.

Allowing herself to be maneuvered on top of him, Jody straddled Vick and eased herself down…

Kaitlyn reached up and turned off the bedside light. She straddled her not-quite-asleep husband.

Dusty ran his hand down his face. "Hey, sugar," he said softly. "What gives?" Katie ground her midsection against Dusty's. "Oh. Jody turning pink?"

She giggled. "Just past that. I guess she likes the top."

"I have no idea where I came up with that," Dusty said as he removed Katie's nightshirt. "I think we need to do more research so I can perfect the scene."

Twenty minutes later, Dusty was gently snoring. Katie felt only slightly bad for keeping him up. "It's your own fault," she said softly as she hit the power button on her e-reader. Dimming the backlight, she returned to the story. She skimmed though the scene with a grin. "Nailed it."

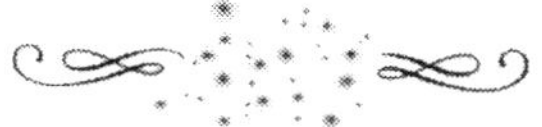

Jody was zipping up her uniform when Vick pressed her against the wall one last time. "I can't tell you how long I've wanted to do this. It won't be the last, Lieutenant."

"Is that an order?"

He stared into her eyes, trying to truly gage her response. Her skin tone hadn't changed, so nothing was being reveled about how she felt. He forgot he couldn't see it in her eyes, either. With their skin color giving away their every deep emotion, there was very little need for facial expressions like those that gave humans away. She finally did break slightly into what he'd started to call her version of a smile. He'd noticed when she'd acquired it several months back.

~*~

Shortly after Jody had joined the Navy, she was recruited onto Vick's ship. She'd explained in great detail over her first weeks how she hated her home planet, especially the rules that fell on females. For her, joining the Academy was the perfect solution to her exile. Science was her passion, something her father had never understood. Being told not to return to Teria was a gift, not a punishment.

He'd joined her at a table in the lounge one day, at a high table for two, where she sat alone. They had a month before they'd reach his second nebula and he'd ordered everyone to take the night off and have some fun. Her skin was so slightly yellow he would have missed her somber mood had he not been trying to gauge her emotions before his approach.

Much to his frustration, he'd found himself falling for a member of his crew. The more they talked, the more certain he was falling hard. She was it. The *one. Damnit*. It took a few drinks to get her to loosen up and discuss something other than work. When she'd motioned to a couple of the women nearby and said she wanted to be more like "earth females," he quickly shot down that thought.

"Trust me, doll. That isn't something to strive for."

"Doll? Isn't that a toy?"

He had often forgotten to watch his use of any slang words with his non-human crew.

"Sorry. It's a term of endearment."

"Why can't you call me Lieutenant Opex?"

"I'd like to not be so formal all the time. Didn't your parents or siblings have a nickname for you?"

"Why would they? My name is Jodessa. Why would they need to call me anything else?"

Vick let out a heavy sigh. "It's just what we do. Take me for example."

Her expression remained blank. "Take you where?"

"No," he said, again with a sigh. "My name. It's actually Victor. Friends call me Vick, though."

"You prefer this?"

"I do. It just sounds less formal. Almost everyone has a nickname. How about I call you Jody?"

"If that's more pleasing to you, I suppose that's fine."

"Pleasing to me isn't the point."

"So calling me 'doll' pleases you?"

He held up a hand, silently begging that part of the conversation to be over. "Let's just get back on track…uh…back on the subject. Don't try so hard to be human. You're perfect the way you are. There are a lot of faults with us. You Terians say things the way they are and your color gives your emotions away. Trust me; I'd take a crew full of your kind over some humans I know any day."

"You want to know what I think?"

"Yes, Jody. I would love to know what you think."

"I think you're a very strange man, Captain Victor Skinnard. I think you will put us all deep in danger someday. I also think that you cannot hold your Terian ale." With that, she got up and left. And took his heart with her.

~*~

"Hello?" Jody waved her hand on front of his face. "Are you having a medical problem?"

He chuckled. "Sorry. I just spaced out."

"Spaced out? We are in space? How does one—"

He stopped her rambling with a hard kiss. The purr-like sound that came from her chest let him know that he wasn't in trouble for doing so. When he broke the kiss, he stroked the side of her face. "I was thinking back to the time I sat with you at the lounge. That's when I fell…that's when I knew I really liked you." He kissed her lips, softer this time. "You're so beautiful, Jody."

"I remember that night. That's when I thought you were a…how would you say? A major pompous ass?"

Grinning, he leaned into her neck and gave her gentle kisses down to the neckline of her uniform, not ready to let her go. "Tell me this isn't all there is, Jody. I—"

The ship was thrown hard to the left, sending them both to the floor. "What the hell was that?" Vick shouted.

A loud voice boomed over the speaker. "Captain! You need to get up here. Immediately."

Vick helped Jody to her feet then ran full bore for the bridge. He didn't even realize she was behind him until she ran into him when he stopped at the door to swipe his ID card.

"Sorry," she said from behind.

"If it's such an emergency, it should have been open."

He had to swipe the card a second time to get the doors to slide open. He hustled over to his first-in-command. "What's going on? Is the debris getting through?"

Lieutenant Xolo Gatron pointed out the viewing window. "No, Captain. We were fired upon."

Victor fought to keep the expression of fear from his face. He knew that ship. It couldn't be her? Could it? Closing his eyes for a moment to gather himself, he took a deep breath. He never imagined this day would come again, although he wasn't sure why he entertained such idiotic thoughts.

When his eyes opened, he was looking out a viewing window once again, but his gaze now fell on his own ship. Something was missing. The blast burn mark from the Delton battle ship that they took last year. It was his ship, but over a year ago. *Dammit! She did it again!* He was now on that Delton battle ship just before the attack! He felt a hand grasp his, he spun to the right.

"Deidre, what on earth are you doing?"

She grinned then leaned forward and kissed him, taking time to lick his lips with her tongue. "I've missed you, Vick. And in case you haven't noticed, we're not on earth."

Chapter Three

Katie woke up at the sound of the alarm. She reached over to rouse Dusty but decided a smack was better. He woke with a start. “Ow! What was that for?”

“You have Deidre trying to kill Vick now?”

Laughing hard, he flopped himself on top of her, pinning her to the bed.

“You read after I went to bed.”

“You snored yourself silly after amazing sex. What choice did I have?”

“Sorry.”

“About Vick or the snoring?”

"Snoring. Trust me; the love of your life makes it through this and lives to see another sequel."

Katie freed her hands and covered her ears. "La la la la la la! Don't give anything away!"

Dusty pulled the covers over their heads, pulled up her shirt and began kissing her chest. He'd just reached her breast when a small voice interrupted them.

"Can I have waffles?" a groggy Alexander asked.

Dusty quickly rolled to the side and popped up from above the cover. "Of course you can, Champ. Anything my main man wants, he gets."

"I want a dirt bike."

Katie picked up a pillow and swatted Dusty. "You even think about putting my baby on one of those things and I'll have your hide." Their son climbed up on the bed, wanting in on the early morning playtime.

"Alyson! Mommy's beating daddy up! Come quick!" He squealed as he was brought into the fray of pillows, sheets, and kisses.

After their daughter joined them for a few more minutes of impromptu playtime, Katie shooed the kids away to get dressed.

"Will you drop the kids off please, Dusty?"

"Sure, Sugar Bear. You don't have to go in today?"

"Nope. Sorry I forgot to tell you. Steve wanted to switch with me. He's taking a long weekend with his new flame. I have his Friday. I hope that's not going to put a damper in any plans."

"Right. 'Cause Dean will have a fit if you don't bring your salad next door to the usual weekend barbeque." He grinned. "Of course it's okay. I gotcha covered, my sweet. Isn't Monday a pretty big surgery day?"

"Normally yes, but I had Karla reschedule a few of my regulars for tomorrow. No sweat."

Dusty climbed out of bed. "You going to spend the day reading?"

"Maybe. The big decision is if I'm going to stay in pajamas all day or put on an actual pair of big people pants."

"Take the entire day off. I'll bring home dinner. How's that sound?"

"Amazing, actually. Boy, I really did ride you well last night."

He laughed. "Yes, you did, but I'm not bringing home any jewelry. I have a dirt bike to save for."

Katie threw a pillow as Dusty ran out of the room.

"Why are we here, Deidre?" Vick demanded answers. This was not the woman he was in love with any more. A few years ago he would have stopped the world for her. She'd saved his life on more than one occasion, but her games became too much to handle. His past with her came back all too clearly…

~*~

Deidre was born a slave. Her one green and one blue eye had set that fate for her.

Athracki laws were strict. Everyone had their place. Bloodline or skill did not determine your role in life, your eye color did. Brown eyes were the most common and therefore built the everyday work force and most common jobs. Everyone was equal. There was no pay, no currency. Your neighbor flew the same vehicle you did, lived in the same style home. If a green-eyed baby was born, it was taken to the capital. These children made up what was the equivalent of government. Senators, governors, and such.

The rarer yet children with purple-hued eyes, no matter who they were born to, were royalty. Only one in over ten thousand children were born this way. Even at that, most were female. When they came of age, they were sent to rule one of the surrounding stars in their colony with the purple-eyed male of their choice. It didn't matter that the purple-eyed males were sterile. The royal couple would be given children when one was produced with the royal eye color. This arrangement insured the queens would never have to bear children. Never lose the figures they fought daily to keep. Never have to cause their breast to be more than things of enjoyment for their men. Sex drive always on high – no distractions. The maternal bond came much as it did for any adoptive parents, but of course there was staff. Lots of staff. Slaves, actually, and Deidre had been one of them. The lowest of all: one blue eye and one green eye.

No exceptions were made to the rules of what eye colors the gods distributed...Except of course when you discover you can time travel. At eighteen, Deidre had discovered she possessed this gift. A gift told only in myths and legends.

She'd taken her chance to escape when Captain Skinnard landed on her planet's moon to pick up supplies. She'd snuck away, hidden on a transport ship, and found her way into his heart. She'd played the part of helpless female well, runaway slave, beaten and abused. He'd hidden her on board his ship, thinking he was saving her from an abusive owner, but quickly fell in love with her. When she knew he trusted her, she'd told him her story.

She had been recently traded to a royal to be used for her owner's pleasure. The deal was arranged sight unseen. Once he got a good look at her, he didn't desire her. He'd complained she was too skinny. With that information, Deidre skipped meals where she could to keep herself that way. His son, however, viewed her differently. Even though he was married, he'd never hidden his intentions with her. He finally arranged to have her delivered to his quarters one night. The mere fear of seeing him naked in his bed, his manhood erect and waiting for her, sent fear and shivers through her from head to toe.

She was unsure what had happened next.

One moment she was staring at the arrogant boy, but after a long blink, willing this not to be happening, she was standing in her own bedroom. She was left wondering if it all been a bad dream. Shaking, she'd crawled in bed. When they woke her up the next morning and told of what was to be done to her that night, she knew without a doubt she'd traveled back in time one day. When she was once again faced with Jabar's manhood hopping at the sight of her, she closed her eyes and willed herself back in time.

When she made it back to the same day yet again, she pinched her eyes tight and tried to go back to another day. Any day; she just wanted out. An hour of trying got her nowhere. She wondered if she would be forced to re-live this day for eternity.

A month of attempting to escape the same fate, night after night, made her question how she could remain sane. Desperate for change, she left later and later each night, anxious to see what would happen. Although arrogant and young, he was handsome. He had always treated her terribly in public, but he was nothing but a gentleman when they were in his chambers. Deciding that there was no way around it, she'd let him take her that night. Much to her surprise, he was gentle and she'd enjoyed it. So much so that when she awoke the next morning in his chambers, she wanted to do it again. When he shoved her out of the bed and called for his guards, she was humiliated.

He called for her again that night. She was both scared and curious as she entered. Instead of sweet talk and caressing, he'd pulled her by the hair and threw her to the bed. When he mounted her from behind and tried to force himself in, she screamed…and returned to his quarters the day before. She found herself as before; shyly smiling at him as he gently caressed her breasts, eagerly waiting to be invited inside her. The fear of his previous touch scared her – sending her into the previous day yet again: staring at his erect penis as he grinned from the bed. It was the day before, yet again. A day before over a month ago? She was losing track of real time.

She shouted "Enough!" at the top of her lungs, clasped both hands over her head, and dropped to her knees. When she opened her eyes, she was in the middle of a forest. It looked familiar to her: it was the forest she'd gone to as a child when she ran away from her first owner. The beating had been severe when she'd been found. The memory of her broken arm sent a scared chill up her spine. She shut her eyes tight. When she opened them, she found herself back in her room.

Standing in confusion and trying to figure out everything that had happened in mere seconds, it finally hit her: fear was her trigger. Every time she'd been afraid, she time traveled. She needed to get a grip and find out what kept happening to her. Above all, she needed to get away from her home planet and find someone to help her stay away. Somewhere she could hide her eye color from others. She needed to get away from the prince once and for all, not just for the night.

Vick had listened to her story of abuse with a heavy heart. He knew the history of several planets and how slavery was still practiced, and any interference from outsiders was dealt with by the harshest punishments. But being the man he was, he still allowed her sanctuary on his ship.

Once he'd convinced her she was safe, she told him about her ability.

At first she used what she called simple "party tricks." Telling him the plays and scores of the earth games he followed before they were played, and writing down the course he would charter the following day, and then showing him what she'd written after he'd made his plans.

She'd truly earned his trust when she warned him about what would happen when he entered his first nebula. He changed his course and sent out a pod to his original destination. When it exploded after being hit, he vowed to never doubt her again. He was enthralled with her beauty and special talent. It had been obvious she'd wanted more; he finally gave in and invited her into his bedroom that night.

Her feelings became instantly clear. "We're meant to be together, Vick. I know it. I can help you in ways you can only imagine."

He'd already been several months into his traveling with no female companionship. The gym onboard could only work off so much energy. Anything she said after she'd removed her blouse was just white noise. Her body was very like a human woman's. The noises that escaped her while they made love, however, were unlike any other.

He had quickly grown accustomed to her popping into his cabin each night. She was more like a sex-granting Genie than a time-traveling woman. Each night after making love, she told him about their next day's adventures.

One night in bed, after they'd made love, he'd whispered to her, "You know, Deidre, this isn't fair. You need to leave some of the guesswork up to me. I'm an explorer. Taking risks is all part of the job. I don't want you to tell me everything and spoil it."

"I promise, lover. But if you're about to be destroyed," she said, grabbing him by his rear end and pulling him close, "I'm going to make you change your course."

"Fair enough."

After over seven months of her popping in like clockwork each night, Vick didn't want to admit that he didn't feel like sex that night. "I've had a hard day," he said to her. "I don't want to sound like a chick, but can we just cuddle tonight?" What he really wanted to say was, "Could you disappear? My dick hurts like a mo-fo."

"Cuddle?" she shrieked like he'd used the words "Let's have a root canal."

He quickly closed in on her. "Come on, sweets. You know I hate being without you. I'm just really wiped out."

She unzipped her dress and let it fall to the floor. She reached forward with a devilish grin and got a handful of crotch. "You'll get enough sleep when you're dead. Now do me, lover. We'll simply go back to yesterday when you're less tired." Within a blink, he found himself already naked and on top of her.

"What's this?" he said, scared and shooting to his feet. Although he never doubted her, she'd never taken him with her before.

"It's yesterday, my darling. Don't you feel refreshed?"

"Refreshed? But everything I've accomplished today…I have to do it all over again!"

"Nonsense. I'll return you when we're finished."

He held his hands out. "Wait a second. When we're finished? You're not a chore of mine to be completed. This relationship goes both ways."

"Relationship? Have I met any of your crew? Have you ever taken me out on a date? Have we ever left this room together? You like to screw me, use me for information, and that's that."

"You know that's not true."

She slinked over to him like a cat in heat. "Do you want to make this a relationship?" Deidre dropped to her knees. This was one fight the mighty Vick Skinnard was not going to win. The way she was working on him made him forget what he was fighting for.

That had been the first of a long string of insane moments with Deidre. He'd gotten by a few more months without asking for a night off from sex, but he'd finally had enough of her crazy ways. He tried to convince her that he was too old for her, that she should start a fresh life with a younger man and have children – that his life was too hectic. She managed to seem calmer, more mature for a few more months, winning him back once again, but sadly it didn't last. Like clockwork her true colors began to show again when he questioned her about some information he'd learned a few days prior. He didn't want to believe it, but the more he learned about her, the more he knew it was true.

"I need to know something, Deidre, and I want the truth."

"Anything for you, my love."

"You murdered that prince, didn't you?"

Her eyes widened with fear as she took a few steps back. She quickly recovered and let out a hard laugh.

"Where did you hear that? You know, they'd make up any lie to bring me back there. I didn't kill him or anyone, I got away by teleporting."

He closed the gap and took her hand in his. "I'm not judging you, Deidre. I would have probably killed him myself for hurting you like that, but I need to know."

"That's twice you've called me Deidre. Where's all my nicknames, dearest love?"

He let go and took a few steps back, awaiting the wrath that was guaranteed to hit. "I asked for the truth. It doesn't matter to me, but I'm concerned for the safety of my crew. They'll come looking for you here. It's only a matter of time before they figure it out."

She turned on her heel, scoffing. "You chicken shit bastard." Turning again she stomped over, pressing her finger hard in his chest. "It's been well over a year. I don't believe for a minute you think they'll search your ship for me. You know I can disappear if they did. You don't want me anymore. Admit it, you coward."

He slowly nodded his head in agreement. "I will admit that this has run its course. We had something special but it's just not working anymore. It's pretty hard to make future plans, dating someone wanted in every galaxy for murdering a prince."

"You know I didn't do it." She grinned devilishly as she closed the gap between them. "I told you, I teleported. I can only imagine it was his wife. She was jealous over the attention he paid me." After stroking her hand down the center of his chest, she rested her hand on his crotch. "I may be wanted all over the galaxies, but you have me."

When he removed her hand and said, "No, Deidre. This is over. For the sake of everyone, I can't see you anymore," she lost it. The blast she left in her departing wake left him unconscious for two days with two broken ribs, and no explanation for the ship's doctor on the how or why…

Which brings them to where they are now. She'd returned him to the first time she saved him from another ship's attack.

"Why are we here, Deidre?" he repeated.

Chapter Four

The neighbor's dog barked. Katie put down the book and rushed to the door. It opened before she'd reached it. Dusty stood there with a bouquet of sunflowers.

"They're beautiful." She greeted her husband with a kiss. "What are you home for?"

"I figured you'd need a nooner if Deidre is in the picture."

She gently jabbed at his chest. "Right. You're hoping I'll go all psycho on you for not putting out and give you a blow job against your will?"

"Only if you insist, babe."

She swatted him again and walked to the kitchen. "Nice touch with the eye color thing. To think it took me years to engrain in your head about calicos almost always being female."

"And males being sterile. You like that touch?"

"I don't know. You make me feel like I've let myself go after two kids. Do I not have the breasts you desire anymore since I've nursed both of your offspring, my love?"

He laughed. "Come on. You know I'll love your breasts when they're dragging on the floor. Can I help it if Athracki males are pigs? Put on forty pounds if you want. You'll see how much I still love you."

"You're still not off the hook for that." Katie opened the fridge. "You want me to heat up leftovers?"

He held up a bag he had hidden behind his back. "I brought your favorite sandwich. I hoped you didn't eat yet."

"Ohhh…you are going for points today. I didn't eat yet. I'm really having a hard time putting this book down."

"It's not too much repeat back story? I'm afraid a lot of that was covered in book one when Deidre first showed up."

"Some of it was, but it's still good, though, hon. It was two books away and you did elaborate a bit more. She is a little more psychotic this time around than I remember her being. I also had to laugh about you saying he tried to break up with her because of her age. Wherever did you get that idea?" Katie grinned wide. Parts of this story could not have played out any closer to their life. Dusty had said that the time-traveling girl he added in his story after what they'd been thorough, had made all the difference in the plot in his first novel. She had to agree. Although his second book had taken a slightly different twist, she was glad to see Deidre back in her full glory.

"What can I say? I'm a genius."

"Humble, too."

Taking her by the waist, he dipped her back. "So, no nooner?"

"I have to get Alex in an hour."

"I don't need a minute over twenty-seven."

Katie laughed hard and tried to pull herself up. "I'm surprised you don't make Vick say that."

"Bastard steals enough of my stuff," he said with a wink as he stood her up. "Come on, sugar cookie. Get naked for your dreamboat."

"You think you'd at least try to woo me with the only name I like that you use," Katie said, crossing her arms.

"I don't need to woo you, you're my wife. I brought flowers and food…baby."

She ginned. "I'm so easy."

"That's what it says on the wall at work."

Again, a love tap met his arm. "I'm afraid we already pushed it last night, but I'm sure I'm ovulating soon. Wear a condom, okay?" She started to head up the stairs.

Catching up to her, he grabbed a handful of her behind. "How about I don't?"

Katie spun so fast on the steps that she almost fell over. "What?"

"How about we don't, babe? Let's play a little roulette."

"But I thought you only wanted two kids?"

"I never said that. You did. I want what you want, except I wouldn't mind another."

A wide smile spread over Katie's face. "Really?"

"Of course. I'd have a million kids with you, baby. Are you ready?"

"Honestly…I don't know. Alex is already four."

"So."

"There's only a year between him and Alyson. Is that too much time?"

"I don't think so." He grasped her shoulders. "I don't want to rush you, though. I'll wear a condom. We can talk about this later. We're cutting into my minutes here." He smiled and gave her a reassuring kiss.

"No, I don't want to. I love you, Dusty. Let's make another mini-us."

Dusty hustled out the door with his sandwich. He'd have to eat it on the way back to the office. They'd gone into what Katie teased was "overtime." As much as she picked on him about coming home for lunch and "nooners," she was always glad when he did. They didn't have much alone time without the kids, not that she was complaining. Dusty was a better father than she could have ever wished for. Every day was playtime with him around. She laughed, thinking she already had three kids.

She wasn't one for reading erotica like Courtney. Dusty had made a science fiction fan of her, and his books had all the heat she could to handle.

"I don't need to read about people having sex, Court. Dusty keeps me more than satisfied."

"It's not about not being satisfied, hon," Courtney had said. "Everyone can use a good 'bean flicker' every now and then."

That had sent Katie's beer flying, and the vowing of trying to never discuss erotica again any time soon. The things that came out of Courtney's mouth never ceased to shock and amaze Katie.

Laughing about the time she'd actually found a beer with the name "Bean Flicker," she grabbed her sandwich and returned to Dusty's book.

"Answer me, Deidre. What am I doing here?" Vick demanded.

"Do you love her?" Deidre's hand hovered dangerously close to the firing button.

"Love her? Jody? You're spying on me? Christ, you psycho Athrackian. We've been over for years. You left me, remember?"

"No. You made me think I was the one who left you. You wanted me gone for a long time."

"That's not true. You know I loved you." He tried to soften his tone and recover from calling her psycho. He couldn't remember really being in love with her. Maybe it was love in the beginning, but it didn't last. Knowing he was far from perfect, he still truly blamed her strange ways for everything falling apart. Whatever the reasons were then, he had to sweet talk his way out of this if he was going to save his crew. He didn't doubt for a minute that she'd blow everyone up.

"You changed, babe. It was best for both us that you left. I really cared for you, but it just didn't work. I'm sorry, but don't take this out on my crew."

"'Babe?' Where's all the sweet tooth names you had for me?"

"I thought you preferred babe."

She shrugged. "I didn't care what you called me, as long as we had a follow-through of outstanding sex."

"We did. Dammit, it was some of the most outstanding sex of my life, but it had to end. You know that as well as I do. You deserved a better life than popping into my bed every night and disappearing each morning."

She swayed her hand over the firing button once again. "You didn't answer me."

"Answer what? Do I love Jody? I don't know. All right? This is something new to me. I have feelings for her, I'll tell you that much. I haven't had much for relationships since you left. I haven't wanted anyone since you."

"Oh bull. You didn't love me so much that you went celibate after I left."

"I never said celibate. I said I never had real feelings for someone. I was confused. I was then and I am now. Why are you doing this?"

"So…a gal in each port?" was her response, instead of answering his question.

He let out a frustrated grunt. "No one who pines away for me, that's for certain. Please, Deidre. Be pissed at me for whatever it is after all this time, but please, leave my crew out of it."

"I'm not pissed at you. I'm in a pickle." Her finger slid away from the trigger.

Despite the situation, he chuckled at her use of the phrase she'd picked up from him. He'd used it only once to describe his approach of a new planet. "Either way I look at it, we're in a pickle, but I have to go in." Of course he had to describe what an actual pickle was and how it was the favorite expression of his uncle Francis. It took a lot of explaining. He easily forgot language barriers with his non-human crew.

"A pickle?" he said. "If you're looking for my help, threatening my crew is a strange way to go about it."

She closed the gap and rested her hands on his shoulders. Within an instant, he knew she'd teleported him. It was a planet unknown to him. It almost had an Earth feel to it. New York, specifically. They were in what was very much like Central Park, with massive modern skyscrapers not too far off and a monorail of sorts, twisting its way overhead. The trees resembled something out of a Dr. Seuss book, though. The twists and turns of the trunks and branches were almost comical. The vibrant colors were unlike any he'd ever seen before, let alone coming from vegetation. A fluffy cat-like creature ran by, chasing an unrecognizable animal twice its size.

"Where are we?"

"My home."

"Home? This isn't Athracki."

"No, but it's where I've been for a couple of years."

"Does it have a name?" he asked, impatiently.

"Einnoc."

"Einnoc?" He hadn't recognized the surroundings, but he knew the name. "Are you crazy? You know how far I am from my ship and crew?"

"I'll get you back there, don't worry."

He raised an eyebrow. "*When* are we?"

"The present. I stopped time traveling, my love. At least, I had stopped until today. I was going to behave myself and just talk to you, but when I popped into your room and saw that Terian, I lost my cool. Going back to the time of the Delton battle ship was all I could think of to get you on a view of your ship."

"A little dramatic. You seriously didn't expect me to be with no one else forever."

"Of course not!" she yelled, and then quickly covered her mouth.

Seeing where her attention went, he glanced over to playground equipment. There were several children playing on what looked a lot like the same colorful, plastic pieces from when he was a child. A small boy with dark brown hair came running over to them. As he got closer, Vick saw his eyes. He had one blue and one green.

"Who's this?" he asked.

She didn't answer him as she gave the boy a hug and sent him back off to play. "We'll go home in a few minutes, sweetheart. Go say goodbye to your friends."

"Okay, Mommy."

Vick was speechless for a moment. "You have a kid?"

She nodded. "As do you. He's your son, Vick."

"My son?" The words hit him like a baseball bat. His eyes followed the little boy as he tripped over the plastic side of the sandbox. Stepping forward like he wanted to run and help, Deidre held him back.

"He's fine."

Sure enough, he'd gotten up, brushed himself off, and hurried over to his friends without so much as a whimper.

Vick turned to her. "He's big for three."

"What can I say? We grow them bigger in my sect of the galaxy."

"Why are you only telling me this now? You pick a funny time to want to come back in my life. I finally got over all the crazy. I'm sorry to be so blunt, but it is what it is, doll. I don't know what kind of life I can offer you two or what exactly you want from me."

Her emotionless eyes met his. "I'm dying, Vick."

"You're dying?" He backed up and sat on a picnic table. He didn't love this woman, but even after what they'd been though, he didn't wish her dead. Especially when she seemed to have gotten her act together and had a child. Holy shit, *his* child.

She sat next to him. "I've known for a while."

"How? I mean…it is cancer or something? I thought your people didn't get things like cancer. You're supposed to live twice our life span." He lowered his head in his hands, elbows resting on his knees. "I'm sorry. I'm sure I sound like an idiot."

"It's the time traveling. It's not natural. I spent too many years abusing my power. Each trip took its toll on me."

"Do you know how much longer you have?"

Deidre wiped a tear that had snuck down her cheek. "Not long. A few weeks at best. I just had to know something and went into the future. I…I shouldn't tell you this."

"I asked. Tell me."

"The rest is something you've asked me not to do."

"I did?"

"Yes. Letting you know something before it happens. You never wanted your knowledge of something to affect your decision later."

Vick stood and took her hands. "You saw me with him."

More tears flowed down her cheeks as she nodded. "You two passed me on the street. I was in a store – you didn't see me. I followed you two to my grave." Her sobbing got louder, he couldn't help but to lean down and give her a strong hug for comfort.

When her crying finally subsided, he sat next to her. "Of course I'll be there for my son, sweetheart. I admit I have no clue what to do with a child. My lifestyle isn't the most inviting for a toddler." He paused. "But I suppose I'm long overdue for a change."

It was obvious his words shocked her. "Are you really ready to give it up, Vick?"

He gave her hand a reassuring squeeze. "I'm ready to do what I have to. Can you send me back? Give me a few days to figure this out?"

Flopping into his chest, she allowed more gentle sobs to release. "Your ship is your life. All your dreams—"

He cut her off. "Have just been altered a bit. I'll get new ones, with my son at my side."

"He'll be despised. Athrackians with his eye color are still looked upon as slaves on some planets."

"It wasn't long ago on earth that people argued among themselves over everything. They tried to outlaw marriages for people that were different colors. Even same sex marriages were fought in lengthy battles in our courts. If we can overcome that, surely a galaxy or two will accept an Athracki boy and his human father."

"I'm sorry that I threatened your ship. I wasn't really going to do anything."

"I know," he said, wrapping an arm around her shoulder. "I'm sorry things ended the way they did. I wish you had come to me sooner about him."

"I couldn't. You had to map your nebulas. I wasn't going to take that from you. I saw what greatness you would achieve. You were going to do it without me warning you about danger. I honestly knew you preferred it that way."

Victor kissed the back of her hand. "What's his name?"

"Aiden. Aiden Victor."

"You named him after my father?"

She gave him a one-shoulder shrug. "I knew you'd meet him someday. Parental ties aren't the same to us, obviously."

Vick stood, wanting a better view of the boy, who was busy running around the play area chasing a friend. "Do I get to meet him before I go?"

"Of course. I want you to get to know him before…" She bit her bottom lip.

"You don't know exactly when you die, do you?"

"No. I'm afraid to go forward again and find out. I think this is one slight uncertainty I need to deal with. I—"

A red circle of light was suddenly on her chest. Vick saw it a second too late. Where it had been was now replaced with a gaping hole. Deidre fell back as he shouted, "No!"

Katie flung her e-reader into the couch as if she'd been shot. "You bastard." She dashed to the bowl on the counter to grab her keys when the phone rang. She smiled when she saw Courtney's name.

"I was just thinking about you."

"How awesome I am?" Courtney said.

"Something like that."

"Yeah, right. But I am. I'm going to grab Alex then kill time with him and get Ali. Is that ok?"

"Of course it's okay. What's the occasion?"

"Just feeling like the world's best Godmother, that's all."

Katie grinned. "You're craving ice cream and don't want to go alone."

"Bingo!" she said with a giggle. "I'll see you in two hours. Holler if you need me to grab anything for you."

"Will do. Love you."

"Back atacha."

Turning around, Katie was brought to a screeching halt at the sight of a man standing in the kitchen.

"Frank? I mean…Dusty?"

"Hiya, pop-tart."

Chapter Five

Instead of being frightened, Katie crossed her arms over her chest. "He gave in too easily."

"Who gave in too easily?" the older Dusty asked.

"Vick, jackass. Oh, here's your kid. Okay, I'll just give up traipsing the galaxy now. No problem. Feel free to die now. Ahhhhh!!" Her hands dropped at her side.

"I'm glad to see you, too."

"Seriously, Dusty. Make him work for it a little."

"You're yelling at the wrong 'me,' doll face."

"Oh, you'll get it when you get home."

"How about I get it now," he said, waggling his eyebrows.

Katie scrunched her eyebrows. "Gawd. Even at your age you're still this way? I'm not sleeping with the seventy year old you, Dusty."

"Why not? The almost eighty year old you doesn't mind."

That sent her laughing until she snorted. "God, I love you."

"Annnnd I see you still call me God."

"Stop it," She finally walked over and gave him a strong hug. "Should I be worried that you're here? Please don't make me or you travel through time again. We're so happy."

He clasped both of her hands tight. "No way. I just thought now was a good time to come see you."

"I know there's more to this. You showing up is never a good thing."

"Is too. Last time I showed up, I called me, if you recall. I saved Courtney's life."

"I know…but…I've just gotten used to the stories. I think I actually know which life is mine. Which 'you' I won over and when."

"You mean which '*me*' won *you* over."

"Whatever. I love you but please go."

"Can't you even spare a cup of coffee?"

She crossed her arms and squinted for a moment before she answered. "Fine. But you go before you come home."

"Deal."

They sat together on the porch swing out back. Dusty finally spoke up after a far too uncomfortable silence.

"I lied. I did come for a reason."

Katie stood. "I knew it. What? What happens? Is it one of the kids?"

The older Dusty took her hand and sat her back down. "They're fine. You know I'm not going to give you any details, but everyone is fine. If my math is right, we're planning a number three right about now."

Katie's eyes lit up. "Today actually." Her hands went to her stomach. "I just know I'm ovulating. I hope we get pregnant right away."

His wrinkled hand rested on hers. "It's not in our cards, cupcake."

"What do you mean?"

"I wanted to tell you now. I can't bear the thought of you going through what you did over the next two years."

"What do I go through? Why can't we have another baby, Dusty?"

"There's a ton of medical mumbo jumbo for it. You take every test twice, fight them every step of the way and do expensive procedures everyone tells you that there's barely a ten percent chance of working."

Her lip started to quiver; he pulled her in for a tight embrace. "I loved you every step of the way, but they were the hardest years we've ever had. You're so hard on yourself. I needed to come back and tell you. I'm begging you to let it go. It doesn't happen."

The lip quiver turned into a full-blown cry. "Why?"

"Shhhh, baby. You're a wonderful mother. You're not done being a mom just because you're not having another baby. Ali and Alex need you. Let them be enough of our own seeds."

Her tear-filled eyes met his. "Are you sure?"

"I wouldn't come here to lie to you, darlin'. I know it sounds bad now, but it's not as pickled as you think. It'll work out in the end. Be happy." He wiped away the tears that had made their way out. "Until a few hours ago, you thought we were done. Let our two be enough." He kissed the top of her head. "I'm going to skedaddle before I get home and want to kick my ass again."

She let out a soft laugh.

"Be sure to holler at me about Skinnard and the kid, okay?"

A nod was her only response. He turned to walk away but she cried out, "Wait!"

"What is it?"

"Can I tell you?"

"Please do. I'll understand. I only ever wanted what you wanted, baby. We're a family. A wonderful family. Be happy like I know we've been and will continue to be."

"I'll try."

"There is no try. Only do."

"Good lord. Tell me you don't quote Yoda in the book."

He walked away, laughing hard. "No promises, puddin'."

When Dusty got home, Katie told him about her visitor after she told him her thoughts on the book.

"I wish I was here."

"So you could kick the crap out of yourself?"

He grinned. "Maybe. What do you think, babe? Do we trust me?"

"I don't think you'd risk coming back to lie to me, hon."

"Risk? Risk what?"

"I don't know. Don't you think it has to be bad for you? I mean, on some level you must. You killed off Deidre with time traveling."

"No, the laser got her."

"Yeah, but you *were* going to kill her off with it. She thought you were, anyway."

"Kill who off, Mommy?"

Alyson joined them in the kitchen with her brother close behind. "One of Daddy's character's, honey."

"Killing people is bad," Alex reprimanded his father.

"It's the worst thing ever, pal. But sometimes in a story, writers do that to make people like your mommy mad."

Alex smiled wide. "You're teasing me."

"Actually, he's not. Mommy's mad at Daddy's story," Katie said with a poke to her son's stomach. The move caused the usual fit of laughter. "You two go clean up. Supper will be ready soon."

The pair happily ran off together. Kaitlyn hopped up on the island. "Maybe we shouldn't have thought about another. Those two are so close, just like we thought they would be with them being only eleven months apart."

Dusty closed in on her, resting his forehead to hers. "You know if we could, we would, and they'd all be great together."

A heavy sigh escaped her. "I know."

"Give it time to sink in. We were so happy this morning, love muffin. Don't let a rash decision in the heat of anticipating a nooner change how you feel about our life. Hey!" he said, slapping his hand on her knee. "Maybe it's time for another shot at a puppy."

Slumping even further, Katie groaned. "I don't want a puppy. I want a baby, Dusty."

He reached into the fridge and pulled out a beer. "So we'll adopt." After removing the cap he offered it to her. She declined.

"Adopt? You'd want to do that?"

"Why not?"

"It's expensive, they make you jump through hoops, it's nerve-wracking, expensive…"

"You said that already. We do more than okay. There has to be someone insane enough to let us raise their kid."

"Right. I'm sure Courtney will let us have Dean."

Dusty sprayed his beer, and then spent a minute coughing. "That's funny, but I'm thinking a little smaller. Maybe he has a lawyer buddy who handles adoptions. I'll go over and ask him."

"You can't yet."

"Why not?"

"Because technically I don't know I can't get pregnant yet. Courtney will know that I haven't had appointments. I would have talked to her about it."

"So go make an appointment. Tell your OB/GYN that we've been trying for a while. Then I'll talk with Dean-O. Another week won't matter. Since you said I told you we'd been trying for two years, we'll be well ahead of the game."

"Good lord."

"What now?"

"Now I know why Captain Skinnard is so agreeable. He's you."

"He is not," Dusty argued.

"He totally is. You know…if some woman showed up and said some strange boy was yours, you'd so just say 'okay, thanks. I'll raise him now.'"

"What else would I do? You want another kid. Want me to go knock up someone?"

"You'd better go write your article before I hurt you." She tried swatting for him but he was already out of reach and hustling to his den. "I'll call you when dinner is ready, Captain."

Vick tried to keep his son from seeing his mother like that, but Aiden had been on his way back over and saw the hole blown into her. He rushed over and scooped up the screaming child.

"It's going to be okay. I'm your daddy, Aiden. Your mommy found me and brought me here to be with you. It's going to be okay, son."

Whether or not the three year old had understood, he'd accepted the comforting hug while Vick had continually scanned the area for the shooter. Despite the area quickly being cleared by authorities, Vick and Aiden were taken into protective custody. Although worried about vanishing from his ship with no explanation, Vick couldn't protest.

Two days later, standing at the grave, Victor Skinnard held his son's hand, unsure how much the boy truly understood. *His son's hand.* That was going to take some time to get used to. He longed for the days he was deprived of, getting to know his son with his mother around, reassuring him Vick was who he should be with. Luckily she'd already set the plan in motion. Aiden's nanny had also been at the park, knew about Vick, and where all the documents with Deidre's plans were safely stored.

"I begged her to let me keep him," the nanny said. "Your life is not one for this wonderful child. A life in space isn't normal."

"I'm going to make accommodations for him. We'll be settled in our own place soon." He tried to sound assuring, but he wasn't sure if it was for her or for him.

"Is that where mommy lives now?" Aiden pointed to the grave.

"That's where her body is resting. Most people like to believe that she's somewhere better now. The people of earth say there's a heaven and when we die, we go there. Nothing can hurt your mommy anymore."

"Can I go there and see her?"

"It'll be a long time before you can see her again, buddy. Only good people that die can go there. I know she wants to see you again, but she also wants you to take your time getting there. She'll be waiting for you."

Tears formed in those big eyes. The one blue and the one green, big, beautiful eyes. Vick picked him up and stared hard into them. He noticed a small fleck of brown in each. A smile spread over his face. "You have a little of my eyes in you too, son. Did you notice that?"

Aiden shook his head. "I miss my mommy."

"Me too, son."

"I want to go home."

"Home is with me now. Are you ready for an adventure?"

He shook his head again, harder this time. "I want to go home."

Vick turned to the nanny for assistance.

She walked over and began stroking Aiden's back. "I wish you could stay a few days in his home. This is such a shock to him and you want to leave right away. That will only make things worse."

"We have no idea yet who did this and why. The authorities think it's best and so do I. I refuse to hang around so they can take pop-shots at Aiden, or kidnap him. We're leaving tonight." With Aiden right there to hear them, he regretted his words instantly.

Aiden's head buried deeper into Vick's neck. Tears had started to fall again, leaving Victor Skinnard feeling very much at a loss.

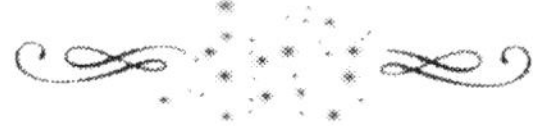

"Excuse me. You're where?"

Vick knew Jody would blow her top, but he had to make the call. He'd only managed to deliver a brief message about leaving the ship to his first-in-command the night of Deidre's death. He gave no details of how or why he left, or when he'd return. He and Aiden were on the second leg of the long journey back to his ship. He got on the video phone as soon as he felt they were a safe distance from Einnoc.

"You heard me."

"Exactly how did you get there so fast?"

"Honestly, you wouldn't believe me if I told you."

"Try me. You can start with how you disappeared from your quarters without waking me."

Vick sighed. He didn't have time for this. "I promise I'll explain it all later." He'd worried that Deidre had lied and brought him to a different time, despite what she had told him. He had mixed feelings about the timing. Jody had no memory of the attack, but now she thought she had been abandoned after sex. He wasn't sure what was worse. "I need you to take my pod to come get me."

"Get you? Are you crazy? I'm supposed to just leave Xolo in charge of your ship and crew?"

"The ship will be fine is his care. As long as he doesn't get any crazy ideas about trying to go anywhere, everything will be okay. Look, I'm sorry. I can only get as far as the seventh Kilgent star."

"I can't believe you want me to go all the way to the Pandora Galaxy for you. That'll take the better part of five days to get to Simian's orbit, *if* the hyper drive doesn't break down again and *if* I don't get stopped for going through the green zone."

"I'll call in a favor. You won't get stopped. Not my travel pod."

"And then rent a ship with a kick ass warp drive—"

"I'll take care of the details."

Jody was silent for a moment. Vick could hear her fingernails tapping away at the keyboard.

"Captain…I've run all the numbers. There's no way you can be in—"

"Jody, you're going to have to trust me. I'll fill you in with everything later. I promise. If you won't come get me, I'll get Xolo on the line. You've had a hard-on for that captain's chair since the day we met; now will be your chance." He knew that wasn't the case, but he figured pissing her off would be the one sure way to get her to do what he needed.

"It's not about the fucking chair, Skinnard!" He watched as she looked over her shoulder as if she was making sure no one had heard her. "I wake up in your chamber, naked in your bed, and you're gone. Just gone. Now you tell me you're billions of stars away, wanting a ride back?"

Jody turned bright orange. She didn't have to drop an F-bomb for him to realize how pissed she was. It surprised him she was using it properly. He recalled the way she'd cursed when she first tried.

"Go shit your stupid face, jerk knocker" or "yank your assmuch off" were a few that came to mind.

"There are only so many ways I can say I'm sorry and I'll explain later, Lieutenant. Will you come get me or not?"

"So, we're back to Lieutenant?"

"Don't bust my balls, dammit, Jody! I'm not doing this now."

Shooting off her chair, now glowing crimson, she slammed her hand next to the monitor. "See you in a few days, scrod-nut-muncher." With that, the screen went blank.

Turning away from the screen, his eyes went to his son. Thankfully he was still busy playing in the corner. Aiden spoke very well for a three year old. Not that he'd had a lot of experience with human babies, but Aiden seemed to be a lot more advanced than Vick would have expected.

He'd have to do a little research on Athrackians. So far his knowledge was limited to females of the species, their high sex drive, and the noises they made while making love. He didn't think that would be too helpful in raising his son.

A lot more investigating needed to be done first. Specifically, who killed his son's mother and why. Vick had known she was a wanted fugitive when they'd been sleeping together, but it couldn't still be over that. After she'd left him, Deidre had returned to her home planet. He'd learned that she'd cleared her name. She'd never given him the details, but he was sure she'd used her time-traveling ability to change her fate. He read the new version of the story: The *real* murderer of the prince who had tried to rape her had been caught and put to death. The king had been killed in battle and the queen murdered a few years prior when it was discovered she was pregnant. It wasn't hard to figure out she'd had an affair, since her husband was sterile. The prince's young wife now had the throne. She'd abolished slavery. No longer were the one blue eye and one green eyed Athrackian babies given over as slaves to the royals, and everyone currently in slavery was free.

Searching through the intergalactic journals, he found nothing about Athracki children being half-human. Everything he read said it was improbable; nothing said impossible. He couldn't have been the only man charmed by a beauty like Deidre, could he? Vick always found his taste leaning toward females who were not human, but he didn't think he was unique. A lot of his crew had far more eclectic taste than he did. Deidre had said that he was the only human she'd ever looked twice at. Athrackians and humans rarely mingled. They were taught humans were "foul and unclean." Maybe in her desperation to be rescued, she'd looked past the hatred that she'd been taught, judged humans for herself, and given in to her desires. Could his son really be the first of his kind?

"Dammit, woman. You picked a fine time to leave."

Aiden's head popped up. "You say something?"

"Sorry, son. Just talking to myself. How about you go brush your teeth? It'll be bedtime soon."

Although curious over the woman who had once stolen his heart, he had never tried to reconnect with her, not even when he'd found himself once again on the Athracki moon for supplies. He'd feared if he tried to contact her, it would once again bring her wild ways, games, and tricks back into his life.

He was at a loss for where to begin to looking for whom she'd angered enough to want her dead. More likely, the list would be too long to narrow down once he got digging. If she'd let her powers be known and agreed to help the wrong type of people, she would have been contracted out to the lowest bidding hit-man.

A buzz of the door shook him out of his brainstorming. Retrieving his gun from his dresser drawer, he closed the door behind him after telling his son to stay put and that he'd be right back.

"Who's there?" he said through the intercom.

"A delivery, Captain."

"I didn't order anything. I've got a U-14 pointed at the center of the door, ready to blow a hole in you. No one knows I'm here. What do you want?"

"Honestly, Captain. I have something that belongs to your son. Don't shoot me. I've been trying to catch up to you since Delta 12. Your wife left him something. It's my job to get it to him."

More curious than worried, he unlocked the door and pulled it open in one swift motion, and pointed his gun at the intruder's head. "How did you find me?"

"I told you. I've been tracking you. I'm a Graneau. I've been tasked to Aiden."

A Graneau. Great. He couldn't shake this particular alien if he traveled from galaxy to galaxy continually for the next thirty years. Once they had a lock on you, they followed you until they dropped dead.

"She wasn't my wife."

"Doesn't matter. By Athracki slave laws, she was yours."

"She was no longer a slave."

"Again, it doesn't matter. She bore your son. She was your wife. You were her only mate."

"I wasn't her only mate. She'd been forced into an encounter by her first owner's son."

"A non-chosen 'encounter' as you want to call it does not place ownership. He could have abused her for years, but her heart was yours."

"You're talking in circles. We weren't in love. As a matter of fact, we pretty much hated each other up until the day she died."

"I don't make the rules." The Graneau held up a small box. "This is your son's."

Ripping the lid off, Captain Skinnard stared at the four-inch square black shiny object with a band. "What the hell am I supposed to do with this? It looks like a bad knock-off of a cheap watch from the twenty first century."

"My job is not to tell you what to do with it, just to get it to you. Good luck to you, Captain." With a nod, the Graneau left him.

Chapter Six

"Nice subtle attempt, Dusty. You trying to hint to me that you want an Apple watch?"

He took the e-reader out of her hands and placed it on the coffee table. "Is that what you picture?"

"Isn't it? That's what it sounds like to me."

"That's sort of exactly what I was going for; I guess I just didn't think of the actual object. You know, it's hard for sci-fi authors these days to come up with stuff. All the cool gadgets are starting to really exist."

"So, no on the watch?"

"No, sugar tits. I don't want a new watch or gadget."

"You must still be good from this afternoon. You certainly aren't getting sex with that name."

"I haven't used it in years. Cut me some slack. And no, I'm still good from our lunch date."

"Dustin Charles. You've got another thing coming if you think that's my idea of a date."

"It's think coming."

"What's 'think coming?'"

"The phrase. It's think coming, not thing coming."

"Really? That sounds wrong."

"I remember that from school. Guess your teachers were more concerned with being able to spell out drug names and diarrhea rather than perfect your grammar. Sorry babe, editor thing."

"I could care less about shit like that."

"Couldn't care less."

"I'm going to fucking beat you. I forget how you love to torture your father with things like *sans*. I think I understand why he hates you." Katie got off the couch.

Dusty hustled after her. "I'm sorry. I was just teasing."

"I know," she said with a smirk. "I was teasing, too. I'm not ready for bed yet. You go ahead; I'll be up after a bit."

"You still upset about the baby thing or do you just want to read some more?"

"Yes, to both."

"Do we need to talk about it?"

"There's nothing else to talk about. It is what it is. I guess it's still sinking in. I need to get used to the idea that we're done. Your book is a good distraction right now. Besides, when I find you've stolen one more plot point from our lives, you'll be buying me more than an Apple watch."

Laughing, he tightened his hold on her and kissed the top of her head. "Take all the time you need, babe. I'll get up with the kids. You can sleep in."

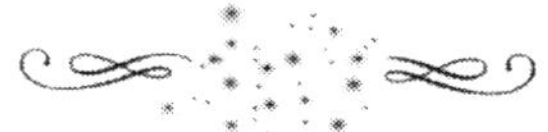

Unable to concentrate on anything but the long trip ahead, Victor tucked the device away to inspect it later on his ship. Before they departed Athracki, he'd purchased a small travel bag, the bare necessities for toiletries, and a few changes of clothes. Being dressed as a captain of a discovery vessel wouldn't be wise for a few of the ports where they'd be docking. It would be earth's equivalent to a millionaire's child walking through a slum – begging to be kidnapped and held for random. Having a bi-color-eyed Athrackian child in tow made it that much more dangerous. Unfortunately, not all galaxies had been so quick to adopt the rule that they were no longer slaves. The thought of having Aiden stolen from him to be sold kept him on constant high alert, making for long, restless nights.

No longer feeling safe, he packed up what little he had acquired and dropped his bag by the door. He stood there for a long moment, contemplating how different his life would be now. No longer would a small overnight bag suffice. He now had to pack a bag of toys, a large suitcase, and a small carry-on for the toddler also in tow. *His son.* No matter how many times he said that, it sounded foreign to him.

Luck was with him when he boarded the next ship; Aiden was sound asleep on his shoulder. He didn't have to worry about anyone making eye contact with the boy and questioning whether or not he had the right papers. Even traveling on the most questionable of ships and in the worst possible storage area not meant for human travel, someone was bound to want to see your documents. With Captain Skinnard in near paupers' clothes, an exhausted toddler in one arm, two bags over the shoulder, and a large suitcase in his other hand, he was simply waved through and pointed to his closet of a cabin. He hoped the rest of the trip would be as uneventful.

After getting Aiden settled on the makeshift bed, he paced for a good twenty minutes before finally giving in and retrieving the watch-like device from his bag. He flipped it around, examining it from every angle that he could in the poor lighting. A loud screeching came from it, after he pressed a silver button on the right side. It woke Aiden with a start. He ran up and snatched the device from his hand. Aiden placed his thumb on the top screen; a keyboard of only lights and lines appeared just above it, mid-air. He keyed in what looked like a password. Within another second, the terrible noise stopped.

"When did you get my Hawkeye?" Aiden asked as he slipped it on his tiny wrist.

"I'm sorry I didn't tell you sooner. I've been busy packing and unpacking. A friend of your mommy brought it to me a little while ago. It's called a Hawkeye?"

"No. It has some long name. I call it my Hawkeye because it can do this." Pulling up the keypad again, he keyed in another code. He faced his father with a wide smile and pointed to his eyes. "Look, sir."

Victor had been squatting. He was about to correct Aiden for calling him sir, but when he saw that his son's eyes were now brown; he fell to his ass hard.

"You can change your eye color?"

"Uh-huh. Want to see me make them purple?"

Vick quickly grasped his son's arm. "No, buddy. Don't do that. You know what purple eyes mean to someone of your…" He caught himself, unsure of how to word what he wanted to say. He didn't want to say "race" since he was half human as well. "Someone who comes from where you do."

"It means I'm special."

"No, buddy. You are special no matter what your eye color is. But on the planet your mom is from, that means you get to run the show someday."

"Show?"

"A planet, son. Men with purple eyes are kings."

"Oh, I know that."

"You do? Do you know what all the eye colors mean?"

"I know a lot of things." He pulled up the keypad. "Do you want me to look like I'm an angry Terian?"

"No!" He quickly grasped his son's arm again. "Let's not go changing colors. Uh…you'll confuse people that saw you come on as you are."

"Should I change my eyes back?"

"Actually, leaving them brown for now may not be such a bad idea."

"Okay." He sighed and looked around. "How long do we have to stay in here?"

"We can go out after a while and look for food if you're hungry, but I'm afraid for the most part, we need to stay in here. I don't want to scare you, but the men on these types of ships don't take kindly to children. Or most other men for that matter. Sorry again, buddy. The trip is at least three days."

"Then your friend picks us up?"

"Yes. She'll probably beat us there since we have to make one more stop."

"Can you call her?"

"No, I can't." He brought his son onto his lap. He didn't know where to begin. Did Aiden know what his mother was capable of? Can a three year old even comprehend the idea of time and inter-galaxy travel at will?

"When your mommy brought me to your planet, I didn't have my communicator with me. I was lucky to be able to call my friend from the room we had."

"We can call her on my Hawkeye if you want."

"It can do that?"

"Uh-huh." Aiden keyed away on the small device and called up a keypad above his head again. Vick shifted him so he could enter what he needed to call Jody on his pod. Aiden scooted off his lap while he did so.

While Vick was waiting for the connection, he watched as Aiden brought their bags closer to him.

"What are you doing, pal?"

"I don't want to wait three days in here. I don't like it."

"I'm afraid we don't have a choice, little man. We're sort of stuck here."

"No, we're not." His tone wasn't sassy, it was quite matter-of-fact.

"Son, I promise you—"

Jody answering cut him off. "I'm on my way, dicker-head. What the dirt do you want?"

There was nothing but silence as they were surrounded by darkness. Skinnard reached for Aiden and found him. The second their hands clasped, everything became light once again. He was now staring at Jody, only she was right in front of him, not on a screen.

"What the crapper happened?" Jody shrieked. "How did you…" Her eyes fell to Aiden.

Vick wondered if she knew enough not to use her attempts at swearing in front of him.

"Who's the kid?"

He held up his hand, stopping her, and pulled his son to him. "Did you do this?"

"Yes. That ship smelled. Can I get something to eat now?"

"Aiden…were you aware of what your mother could do? You can do that?"

He shook his head hard. "I'm not like Mommy. Mommy could go to tomorrow and yesterday. I can only move *today*." He emphasized the word as if the feat was as special as taking out the trash.

"You can move today?" Skinnard spun around and noticed that all of their belongings had come with them. "You brought our stuff, too?"

"It's my stuff. Can I get something to eat now?"

"Whoa! *He* teleported you?" Jody said, sitting down hard.

If Vick wasn't in such shock himself, he would have taken humor in the fact that the color green seemed to be universal for "about to puke." He hurried over to be sure she didn't have a side-order of "pass out" with that.

"There are some meal bars in that back cabinet, little guy. Help yourself. I'm going to talk to my friend here for a minute, okay?"

"She's pretty," he said with a smile as he walked away. "Even green."

Victor gave his communications officer a few minutes to gather herself. After a minute, she shrugged off his touch, her color shifting from green to her more normal olive shade. "Let go of me."

"Don't be mad. I have a million things running through my head right now. You being angry over the fact that I left that night isn't going to help."

"Is he why you had to leave?"

"Yes, but I didn't know that when I was taken to Einnoc."

"Wait…climax again?"

He couldn't help his laugh. "The phrase is 'come again.'"

She crossed her arms and started to turn orange. Not quite mad, but getting there. "I hate English!"

"I'm sorry. I didn't mean to laugh. You already hate me so I'm going to give this all to you at once." He almost said "Lay it all out there," but she could have been translated that as something sexual as well. Damn English indeed.

"I'm waiting."

"Aiden is my son."

Magenta. The color of a Terian passing out is deep magenta.

Victor was at her side when she came to ten minutes later. He'd placed her on the small couch in the travel pod. She tried to sit up but he pushed her back down. "Take it easy there, cupcake."

"Cupcake? Back off you oversexed nut-sack."

"Shhh. I have Aiden listening to music so we can talk."

He gave her a moment to gather herself. She stared at Aiden for a moment before she spoke.

"He's Athrackian."

"Yes, and half human. My half."

"And you never told me?"

"I just found out. You've already seen what he can do. His mother…that's a whole other story."

"Athrackians don't have mysterious powers. Not like the Graneau who can track you across the galaxy. Or Venar—" His hand was now over her mouth, effectively cutting her off.

"I don't need an intergalactic roll call. His mother was special. She time traveled and never understood it herself. Aiden has some of that, too, only I didn't know it until he brought us here. I have no idea if he's born with it or if it's because of that device on his wrist."

Once again she glanced over her shoulder at him. "Looks like a twenty-first century knock-off."

He grinned then dared give her a quick kiss while Aiden's attention was elsewhere.

"That's not the most welcome right now."

"Tough shit."

"Why is this excrement always so hard on you humans?"

This time, he didn't let the kiss be short. He couldn't help himself. Despite everything that was happening, he knew he didn't want to be anywhere but with Jody at this very moment. He loved her. Every color she had, every funny twisted phrase she said. It all only made her more beautiful to him.

Although she had accepted his tongue and returned the kiss, she pushed him away after a moment.

"We'll talk about this later, Captain." Her eyes widened; Vick quickly turned, staring into the big, currently brown, eyes of his son.

"Hey, buddy. You okay?"

"Can we go to your home now?"

"We're on our way. After I got my friend Jody here set up, I changed the course back to my ship. You bringing us here saved a lot of time. We'll be there in just under a couple days now."

"Can you show me the course to your ship?"

"Of course." Vick scruffed his son's hair. "You sure are a smart lad for being three."

"Athracki children are one of the smartest races there are, Victor. You impregnated his mother and didn't know this?"

He placed his hands over Aiden's ears. "Could you be a little more sensitive? There's not a lot we've had time to cover," he whispered.

She mouthed, "Sorry."

Aiden reached up, taking Jody's necklace in his hands. Vick watched as he rolled the opal-like glass bead in tiny fingers.

"This is very pretty."

"Thank you. It's a piece of my home planet. It actually looks very much like it does from space." She took his index finger and moved it from one black bump to the next. "These are our surrounding moons and their position. No matter where I am, I'll always know how to get back home."

"That's cool." He took another minute studying it, then let go.

After walking Aiden to the control panel, Vick pulled up the coordinates of his ship. "That's where my ship is."

"You're right next to a nebula?"

"My, you are a smart one. Yes. My ship is an exploration vessel. This is the third nebula we've gone to. We were going to go in, but I'm not so sure now."

Aiden keyed away at his wrist device. "Why? There's nothing wrong with the Andromeda Nebula."

Skinnard knelt down in front of him. "Son, I—"

Once again everything went black. It was like a bad case of déjà vu. He reached for his son, made contact with him, and then everything was light again. The ship jostled slightly and went stationary.

Jody ran over to them and held Aiden's face in her hands. "Honey bee, what did you do?"

"I've never been so close to a nebula. I didn't want to wait another day. And I want real food, not a meal bar. Can I get something to eat now?"

Jody lowered her hands and ran to the starboard porthole. "Holy feces on thin toasted bread. We're docked to your ship, Captain."

Chapter Seven

Katie couldn't help it. She was still snorting when she climbed into bed. Dusty groaned and reached up for her to lie down on his chest. He cleared his throat before he asked, "What's up, babe? You okay?"

"It took me a minute to figure out Jody was saying holy crap on a cracker."

His chest rose and fell slightly. It was a silent Dusty "I'm still asleep" chuckle. "I don't know where that comes from, but I love her."

"You're probably channeling your inner Dean. I remember the way he used to butcher sorority names."

"Maybe that's it."

"I also like all the names Vick has for Aiden. I told you he's you."

"Babe?"

"What?"

"I'll give you a million bucks if you let me go back to sleep."

"What an old married couple we are. You used to offer me that for sex."

He pushed her off and rolled over.

"Nice touch with the couch, too. You didn't even buy her a caramel latte before you slipped her the tongue."

"I swear to God, woman. Let me go back to bed or I'll let go of this fart I've been holding back."

"Don't do that, Vick. You'll implode the ship."

"Go to bed or I'll burn your reader."

"No!" Katie took off downstairs for the coffee table. She clutched her e-reader to her chest and dropped into the chair, waiting for Dusty to come wrestle her for it. When he didn't follow, she opened it up again. "Burn it my ass."

A throat clearing caused her to jump. "So you did decide to—"

"Decide to what?" the seventy year-old Dusty asked.

"Join me."

"I left beautiful you down here alone? What the hell is wrong with me?"

"Apparently, dinner."

"Ah," he nodded in understanding. "You're too good to me. I give you permission to go easy on the red peppers over the next forty years."

"Like I could convince you that *you* told me this."

He shrugged. "You can try." His eyes motioned to her reader. "Going to yell at me about something?"

"I just did. Not yell really, I'm just seeing how much of this book is us. It's funny more of us wasn't in the first one."

"The first one was almost done when we met. The only addition was Deidre. The time traveling added what the story was initially missing."

"I suppose you're right."

"Oh, say that again. I think that makes it twice for our entire marriage."

"Stop it, Dusty. You're making it very hard to make you want to go away."

"You want me to go away?"

"Yes. It scares me when you show up. Like you're going to whisk me away again. Or yourself. Is something else wrong now?"

"No, my sweet. It's just funny, that's all."

"What's funny?"

"I know how this all works." He motioned between them. "You went back and changed the details of when we got together. Even caused you to relive a few keys years of your life somehow. I went back and did kind of the same thing when I saved Courtney. Now…"

Katie bolted up and stood in front of him. "Dammit! Don't do this to me! What? What have you done now?"

"Whoa, cupcake." He led Kaitlyn to the couch and sat down with her. "Everything is fine. Beyond peachy."

Her eyebrows scrunched. "Since when do you say peachy?"

"I don't know," he said with a slight shrug. "It just came to me. Anyway, when I came here yesterday and told you about our situation, I guess I wasn't thinking about the effect it would have on us now. In my time. I thought we were done with changing our history. Guess I was wrong."

Katie was certain if she were a Terian, she would be turning magenta. The desire to faint hit her hard. She hadn't fainted since the first time she met Dusty. Dusty had to have noticed.

"I'm sorry. I don't want to scare you. It's not bad news."

Dropping her head to her knees, Katie mumbled into her legs. "Then why do I want to vomit? You're scaring the shit out of me, Dusty."

"I'm sorry, babe." He stroked her back. "I can't tell you what it is, but I just had to come back and tell you how much I love you."

She turned sideways just enough to be able to look at him. "Is this going to be a normal occurrence from now on?"

Shaking his head, Dusty said, "No. It's not like I have an unlimited chance to do this. Things were just still open from yesterday, so I popped back over."

"Wait. There's like some portal or something you just zip through when you want?"

He grinned. "My sweet, Aiden isn't there, tugging me around the universe. I really can't explain this to you. You'll tell me, I'll use it, and cheat in my book."

Motioning to the watch on his wrist, she scoffed. "Liar. You did want one."

Grinning again, he covered it with his sleeve. "Retirement gift."

"What the fuck are you doing here?"

Both Katie and the seventy year-old Dusty's heads whipped over to the stairs. Dusty was coming down them two at a time. Katie stood in front of Frank/Dusty protectively.

She blurted out, "Don't you dare touch yourself!" It couldn't be helped. The three of them burst into laughter.

"Sounds like something you'll be saying to Alex soon, honey buns," seventy year-old Dusty said.

Young Dusty frowned. "Good lord. Is that how stupid I sound?"

"Worse," Katie and older Dusty said in unison.

"Get out," Dusty pointed to the door. "However it is you…I show up, get out. No one is going anywhere. I won't have it."

Frank/Dusty held up his hand. "No problem, young feller. I was just on my way out." He dared give Katie a lingering kiss on her cheek. “All’s well, my sweet. Just keep doing what you’re doing. I’ll see you again in forty years or so.”

“Kiss my wife again and I’ll deck you.”

“I’d like to see you try, Andrews.”

Katie sped over to her husband and wrapped her arms around his waist until she heard the door shut.

“You weren’t telling me anything or about to send me anywhere. I really don’t know why you were here. I’m kind of confused.”

Dusty ran his hand down his face. “Do you have any idea what this is like? Seeing yourself that old and wanting to kick the crap out of yourself to boot?”

Katie gave a slight laugh. “I’m happy to say no. It’s kind of funny that you get so jealous over yourself. I could have banged him and had a free pass. He’s you, you big dummy.”

“You’d bang seventy year-old me?”

“Depends.”

“On what?”

“How much money do you think we have in forty years?” She could barely say it with a straight face. They both burst into laughter.

“I remember getting pissed off before when you slept with a different me. It’s me, but I’d still get upset. Sue me.” He swayed with her hip to hip for a while. “I just don’t get any man that could cheat on his wife. If I live as long as a Terian, my eyes will never stray, my love.”

“Unless seventy year-old me shows up?”

“You’d still turn me on.” He kissed the top of her head. “Can I drag you back to bed now? Bed-bed, not sex. I just miss you when you’re not next to me. If you say no, I’ll never start book number four.”

“Don’t you dare threaten me with that,” she said as she tugged him toward the stairs.

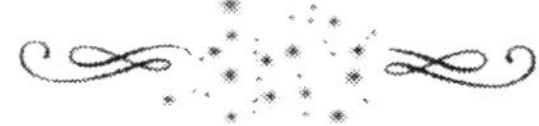

As Jody keyed away at the pad to open the pod's door, Vick picked up Aiden.

"Are you ready to explain him to your crew, Captain?" she asked.

"I find the truth works best. I can't command respect from them if I'm proven a liar myself. There's no way I'd try to hide him." He tapped at Aiden's device. "Change your eyes back, pal. There's no shame here in showing who you really are."

Victor watched Jody's expression as Aiden's eyes went from brown to one blue and one green.

She turned to him wide-eyed. "His mother was a slave?"

The door opened and they stepped onto the ship. Vick wanted to head to his cabin and get Aiden fed and settled in before he called a meeting with his bridge crew.

"*Was* being the key word. And you don't know that. You know how their system works. It doesn't matter who his mother was, his own eyes that would determine his place on Athracki. We need to cover this later, okay?" His head motioned only slightly to Aiden. She understood and nodded. "And the term is just honey, by the way."

"What term?"

"You said 'honey bee' to him. It's just honey."

Again a slight tint of red came over her. He was an ass for forgetting how much she hated being corrected. "You humans and your craving for sweet things and the need to call each other as such. That and helpless infants. Baby? Who would call someone such things?"

He couldn't help his smirk. "I'll try to find something you like."

"I thought at the moment, you liked Lieutenant."

"We're not done talking."

Jody's communicator went off. Xolo's voice boomed over it. "You're back already, Lieutenant?"

She quickly pulled it off her belt. "Uh, yes. Sorry. Things happened a little faster than I anticipated. There was no time to—"

Vick took it from her hands. “I’ll be up shortly to explain, Xolo.”

There was silence for a minute. “Captain? I thought you were in—”

He cut his first-in-command off. “I’ll be up shortly and explain. Captain out.”

His gaze met Jody’s. “This is going to be difficult.”

“That is the most sense you’ve made all day.”

Wanting to include his son in the conversation, he set him down. “How do you like the ship so far, bud?”

“This is really awesome. I’ve never been on a ship this big before.”

“Even with that device you have there?” Vick motioned to his wrist.

“I was never allowed to use it to do the things I wanted.”

Vick stopped dead in his tracks. “Buddy…you made an entire ship transport. You’ve never done that before?”

“No, but I knew how. It was just a pod. Uncle Frank had been teaching me.”

“Uncle Frank? Who is this Uncle Frank?”

“He was a friend of Mommy’s.”

Skinnard wanted to know more, but he didn’t want to press his son right now out in the hall. They’d reached his cabin after a few moments. “This is it, pal.” Hey keyed his passcode and walked them in. “This is going to be home for a while. I hope you like it.”

Aiden darted around, checking every nook and cranny. “It’s pretty cool.” He walked back over and wrapped his arms around his father’s thigh. “Thanks for bringing me here.”

“Hey.” He bent down. “I’m your dad. We’re a team now. Got it?” He tapped at his son’s chin.

Aiden nodded then turned to Jody. “Is there food here?”

After glancing at Vick she said, “If I know your dad, probably not. I’ll take you to the cafeteria, kid. Your dad has some explaining to do to his crew. He’s in charge around here, you know.”

"He is?" Aiden beamed with pride.

"Yes, he is. He loved you enough to disappear on us. Now he has to catch everyone up on why." She extended her hand. "Come on. We'll go find you something that you like."

To say Vick was surprised at how Jody was acting would have been an understatement. He was still sure she was angry enough to take a knife to his throat given the chance, but apparently somewhere deep down in one of her Terian hearts, she liked the kid. Vick gave his son's shoulder a squeeze.

"You mind going with her, buddy? I won't be long."

"If you kissed her, I know you like her and she must be okay."

"Um…that has to be our secret all right?"

"Why?"

Jody bent down. "We want it to be a surprise. Can you help us with that? It's a pretty important job."

"I can keep good secrets. I had to all the time with Mommy and Uncle Frank."

"I knew you could. You're such a big boy." She stood. "I'll give you a second to say good bye to your dad then we'll go find you some food."

As soon as the door clicked behind her, Vick stood and brought his son to his chest. "You are such a big, brave boy. We've hardly had time to get to know each other. I'm sorry I have to leave you already."

"That's okay. I like Jody." He wrapped his arms around Vick's neck. "Can I call you Daddy?"

"Of course you can, buddy. Is there something special you want me to call you?"

"No. I like all the names you have for me. You can call me anything you want. Even those sugar names Jody said."

Chuckling, Vick said, "Okay. Run along now. I'll see you soon."

Chapter Eight

"You brought what onto the ship?" Captain Skinnard's first mate said.

"You heard correctly. My son."

"Your Athrackian son?" he said again, as if there was no way he was hearing it correctly.

Vick held his hands up. "Look, Xolo, I don't need the lecture of how this is no place for a kid. I don't have a choice right now. It was sort of sprung on me, too."

"Besides that," he said, stopping the captain. "Lieutenant Opex wasn't gone long enough to go anywhere to get you. I would have known if there were a ship in the area. You mind explaining that?"

"When I can, I will."

"You risked sending her out through this blanket of debris and return with a child? Dammit, Skinnard. Have you lost your mind?"

"Look, I'll take this crap from you now, but I won't have you talking to me like this when the rest of the bridge crew gets here. I'll wipe your Forengi ass all over the place if you don't put a lid on it."

"Vick, come on. You know better than that; we've been friends too long. I just…a little heads up on the kid would have been nice."

"Trust me, I had no warning myself."

Xolo snapped his fingers. "Wait a second! Deidre? You knocked up Deidre?"

"Fuck if your mind isn't like a damn steel trap. You walk in on me one time…"

"Two times. You can't tell me I have free reign of your Terian ale, give me your passcode, and not expect me to use it."

Vick had to explain Deidre to Xolo after that night, but he hadn't told him the whole story. He explained she was a runaway, but that was all. The ship docked for supplies a few days later and he'd lied about her leaving the ship at that time.

"So what happened? How does she even still have her kid? Unless he's a slave, too. But wouldn't he still have been passed on to his proper place in their society? Mothers almost never keep their own children."

"Yes, his eyes are same as hers and hello… Don't you keep up? There's no more slavery on Athracki."

Xolo rubbed his chin. "Yeah, guess I know that. You still think he would have been taken somewhere else. What if his eyes had been purple?"

"We didn't have time for any details, but I can assure you she most certainly didn't have him on her home planet."

He stared hard at Vick. "That hasn't mattered with their history."

"Apparently she got very good at hiding."

"You sure you're the father? I mean, can they even reproduce with humans? I've never heard of it."

"He's got brown flecks in his eyes like I've never seen in an Athrackian. Kinda looks like me now that you ask. But besides that, Deidre was a whack-job toward the end, but I trust her. The kid is mine. There's no reason to believe that we wouldn't be compatible reproduction-wise. Humans disgust them as a general rule, so maybe it's never come up."

He nodded in agreement at Vick's comment. "So what happened? Why do you have him?"

"She was murdered."

"Murdered? You know by whom?"

"No clue. But I have a feeling I need to find the answer to that. I'm afraid they'll come looking for Aiden."

"He's named after your dad?"

"That's what you take from this conversation? Xolo…someone could come after my son."

He motioned out the viewing window. "Not in that nebula they won't."

"You know, you're a pain in my ass, but maybe you have a point."

Xolo's expression became more serious. "Are you finally ready to go in?"

Although he was still dragging his feet, Vick said, "Why not? I believe it's safe. All the readings say so. I'll admit I hesitated a little at this debris field, but I'm ready if you are."

Now Xolo grinned. "I was born ready. Let's do this."

"I'm glad you're on board, but I honestly wouldn't have appointed you my second in command if I didn't think you were a little on the crazy side."

Abruptly switching subjects, Xolo said, "What's Jody say about the kid?"

"Jody?" That took Vick off guard. "Why do you ask about Jody?"

"Please. I wish you two would just bang and get it over with already."

Vick's expression must have given him away. Xolo leaned against the table and crossed his arms over his chest. "You did. When?"

"Hey, don't ask me to say anything. She'll serve my dick on toast."

He grinned. "You prick. When things are settled, I want details."

"She's with Aiden now. He likes her and unless I've lost my ability to read her colors, she likes him. We're not designing wedding invitations, I can guarantee you that. Can we stop this, please? I can only handle one thing at a time."

"Fine. I'll quit busting your balls. I got your back with the rest of the crew. Their job is to do as they are told, and not ask questions, although you are relying on that a little heavily here. You just let me know when I can be of help regarding his mother. I can do some digging when you're ready. I still have a connection or two at Lawton-8. You want me to contact him now to listen to chatter?"

"I'm not sure what you'll get from the Eighth Quadrant's legal star, but I guess nothing can hurt. If you let wind of this get to my dad…"

"I know. My ass will make a nice side dish to go with your dick. I'll keep it on the down-low. Can I let everyone else in here now?"

"Yeah. Better get this over with. I need to get back to the kid."

The meeting with the rest of the bridge crew went well over an hour. Vick explained Aiden's presence on board and his current stand on when to enter the nebula. He left them with the question of "when and how" Aiden got here, but they let it go at the excitement of finally moving forward.

With that done, he headed back to his cabin in search of Jody and Aiden. When he found her asleep on the couch with him on her chest, he stopped dead in his tracks. He couldn't help staring at them. Never in a hundred years would he have imagined his communications officer to be like this with any child.

It was as if she'd felt his eyes on her. Her eyes opened and met his. Instead of squinting and burning with anger, she smiled at him with that practiced smile of hers.

"He asked me to sit with him. Poor kid is really missing his mother," she whispered as she sat up carefully, trying to jostle him as little as possible.

Vick took his son from her with less grace. He quickly discovered Aiden could probably sleep through the ship being hit by an asteroid. Laughing softly he said, "I'll go lay him down in the room."

When he came back out, Jody was drinking his Terian ale. She offered him one.

"I hope you don't mind. I believe I've earned this."

"You've more than earned it. Thanks for the help with him. I'll try to come up with a more permanent solution. Xolo is on board with this but I can't abandon the bridge all together tomorrow."

She sat back on the couch. "So…your first in command isn't planning a mutiny?"

Vick grinned. "No."

"What's that grin for?"

"I could tell you…but then you'd kill me."

She turned a deep red before she said, "You told him about us?"

Rushing to her side, he said, "No. I swear I didn't. He knew though. I made him drop it. I'm sorry."

Throwing her head back, she let out an odd call. He'd heard it from her before. He imagined it was a sound her race emitted in their ancient days, just before a kill. Seeing as how he was screwed anyway, when she came back up, he kissed her. Not giving her the chance to push him away, he blindly placed both of their beers on the table beside the couch and pulled her closer to him. Her arms went around his neck and she returned the kisses. Not expecting her to let him, he'd almost gotten lost in the action. His hands were stroking her sides when he finally pulled away.

"Damn."

"Damn what?" she asked. Her expression was truly surprise that he'd stopped.

"I'm not sure I could explain us being naked to the kid if he walked out here."

Once again her head leaned back against the couch. This time it was more disappointment than anger.

"I've only been placed by you once, and already there are stipulations."

"Laid, my sweet, not placed. And I wouldn't call it that."

"Why not?"

"Because that sounds cheap. You're not just a lay to me. I need to know that we are on the same page here. I know you think I'm not right for you, but that's not true."

"Skinnard…I wanted to bitch you out, then we ended up in bed. I wake up alone and get zapped into your presence with you and your teleporting Athrackian son."

"What bothers you more? The fact that I have a son or the fact that he teleports?"

"I don't even know where to begin with this."

"I know this is a lot to deal with but we've fought this for so long. Teleporting son aside, can't we just see where it's going?"

"You're amazing. You know that, right?"

He smiled and stroked her cheek. "I know. Or so you said in the throes of passion. It's a good thing I don't have neighbors."

She shoved his hand away. "Not that, you gnat."

"Nit."

"Whatever! I'm not talking about sex. You have no idea what your boy is capable of or who killed his mother, but all you can think about is bragging to Lieutenant Gatron that you're…hammering me. Screwing me. Whatever."

"Technically, they are both right. You could throw in drilling, too. Nailed as well. Until just now, I didn't realize there were so many earth terms for making love that involved construction."

"Making love?" Her eyes widened.

He slid closer and grasped her by her waist. "Yes, Lieutenant. Making love. No more games. Aiden saw us kiss. I need him to know how important you are to me. That as his father, I won't be traipsing woman after woman in here who will walk in and out of his life. It's going to be hard on him, having just lost his mother. It would be nice if you were here for him, too."

Beaming so red she could have flagged down a passing ship, Jody shot to her feet. "We've been together once. Now you want me to step up and be his mother? Just like that? What the fucker is wrong with you?"

Not daring to correct her grammar, he stood and clasped her hands. "Whoa. Wait a minute. You took that wrong. That's not what I meant."

"How am I supposed to take that? One minute you stop sex, the next you're spouting how I need to be the woman presence in your son's life."

"That just got jumbled up. That's not what I meant."

She shook free of his hold. "Goldstein taught me some of your English, too. You can kiss my Terian ass, you schmuck."

Shaking Dusty, Katie said, "Does Goldstein know you used his name in a book?"

Laughing as he rubbed at his eyes, Dusty said, "Yeah. I don't have many Jewish friends. He was tickled. I said I'd put him in the credits."

"Calls you a schmuck often, does he?"

"Often enough." Pulling her onto his chest with a grunt, Dusty asked, "What time is it?"

"Six-thirty."

"Geez, Woman. What time did you get up?"

"Five. I couldn't sleep. I wanted to read some more."

He gave her a gentle kiss. "I'd say I'm sorry, but I'd be lying. I hope the book is that good and it's not just my adoring wife, trying to be kind to the shitty writer."

"Puh-lease, Dusty. I don't recall you ever being insecure about your writing."

"Maybe. But you never know. You know how more often than not, a series goes downhill after everyone falls in love with the first one."

"That's not true for you. You know I love your work, but honestly, I think each one gets better, not the other way around."

"Baby, if you're trying to give me morning wood, it's working."

"Best cool off there, big guy. The kids will be up any minute. I hope you haven't forgotten that they're all yours today."

"I didn't forget. Alex will have to hang with me for a little bit after I get Ali dropped off but he'll be fine. I already okayed it with the daycare at work. Lindsay is excited to see him again. I kinda got yelled at for not bringing him by sooner."

"She's so sweet. I'll have to make a point to visit her with him again soon."

"Do that. She actually got overly weepy about it if you ask me."

"Overly weepy? What do you mean?"

"You'll smack me, but I don't know how else to put it. She went…hysterical bitch on me."

As predicted, Katie smacked his arm gently. "You know I hate that."

"It's true though, babe. She's been really moody lately. I've been going out of my way to be nice. I brought her coffee one morning and she about bit my face off, saying how she couldn't have caffeine anymore."

"Why couldn't she…wait, is she pregnant?"

"Not that she's show—" Dusty snapped his fingers. "Holy shit. I think you're right."

Katie crossed her arms. "You are so transparent. You just realized her boobs are bigger. Am I right?"

Dusty's grin gave it away. "It's not like I'm looking. I'm not about to say, 'Hey, Lindsay. How about I give you a raise and you go buy yourself some blouses that fit.'" He paused for a minute, taking in her expression. "Don't look at me in that tone of voice."

"Do you even hear yourself sometimes?"

"I'm serious. I've never noticed her boobs until recently. They weren't there, then they were. I didn't even think about her having enhancement surgery. Only your nagging is making me ponder it."

"Nagging?" Katie gave him a gentle shove.

"The only boobs I'm interested in are yours. You know that." He paused for a minute. "Well, shit. Do you think I should ask her if she's pregnant?"

"Do you want to get slapped for real? You know better than that. If she's not and has just put on a few pounds, she'll kill you."

"Maybe she's on some meds and gained a little weight and can't have caffeine? Who knows? This isn't any of our business. I'm just happy I was able to make her smile with the news of Alex coming in."

"He's been asking to go to the zoo. I was hoping you'd get a nice day in with him not just abuse your daycare at work."

"We can go on another day. All of us. You know how it is with my deadlines this time of the year."

The conversation was interrupted by a bunny being flopped onto Katie's back. "Scoot over, Mommy. I want to squish Daddy, too."

With his free arm, Dusty helped his daughter onto the bed. "I'll take a squishing from you any time, mini-cupcake."

Chapter Nine

After three hours of going from the waiting room, the doctor's office, and to the lab and back again, Katie was ready for a few beers with Courtney, whether her pregnant friend could join her in having them or not. Even though she knew what the results were going to be, a long session of tears followed the news. Knowing test results in advance is one thing, but actually hearing it come from a doctor was another thing altogether.

She swung by a liquor store for a mixed case of her and Dusty's favorite beer, and then headed to Dusty's workplace to get Alex. She popped into his office first.

He looked up from his desk and took in her expression. He immediately went over to her and held her in a tight embrace. "I can tell by your face how things went. I'm sorry, baby."

"I knew what he was going to say, but it still stung." The last few words were cracking as she fought tears.

"Shhh. We already have a plan B and are ahead of the game. You okay? You want me to take off?"

She stepped out of his hold. "I'm okay. I'm going to get drunk with Courtney. Well, I'll get drunk, she can watch the kids."

"I'll leave early enough to get the grill going. Sound good?"

She shrugged. "Sure. See you then." After turning to leave, she spun back around to give him a quick kiss goodbye. "I'm really okay."

"No you're not." He held her chin with his forefinger. "I love you."

"I know. I love you, too. See you at home, Captain."

He gave her a playful swat on the behind as she walked out.

Once Katie stepped into the daycare, she noticed right away that Lindsay not only looked heaver, she looked pregnant without a doubt. *How could men be so oblivious?* Lindsay's eyes lit up at the sight of Katie and she rushed right over, giving her a tight hug.

"It's so good to see you!" Lindsay said, sounding like she was fighting tears.

"You too. I'm glad I needed your help with Alex today. I should have stopped by sooner. I'm sorry. I've missed you."

"Don't be silly. We all get busy." She looked down and rubbed her belly. "I'm sure Dusty said something. I was just having a bad day. You know how the hormones can be."

"All too well," Katie replied. She wasn't about to get weepy about how she'll never be able to feel that again. "I'm a little mad Dusty didn't tell me sooner. I'm so happy for you."

"I haven't told anyone, Katie. In all honesty, I've been hiding it. I just sort of popped out the past few days. Either no one notices or is afraid I'm just getting fat and they're afraid to say anything."

Katie couldn't help her laugh. "That pretty much summed up our conversation this morning." She immediately felt bad insinuating that they talked about her. Placing her hand on Lindsay's arm, she explained. "Dusty did mention he'd upset you a bit ago. He was worried about you."

"Yeah…that was a bad day. I tried to apologize."

"Don't worry about it. You know Dusty."

"I do. He had Alex give me flowers this morning. He's really trying to cover his ass." She laughed as she motioned to the beautiful bouquet of colored daisies.

Katie smiled. She sure had a keeper. "Hold on a second. Why are you hiding the pregnancy? Aren't you happy?"

Lindsay tugged Katie away from the door and into the corner of the daycare. Alex had yet to spot her, she was grateful.

"I guess I'd be happier if I *tried* to be in the family way."

"Sweetie, not many of us can truly decide when we want to have our babies. It all works out. I never dreamed I'd have mine so close, but it works. You'll be okay."

"No, Katie. I'm not with anyone. I know it'll sound terrible, but this couldn't be more of an accident. I barely get by as it is. I can't handle a baby."

"Not with anyone? You weren't…you know…were you?" Katie couldn't even bring herself to say 'raped.'

"I wasn't raped, just drunk and stupid."

"Does the father know?"

"No. Definitely no. If I could even find him again, I certainly wouldn't tell him."

"Find him again? What do you mean?" Katie checked to make sure Alex was still occupied. This was one conversation she needed to finish. The other daycare attendant was doing a great job of keeping all the kids busy. Returning her attention to Lindsay, she found her eyes pooled with tears.

"I was stupid, okay? Just drunk and stupid. He was hot, I was horny. The fancy car we left in had Ohio plates. He was just passing through town and had a hotel room at the Embassy Suites."

"I'm sure you can trace him from that."

"No, Katie. I don't remember the room number and I don't want to do that."

"Why not? Maybe he wants to know."

"Trust me. He was the hottest, most sought after dude in the bar. He's a player. There's no way he wants a kid in tow."

Katie gave her hand a gentle squeeze. "I wish you had called me sooner. This is a hell of a burden to take on alone."

"I didn't know what to say. Saying it out loud now…I sound terrible."

"No you don't. You sound scared. You have any plans at all? Don't you have family who can help?"

"I can't tell my parents. Dad would kill me. Mom would light candles for the next ten years for my sins."

"Catholic?"

"Hell yeah. Very old school. They'd never forgive me."

"But a grandbaby—"

"Trust me. It wouldn't matter. I'm glad they're states away. I can claim busy enough to fudge a few months of not visiting them. I was just there, preparing for this."

"So you've decided then. You're going to put the baby up for adoption?"

"I didn't want to put it in words yet. But I guess that's what I'm saying." She leaned into Katie, Katie's arms wrapped around her tight.

Katie left Dusty's office building in an even worse mood than when she'd arrived. She ached for the young girl she'd befriended just a few years ago. They didn't need to use daycare much, but knowing the kids were in such good hands make it easier on her. Holding onto her son a little too tightly before buckling him in brought a slight protest.

"You're squishing me, Mommy."

"I'm your mother, I'm entitled. You're only going to be little once, you know. I have to get my squeezes in where I can."

"You're silly."

Courtney had sent a text that she was getting Ali again so Katie headed straight home. Immediately after pulling up, Katie was confused by a constant barking coming from her back yard.

"If your daddy brought home a puppy, he's in big trouble."

"A puppy! Cool!" Alex took off running for the back gate.

When Katie finally caught up, she was surprised to find Courtney there with Alyson and a Dalmatian puppy about four months old.

"What's with the puppy?" she asked her best friend. "I thought Dean didn't want a dog."

"I didn't do it on purpose. He claims he's allergic, but I think he's full of shit."

"Auntie Courtney!" Ali reprimanded.

"Sorry, honey." She turned to Katie again. "I found it on the road. Poor thing would have been hit. I called the humane society, but so far no one has reported a missing Dalmatian."

Together they watched as the dog wandered around the yard, sniffing everything. It barked at a passing bird and ran after it but ignored Courtney's pleas to stop.

"Damn thing doesn't listen for shit either." She promptly covered her mouth. The kids were busy running after the puppy; there was no reprimand.

"It's probably deaf," Katie said.

"Deaf? How can you tell that already?"

"Are her eyes blue?"

"Damn, girl. What are you? Super vet? I didn't even bother to check the sex on the thing."

"There's a pretty easy visual check for that kind of thing. Even from this distance."

Courtney laughed. "I did notice her eyes. Yes, they are blue."

"Then she has a double whammy. White coat and blue eyes. She probably got dumped for being unruly. The breeders who sold her probably never explained the chance she was deaf. Or they dumped her because very few people would take that on."

"That's so sad."

"It's the worst part of my job. Trying to convince breeders when not to breed. Don't even start me on hip dysplasia."

As if just noticing Katie, the puppy came running over to her. She jumped up and pawed at her legs. Katie bent down. "Hi, honey. You poor thin—"

"What is it?" Courtney asked.

"She has one blue and one green eye."

"Really? Guess I only caught a glimpse of one." She bent down. "Hey, that's pretty cool."

"Freaky is what it is. Dusty has a race of characters in his books like that."

"There's more like Deidre in the new one? Sweet! I can't wait to read it. Well, there you go. She's meant to be yours and even has a name."

"Not so fast there, Court."

"Would she still be deaf? Would the green eye help?"

"Let's see. Hold her still for a second." Courtney held her facing the fence as Katie removed her keys from her purse and shook them behind the dog. The keys let out an obnoxious jingle but the dog never budged. "Deaf as a doornail," Katie proclaimed before the puppy took off running again.

"Wow, vet. That's a pretty high tech device you got there."

She shrugged. "Sometimes simple works. That'll be eighty-five dollars please."

Courtney laughed and gave her a nudge with her shoulder. "Hey! How did your appointment go?"

Katie's hands covered her stomach. "Barren as…one of those really barren things." Her arms dropped. "Where's my wonderful-with-words hubby when I need him?"

"Aw, hon." Courtney gave her a strong hug. "I'm so sorry." After letting go she said, "But don't let it kill you. You have a wonderful family. I know it's not what you wanted to hear, but at least you have these guys."

"I know. It would be harder not having any at all. It's easier to convince the brain than it is the heart right now." Her eyes lowered to Courtney's belly. "Can I?"

"Of course!"

Katie placed her hand flat on her friend's stomach, and then added the second. "God I'm going to miss peeing every five minutes, fits of hormones, and wanting blue cheese on everything."

Courtney placed her hands on Katie's. "If I could give them to you for even just five minutes, I would."

That made Katie smile. "I was going to have a beer, but I guess I'm running for puppy food."

"I already called Dean. He's grabbing some on his way home. So, you're going to keep her?"

"I didn't say that, but I'm not going to let the poor thing starve."

Dusty was having too much fun with the puppy for Katie to tell him no. The kids had already been wearing her down, but his expressions and pleading were all she could take. It could have been the beer talking, but she finally said, "Okay. If no one claims her, and if I don't find an ID chip, annnnd, if she doesn't terrorize Blue and Felecia, we can keep her." After a hug that took her off her feet she said, "A deaf dog is more work. All of you will have to be diligent about training her."

"I'll print up stuff tonight, babe," Dusty said. "I'll take charge of teaching the kids her sign language or whatever. It'll be good discipline for them, too."

"You are on your best behavior aren't you?"

"Whatever do you mean, sweets?"

She gave him a shove and headed over to Courtney. "I ought to hurt you."

"Come on. You wouldn't have left her, either. Helloooo. I know how you ended up with both of your cats."

Katie grinned. Courtney only knew part of it. Both of those cats played a big part of her and Dusty's time-traveling escapades. They were both rescues as well. The more she thought about it, the more she thought Deidre would be an excellent fit to the family. Crap. She just thought of it by her name. Yup, she was hooked.

Chapter Ten

"So, can't we ask her if we can adopt her baby?" Dusty asked that night in bed after Katie explained about Lindsay.

"Are you insane? You have any idea how that would sound?"

"Why is that crazy? She likes us."

"Dusty…this is a very hard decision for a woman to make. How do you think she'd feel if you dropped our adopted baby – her baby – to her at the daycare?"

"I guess I didn't think about that. It just made sense. Her kid needs a home and we're dying to give a kid a good home."

"Please, don't you dare mention anything about us wanting to adopt a child. That would place a terrible elephant in the room every time you see her."

"All right. I may be the writer in the house, but you've got that female brain that makes sense of things, I suppose." Katie hiccupped, Dusty laughed. "One too many?"

"I'm entitled."

"Yes, yes you are. It's been a big day for you. Can I thank you again for the puppy?"

"You can thank me by being the one to get up at two a.m. when she wants out."

"I promise."

She knew he meant it, but one beer too many or not, Dusty still slept through the puppy's whining. Katie got up and hustled to the laundry room where they had her gated in, hoping to catch her in time.

"Hi, sweetheart. Gotta go potty?" A violent wag of her tail greeted Katie. "I'm talking to you and you can't hear a word." She reached over and picked up the puppy. Katie was thanked with non-stop kisses to her chin until she placed the dog in the backyard. Deidre relieved herself immediately, and then continued sniffing around.

"Don't bother looking for a chip. Deidre there doesn't have one."

Katie didn't jump at the familiar voice. How she could get used to this was beyond her.

"I thought you said it was a fluke that you were able to come back the other day."

"I might have lied."

"Is this going to be a nightly occurrence?" she asked as she dropped onto the glider in the yard.

"Not likely.

"Is there something I should know? Did I just mess something up, agreeing to this puppy?"

"Nope. You're right on track with her. And I'm right on track for getting yelled at for sleeping through letting her out."

“It’s not a big deal. If we had a baby…”

Frank/Dusty sat next to her and cupped her hand. “You’ll be fine, babycakes. Just wait and see.”

“Why do you keep coming back if everything is fine? Why don’t I come back and visit Dusty? Am I dead?”

He chuckled. “You’re not dead. Beyond that, I’m not saying anything. You know I can’t give anything away.”

“This is all so strange. It’s a bizarre coincidence for your book and this puppy with the eye thing. You sure you don’t tell yourself things?”

“You’re kidding, right? You see how I react at the sight of me.”

Katie’s hand went to her forehead. “Talking like this is making my head spin.”

“Don’t mean to, puddin’.” The puppy came running over and managed to get on the older Dusty’s lap in one leap. He was greeted with the chin kisses that Katie was.

“You won’t regret her. I promise. The kids love her and…”

“And what?”

“I’m not saying anything. I will tell you she’s smart. Being deaf is no handicap for our furry kid.”

Removing the puppy from his arms, she stood. “Well, thanks for that. You didn’t need to come here to convince me, though. I was already hooked.” She placed the puppy on the ground. She happily ran off to explore again.

“It wasn’t just that. I didn’t want you hurt tomorrow taking her in, checking for a chip.”

“Hurt? I got hurt?”

“Hey…you saved me from a broken leg once; I was just returning the favor. I convinced you to let us keep her. You know the guilt that brought me?”

“Dusty—”

A light coming on in the hall sent both their heads in that direction.

“And that’s my cue to leave. See ya, toots.”

He was out the side gate before Dusty opened the door. "Why didn't you wake me? I would have gotten up."

"It's okay. You know I can't sleep for shit when I drink, anyway."

"Did she wake you or you just get up to check?"

"She was whining to get out. I can't imagine someone going through the trouble to housebreak her to just dump her."

"People are strange creatures, babe. You know that. Shelters are full of purebreds as well as mutts."

"But just letting her fend for herself? She could've been hit."

Dusty shrugged. "Some people just don't care. Maybe she's not papered and just a really good knock-off."

Katie nudged into him. "You're terrible, but you could be right. Not that it gives them any more right to abandon her, but I see this a lot. Shelters are full, so people just abandon their animals." She watched the puppy running around. "I don't see a mix in her but I don't care enough to do a DNA test on her. I'll spay her in a month. Two tops."

"If you don't find a chip in her tomorrow and if no one claims her."

"Right." She couldn't tell him about Frank/Dusty visiting again. "I asked Karla to swing by with the wand. I don't need to put her through another car ride for that."

Dusty cupped her cheek in his hand. "Softie."

"This is it, Dustin Charles. You show up with a stray goat and we're having it for dinner."

He laughed hard. "This one wasn't my fault, it was Courtney's."

"Still." Katie called for the puppy, but caught herself. She walked over to where Deidre was sniffing and went toward her head, so she wouldn't startle her. Once the puppy looked up, Katie patted at her legs. The puppy ran over. "Come on, girl. Back to bed for everyone."

Knowing it was best to just let Jody cool down for a while, Vick didn't try to hunt her down the next day. There were too many other things that had to be taken care of right now. He felt like hell for having to leave Aiden alone again already, but it couldn't be helped.

There was no daycare in the plans for the ship since children weren't allowed on a research vessel, but men and women being what they are, there was an unofficial daycare improvised from an infirmary. It currently housed two children less than eight weeks old. The crew had been underway for eleven months.

"An all-time record," Vick had said when the two women approached him about their condition. "You going to give up the fathers or do I have to wait and pull DNA on the babies?"

"You can't seriously punish us for doing what comes naturally, Captain. We're beings, not robots."

"Right," Officer Rhodan said. "Besides, at the time, we'd been on auxiliary power for almost forty-eight hours. We were bored. Aren't there earth stories of cold winters, power outages, and baby booms?"

Victor held back a laugh. "A few stories come to mind, yes. But you're professionals. You know what is demanded of you physically on this ship. There are several precise ways to prevent this kind of thing."

"Sure, Dad," Officer Jameson said. "Not to be disrespectful, but that speech is a little late. What now? You dump us at the next passing ship?"

Vick shook his head. "No. You're both too valuable to me. You knew of the dangers we could possibly all be putting ourselves in when you signed up for this mission. Now you're willing to bring a new life into this mess. Do you realize what a burden the decision to keep you on board and keep moving is on me?"

"It's our decision, Captain," Officer Rhodan said. "Ours and that of the fathers. We don't want to jeopardize the mission and cause you to change course. We're prepared for any disciplinary action you will throw at us, but we want to see this mission through till the end."

"Would it help if I said we want to be married?" Jameson asked.

"No, it would not. This isn't an ethics issue. Lucky for you I have a self-imposed deadline and need to stay on course. We'll deal with this when the time comes. Now get out of my office."

He could hardly come down on them too hard. Not after what he'd done with Deidre on his first nebula adventure. You couldn't keep men and women from "playing nicely together," no matter what the species. It was just bad timing. By his quick calculations, the women would be giving birth when they were in approach of the nebula. Perfect.

Lenore, a charming Graneau, volunteered for the job of nanny. She was the eldest of the crew and worked in the galley. Her mood was always jolly, she was a little plump, and always trying to be "mom" of the crew, offering a shoulder or cookie, whenever either was needed.

Lenore had approached him when the ship gossip reached her about the pregnant mothers. She stated she was the likely candidate for the job of nanny since she was the easiest to do without.

"Anyone can cook and place dishes in the cleaning unit, Captain. If need be, I can help with prep and clean up after the babies are picked up. You know I'm best suited for the job. If one of the little darlings ever scooted off, who better than me to find them?"

He happily accepted her for the position and never regretted it. Not being much for babies, he didn't visit often. But as Captain, he did need to follow up at every station weekly at minimum. The children had grown on him and he found himself there more often. As infants, you couldn't tell the difference between the mixed half-human races.

"Oh, this little fella goes green when he's dropping a bomb. You best run if you see that tint coming," she'd reminded him more than once. "There no doubting he's half-Terian if you want to narrow down who the father is."

"Thanks, but I'm leaving that information in the hands of their mothers."

He smiled as he walked through the doors of the nursery with Aiden. Lenore dropped the blanket she was carrying. "Goodness me. Who's the little one?"

"Lenore, this is my son, Aiden."

"Your…Captain Skinnard…we're…we've never even docked…how—"

He held his hand up, stopping her stammering. "That's a very long story. I'll sum it up with the fact that we had a shortcut of sorts. Lieutenant Opex is great with the pod."

"But we're…" Catching herself from questioning her superior, she simply quieted down on her own. "I understand." She knelt in front of Aiden. "My you're a handsome devil."

"I'm not a devil, I'm Athrackian. Well, half Athrackian. You're a Graneau. I've met one before. He was really nice."

"I'm sure he thought the same of you, my dear."

Captain Skinnard sensed a hesitation in her when she made eye contact with his son, but she never skipped a beat.

"Are you going to hang out with me here? You'd be the life of the party. These two don't do much but eat, sleep, and poop."

"I'd like that, ma'am."

"None of that ma'am business. Call me Aunt Lenore, sweetheart."

Aiden looked up at Vick with tears in his eyes.

"What's the matter, son?"

"Mommy always called me sweetheart."

Vick bent down and picked up his son. "I'm sorry that I have work to do. If you need me, I will absolutely make arrangements. Do you want me to stay with you today?"

He shook his head. "I'm okay. She's nice."

"All right, buddy." He patted his son's back before putting him down. "I'll try not to be long."

Aiden wandered away to a row of books, Lenore approached the captain.

"Anything I need to know?"

"He watched his mother get murdered a few days ago."

Her hand covered her mouth in shock, and then was quickly dropped. "The poor dear. Are you sure he's okay?"

"I haven't had a lot of time to cover much. We'd only just met moments after the incident. He accepts that I'm his father and has been agreeable to being with me. He's shown no signs of distress or PTSD. Not yet anyway."

"I'll see if I can get him to open up. They are a very mature race, even at that young age. Is the little dear four?"

"Three."

"Three? My goodness." She squinted slightly. "You're sure he's yours?"

"Positive on that. I have to run. This won't be a problem, will it?"

"Not at all, Captain. I look forward to the company."

"Thanks. I'll see you in a few hours."

His walk to the bridge left his brain a horrible pile of mush, choosing between doing what was best for his son and what would horribly upset the crew. A few of them left families behind, hoping to be the one to write the next paper of their findings. It would be unfair to them to simply call off the mission, but he didn't see a way around it. He had already been having this argument with himself since the two women confronted him with their pregnancies. An exploration vessel is no place for children. Although Xolo had made a great point about the fact that they'd be hidden in the nebula from anyone that may be after Aiden, there were still risks. He couldn't chance anything happening to his son or the other children on board.

Chapter Eleven

Dusty carefully removed the e-reader from his wife's sleeping hands.

"Bored you to sleep, did I?" he whispered to himself. She must have read a bit after returning to bed. He'd woken up before the alarm and turned it off, hoping he could let Katie steal a few more minutes of sleep. Hearing the puppy whimper, he hustled out of the room and down the stairs.

He was greeted with an intense tail wagging he thought would fly the dog over the gate. Laughing, he bent down. "Easy, girl. I'll take you outside."

While he waited as the puppy ran around the yard, his daughter came up to him with her arms high, wanting to be picked up.

"Good morning, mini-muffin," he said with a few pats to her back.

"Mornin', Daddy."

"I'm glad you paid attention to the sock, sweetie. Mommy needs a few more minutes sleep."

Much to Katie's protest, Dusty had implemented putting a sock on the doorknob when one of them was sleeping in, taking a nap, not feeling well, or just needing to lie down for a moment to recharge.

"They're going to know what that means someday, Dusty," Katie had said.

"But we don't use it like we did in college. We're never in there together. It's just a good system."

She shook her head. "I think my first instinct was right. You aren't ever going to grow up, are you?"

"God, I hope not."

Ali squealed. No doubt she'd just spotted the puppy. "Forgot about her already, did you?" He laughed and placed her on the patio. She took off after it. "Don't forget she's deaf, baby doll. Let her see you so you don't scare her."

"Okay!"

Dusty turned around to his wife standing there holding their son.

"Buddy. What did I tell you about the sock?"

"I forgotted. I wanted Mommy."

"You forgot," he corrected.

"It's okay, hon. You were up same as me last night." Katie placed Alex down so he could run after the puppy and his sister.

"Let her see you coming," Dusty shouted after him. "Remember she can't hear you."

Giggles were the only response.

Wrapping an arm around Kaitlyn, Dusty gave her a tight squeeze. “Is this enough baby for you right now? Or do you want me to talk to Dean today? They want us over for a barbeque this afternoon.”

“Don’t delay, Dusty. Adoptions take freaking years.”

“Babe…you only swear when you’re stressing. Please don’t start already. We can do this. Who wouldn’t want to give us their baby?” He rocked hip to hip with her. “We’re the world’s greatest freaking people.”

“Time traveling lunatics are what we are. Between the two of us, we can barely piece together somewhat of a history. What if they ask us about when we met?”

“What about it?”

“Well, which version is it? Did you pick my drunken ass up after a baby shower in the cities at that Irish pub, or did we meet in college and I move in with you way too soon?”

“Technically they are both correct, but I think the college thing would go over better on an application, don’t you?”

“Wipe that grin off your face. This isn’t funny.”

“Please, buttercup—”

“Not in the ‘buttercup’ kinda mood here, Dustin Charles.”

“Gumdrop?”

She shoved at his chest. “Why the hell can’t I ever stay upset with you?”

“It’s a gift. Anyway, if you’ll feel better, we’ll sit down and come up with a history we agree on. We’re doing it anyway with Dean and Court.”

“We should stick to this then. You know they’ll probably interview our closest friends.”

“Okay, agreed. I’m sorry that I really don’t understand how things work. I don’t know why we have a few sets of memories. You’d think we’d be limited to our present timeline.”

“Maybe that’s the after effect of the nosebleeds and pain of the memory rushes.”

"Maybe. In any case, I'm happy for them. All of them. The only thing I hated was you scaring me to death in the hospital." He grinned and held her cheek, but tears filled her eyes. Once again he pulled her to him. "We'll get this figured out. You know we will. Didn't I tell you so? The old, jackass me?"

"You didn't tell me anything. You had that same damn shit-eating grin on that you always wear. I have no idea if that means we adopted twins or if I was going to walk into a massive fart."

He laughed hard enough that the kids came running over. "What's so funny, Daddy?" Ali asked.

"Your mommy is just funny sometimes, peanut. I'll go start breakfast. You go play with the puppy some more. I'll call you when it's time to come in."

Dusty kissed Katie's cheek then started to walk away. She grabbed his hand, stopping him.

"Talk to your dad, Dusty. I want more lawyer asshole than even Dean can be."

"Babe…no. I love you, but no."

"Why not? You know he'd make anything you want happen."

"No, he'd make anything *you* want happen."

"What's the difference? We both want it."

"Yes, but anything from him always has stipulations. You know the saying. All magic comes with a price."

Katie laughed. "This isn't movie quote time. It's not magic, it's favors."

"Exactly. I don't want to owe my dad any."

"Come on, Dusty. You hardly ever fight with your dad anymore. He's a wonderful grandfather."

Dusty closed the gap between them and took Katie's hands in his. "Please just trust me on this. If we hit a few walls with Dean, we'll give Dad a call. You know what Dean can do when he sets his mind to it. Give him a shot before you go selling your soul to the devil, babe."

"Your dad is not the devil."

"He's closer than I want to get."

"You're terrible. I hope you and Alex never fight like that."

"Not gonna happen. My little man already has me right where he wants me."

She glanced over, watching the kids run around after the puppy. "This is true."

He gave her cheek a lingering kiss. "Let me handle it for now. Please?"

"Okay. I'll try to be patient."

Dusty snapped his fingers. "Hey!"

"'Hey' what?"

"Did I bore you last night?"

"Bore me? Oh! The book? Not at all. I was just beat. I'll have to reread a page to get back in the swing of it."

"Looks like you dozed off when Aiden was getting dropped off at daycare."

"You know… Lenore sounds a lot like a Minnesotan to me. All she needs to do is make him a hot dish and bust out a 'yeah, sure, you betcha.'"

Dusty laughed. "I thought I toned that down a bit. I guess that is how I picture her. Maybe I should add that in there."

"How are you going to explain Captain Skinnard spending that much time in the Midwest?"

"Oh, your talented hubby can always come up with something." Dusty stepped back, staring away for a moment in deep thought. "Come to think of it, I don't think I ever gave him a home state."

"Now that you mention it, I don't think you have. When I'm done, I'll skim though the first book for you."

"That'd be great. I know I had an outline of sorts somewhere in college. Heaven knows where it is now." After stealing one last kiss he took off to make breakfast.

After getting the kids settled, Katie filled her plate and took a seat next to Courtney.

"Great night for a barbeque, Court."

"Don't weather talk me, hon. Spill it. Dean told me Dusty asked him about doing some adoption work for him."

"What else is there to spill? We want to get the ball rolling."

"Not that I'm against it, but why the rush? You haven't even looked into doing the fertility thing."

Katie had just taken a big bite of macaroni salad. She held her hand up, silently asking Courtney to hold on a second. "It's not a big rush. I know these things can take time. I just wanted to get the ball rolling."

"But you don't want to try anything else first?"

More than anything, Katie hated lying to her best friend. But there was just no way to explain the entire truth to her. "I'm sort of a special case when it comes to a messed up uterus, Court. I can try all the petri dish sex you want, it isn't going to get me a baby."

Courtney's hand rested on Katie's knee. "You sure?"

"Yes, I'm sure. I'm more than okay with this. Honest. I'm not going to go crazy and run off to some exotic country and buy someone's baby off the black market. I really don't have a preference on any race or country and despite how it sounds, we're not rushing, we just want to get this hell started."

"If you're going into it with the thought that it's hell, why put yourself through it? You have two great kids. You never even talked about wanting more."

Katie shrugged. "I can't explain it. When it hits you, it hits you. I love being a mom a hundred times more than I love being a vet."

"Well, I get that. I just don't want to see my best bud stressing."

"If your hubby does a decent job of it, I won't be." The friends shared a laugh and a shoulder bump before diving back into their plates.

"I'll see what I can do," Courtney said with a mouth full of fresh strawberries. "Did I tell you we did it in the car the other night?"

Her timing could have been better. Katie almost choked on a bite of her burger. "You didn't! Court!"

"We went back to that parking garage. You know, the first time we did it without a condom."

"The one for valet at Chez Pauls?"

"Yup. I don't know what it is. This fat belly really makes him crazy."

"Stop it. You've driven him nuts since the day you met."

"Yeah, yeah…I'm glad I pulled my head out of my ass with him."

Katie had to about bite her lip, knowing the part that Dusty played in making that happen. She'd have to get him to play something on the piano for her later. She was glad at least Alex really enjoys playing, too. He'd tried with Ali, but Katie could tell she mostly did it to please her daddy and isn't into it herself at all.

Remembering the song that sent Courtney running from the restaurant and Dean after her, Katie said, "Maybe I'll get Dusty to play Misty for you after we eat."

"Please. My hormones are out of whack as it is. I don't need a crying fit after a great night."

Katie smiled. "Okay. I'll get him to goof around with the kids with his Kermit impersonations instead."

"That would be better." After a moment Court said, "So…really? You're going to try for a Forengi or something?"

Katie grinned. "Wouldn't that be nice? But yeah, seriously. We want whoever needs us most."

"Or maybe a Terian," Courtney continued to tease. "I'd have to say having a niece or nephew that changes color with their temperament would be pretty cool."

"What was that about changing color with temperament?" Dusty said as he walked up. "Katie telling you about the mood ring I got her?"

"You got her a mood ring? What are you? Twelve?"

"Hell no. It's awesome, right babe?"

Katie knew where this was going and just played along. "Sure."

Dusty continued. "When she happy, it's as blue as a cloudless sky."

Dean came up from behind him and put Dusty in a headlock. "And when she's pissed, it leaves a red mark on your forehead. You need new material, jackass."

Chapter Twelve

"You're going to what?" Lieutenant Xolo Gatron shouted. "I did not just hear that!"

"I'm sorry. I know what we talked about, but I don't have a choice," Victor said.

"Bullshit!"

"Xolo…settle down and listen to me."

"No! I will not let you try to fill my head with any more of your shit. This is an exploration vessel. Every member on this crew knew the dangers when they signed up. In case you weren't aware of this, you have a reputation."

Skinnard grinned. "I'm aware of my—"

"Shut up. You're a hot head and frankly, a dumbass sometimes. And I say that with the most respect possible to my superior. You take unnecessary risks and make some calls that make me want to go slap your mother for not beating you more, but you get the job done. Everyone here would have given anything for the chance to work with you. Hell, some did give up everything. You can't just turn back and take this from them."

"Xolo, there are children on board."

"There have been children on board for the past two months. Their parents haven't changed their stand about being here. You know why? Because they trust and respect you. The only thing that has changed is that your son is on board now. Are you trying to tell me that your crew has more faith in you than you have in yourself?"

Victor sat down hard. It was a moment before he could process what his first-in-command had said. He didn't want to believe Xolo, but he knew he was scared for the first time in his life.

"That's not what this is about."

"Then what is it? We've been studying this nebula for over a year and up close for almost a month. You were determined to find us a way in, now you want to high-tail it out of here like a fucking coward."

"This isn't like the last two nebulas."

"Now I know you're smoking something. There is something different about every nebula or we would have stopped after the first one. You know we're ready for any and everything. It's what we do, Vick. Talk to me."

Vick rested his elbows on his thighs and lowered his head to his hands. "There was a hole…"

"A hole? What are you talking about?"

Suddenly angry, Victor stood, grasped Xolo's jumpsuit, and slammed him against the wall. "Where her fucking hearts should have been! I could see the damn swing set of the playground though her goddamn chest, Xolo! Aiden saw that.

Saw his mother murdered right in front of him!" As if he finally realized what he was doing, he let go of Xolo and took a few steps back.

Vick spoke calmly now. "I'm sorry. I truly am. Funky nebula aside, I'm worried for everyone's safety because of my son. *Because* of him, Xolo, not *only* him. Do you understand? What if she wasn't the only target? What if they want to kill him, too? I'm putting the entire crew at risk having him here."

Xolo led Vick back to a chair and sat him down, leaving a hand on Vick's shoulder.

"No more bullshit. Talk to me. What are you hiding?"

"Jesus, I don't even know where to start."

"Maybe by explaining to me if your son has the same powers as his mother."

Skinnard's head shot up. "You…you knew she time traveled?"

Xolo laughed so hard, he had to take a seat. "You know, you are by far the cheapest date I've ever had. You never could handle your Terian ale and Forengi scotch. Especially when you tried to make your earth version of an Irish Car Bomb."

"I told you about her?"

"Yeah, you told me. I didn't believe it until I caught her popping in one night. I had too many and crashed on your couch. She was surprised to see me and popped right back out. One night I said to you that I knew her secret and you blurted out time traveling. I thought she may have had teleporting abilities."

"But…but I never let you crash when we were together. She showed up every night."

"Yeah, this wasn't that long ago. I honestly didn't know how to bring it up. You didn't remember telling me and she was long gone, or so I thought."

"Wait a second. She tried to pop in on me? When?" He was now on his feet again, frantically pacing the meeting room."

"I dunno. Five months ago? Six? You think it's important?"

"She had to be trying to tell me something."

"With me there or not, you were in no shape to discuss anything that night."

"Crap, I remember. It was six months ago, you asshole. We just left Kilgore after getting Jody."

Xolo snapped his fingers. "That's right! She'd left in a huff and you went back for her. Now I get—"

Vick's hand went up, stifling him. "I went back for her because we needed her."

"Whatever. Can we try to stay on the same page here? Can he or can't he?"

Confused as he could ever be, Vick replied, "Can who what?"

"Can your son time travel? Is he like his mom or did he gets stuck with your unfortunate, sorry ass genes?"

"I don't know that telling you anything is a good idea. The less you know the better off you are."

"If I'm captured and tortured for information, maybe. If it concerns the members of this crew, then I need to know, Vick."

"He doesn't time travel."

Xolo breathed out heavily in obvious relief.

"He teleports within today."

Xolo had to take a seat.

Although Vick grew up hearing people saying how much they could accomplish with another set of arms, he really didn't notice Xolo being more productive than any other member of the crew. They had a task like everyone else and completed it in a timely fashion. Until now, his Forengi first mate's extra set of arms left him not so impressed. Vick watched Xolo steady himself, wipe the sweat from his brow, cover his mouth, and adjust his uniform all at once.

"That's how you got back so quickly," he finally said after a long moment.

Skinnard nodded his head. “Yes. He moved everything. The pod, us…it’s insane. I’ve never heard of such a thing. Have you?”

“Never. But then again I’ve never known anyone to time travel before, either. You sure attract some serious attention to yourself, Captain.”

Skinnard scooted closer. “The thing of it is, he has this device—“

“A device?”

“Yeah. Looks like an old watch. I haven’t spent enough time with the kid to know what it can do. I have no idea if the powers are all him or if it’s the device.”

“So get Jody to take a look at it. Anything electronic is right up her alley.”

“I’m already on thin ice with her.”

“This isn’t about you. I’d bet my fourth nut she’d love to get her hands on a strange device and figure out what makes it tick.”

Vick was shaking his head.

“What? You know that stuff turns her pink with excitement.”

“I know you’re right…it was your fourth nut comment. T—M—I, my friend.”

He grinned. “You have your sayings, we Forengi have ours. Can we get back to business?”

“For the first time in my life, I don’t know where to start.”

“Start by getting the bullshit notion that we’re not going into this nebula out of your head. I’m done watching it, taking samples, and plotting out a course. If you even so much as think it again, I’ll tie you up and send you off in the pod myself.”

“But—”

Xolo held up his hand. “No buts. I promise you I’ll declare a mutiny and have you removed as captain and go in that thing without you.” He stood and walked to the viewing window.

"Look at that thing, Vick. Tell me you can look at it and not want in. We've waited too long for this."

"You're not a father. You have no idea what I'm feeling. It was one thing risking my life, but now I'm responsible for another."

"You were always responsible for more lives. They may not be your blood, but the life of everyone on this ship is in your hands."

"I know that. This just somehow feels different."

"Would you sacrifice my life over Jody's?"

"Of course not."

"A human over a Graneau?"

"Stop being ridiculous."

Now with all four hands on the table in front of his captain, Xolo said, "No, you stop being ridiculous. I understand why you're beating yourself up over this, but I wouldn't be doing my job if I didn't tell you to pull your head out of your ass. You want this. The whole crew wants this. Parents of the two little ones in the nursery included. Take a few days with your son, Vick. Think this over. If you still want to turn back, then you're going alone in the pod. I'll take over and continue this mission."

"I'd sooner ram this ship up your asshole before I let you run it."

Xolo grinned. "Which one?"

Vick dropped his head to the table after pelting out a loud laugh. "Sometimes I really hate you."

"I mean it, Captain. For now, I say we keep this little discussion between the two of us. I'll stall with the crew. Take two days and think about this. I wouldn't mention it to anyone about your son's powers. That kind of info in the wrong hands…" He didn't even need to finish that sentence.

"Yeah, I know. I'd trust any member of this crew with my life but something like this…hell…the possibilities are endless. I'm not sure to what extent he understands what he can do. He was hungry and Bam! He moved us to the food."

"If it's the device that does this, there could be a number of people that would want their hands on it. If he alone operates it, I could see why someone would want him. If your concern boils down to his safety, then what better time than now to go in the nebula. Start thinking about it again as being the safe place for him, not a dangerous one. I'd bet even a Graneau couldn't track him through all that cosmic dust and gas."

Vick finally stood and went to the viewing window. "You do have a point. If all goes as planned, it is an excellent place to hide him."

"As planned? Since when do you have a plan?"

Again Vick laughed. "Okay, smartass. Point made already. I'll take your advice. Give me two days with the kid. Let me see if I can't get to the bottom of any of the scenarios running through my head. Above all, I want him to know he has some stability in having me for a dad."

"What kid wouldn't love the idea of traveling through space with his old man?"

"He's three, genius. He dreams of playgrounds and bedtime stories."

"He was raised Athrackian. Their sense of down-time is not the same. Slave-born or not, there's more to him than you know."

"Then it's time I find out." Vick gave his first mate a slap on the shoulder. "Don't do anything stupid while I'm away."

"Not a chance. That's your department." As Vick headed toward the door, Xolo stopped him. "Hey…you want to get me that device and I can run it by Jody if you're trying to avoid her?"

"Thanks, but no thanks. I'm not trying to avoid her, just trying to stay out of her way."

"There's a difference?"

"Yes. Besides, she knows about it. She was with me, remember? If I have you approach her with it, it'll really look like I'm trying to hide from her."

"Hell hath no fury and all that." Xolo chuckled.

"Yeah, that. I'll deal with her later. First things first. I need to spend time with my boy."

"I have things under control. You know where to find me when you're ready. And by that I mean no more than two days. Your crew is getting antsy, Skinnard. You promised we were going in."

"I got you loud and clear, you twelve toed bastard. You made some great points, now let me chew on it all. It's not going to be easy without a glass of ale to cry over."

"You out already?"

"I'm not going to drink in front of the kid."

"Then I'll be by to take it off your hands."

"You'll be prying it out of my cold, dead hands before that happens." He waved as the door slid open. "Catch you in two days, lieutenant."

Chapter Thirteen

"What are you doing here, beautiful?" Dean said after kissing Katie on the cheek. She'd popped by his office, needing to talk to him. "I didn't think you were leaving the house until you had the old man's book read."

"It's hard to keep my mind in the story with all that's running through my head." She dropped into a plush leather chair in front of his desk as he returned to his overpriced, high-back swiveling desk chair.

He sat back and quirked an eyebrow at her. "What's wrong?"

"This whole adoption thing."

"What about it? Court said you haven't even tried invitro or anything. You having second thoughts on that?"

She shook her head. "No. I know that will be a waste of time and money."

"So what is it? I'm barely through the first round of paperwork. You want me to pull the plug?"

"No! I don't want you to stop, Dean." Her voice was bordering on frantic; she could tell she'd started him. Dean got up again, hustled over to her, and squatted down.

"Whoa. You're a wreck. Settled down, Katie." He stroked her back for a moment. "You know I'll do everything I can. You guys are perfect candidates for adoptive parents. I don't see any reason you'll be rejected, it'll just be a waiting game. You know that all of this is mostly time and paperwork. It makes it easier since you're not waiting on a blue eyed, blonde baby girl or anything specific. You guys not being race specific doesn't surprise me at all. Also, being open to the baby not being a newborn helps, too. You have everything in your favor. I wish you'd relax and trust me."

"But this isn't your specialty."

"I've called in a few favors. I've got the best in the state working on it."

Katie took his hand in hers. "Should I talk to Dusty's dad?"

"Why? He's more into real estate and such. I'm not sure he could do more than what I am. He'd probably say to call my guy."

"Will we need more money? We do okay, but I know—"

Dean put his hand over her mouth. "Katie, stop. I know this whole 'lawyer soaking you for money' bit is a constant joke with Dust, but you know better than that. When I said I called in a favor, that's what I meant. You think I'd gouge you over something like this?"

"I'm sorry, Dean. That's not at all what I meant."

"Well, that's how it sounds. This isn't a cheap thing to do by any means, but it's not going to come from my fees."

Katie's lip began to tremble. The tears that she'd been fighting came flooding out. "I'm so sorry. I'm not trying to direct any of this to you. I promise. I don't doubt you, I just..." crying overtook any more words.

Dean held her tight and gently rocked with her. "Shhhh. We just started, sweetie. Don't go giving up already."

"Dusty told me everything ended up okay, but I still have so much anxiety about going through this."

He stepped back so he could look her in the eyes. "What do you mean he told you it ended up okay?"

Realizing she'd blown it, Katie tried to cover up her flub of saying out loud what the older Dusty had said to her. "I mean...you know Dusty. Always being so positive. He has tremendous faith in you, Dean. He knows it'll be fine and said so. That's all."

"You ever notice how much you two do that?"

"Do what?"

"Say shit like it's in the past tense then run around, talking in circles trying to cover it up. It's like you two are sci-fi characters in that damn book of Dust's. You're freaking time travelers or something, I swear."

Katie forced a laugh a little too hard. "Wouldn't that be great?"

Dean continued, shaking his finger. "If I believed in that shit, I'd ask you for lottery numbers. Even his grandpa—" He stopped talking suddenly, as if he'd screwed up. And he had.

"His grandpa? Dusty's grandpa?"

"Shit. I wasn't supposed to say anything."

"He visited you?" she shrieked. Dusty's grandfather wasn't alive. He could only be talking about Frank. Dusty. God she hated this whole mess.

"I can't get over how much that codger looks like him. You know? If you sat Dust down in one of those make-up artists chairs and told them to do their aging thing, that's what he'd have to look like."

Trying to get him off track, she asked, "Why was he here, Dean? When was he here?"

"It was just a friendly visit a day ago. He wanted to make sure I was on the right track with the adoption. I can't believe I've never met the guy before. I remember seeing him at the hospital when Court was in labor, but we were never introduced. Doesn't he come visit the kids?"

"We…uh…he's usually at his parents place when we go."

"Huh. Still, you'd think Dust would talk about him. I'd swear the codger died when we were in college."

Katie fumbled with a quick cover-up. "Maybe it the one on his mom's side. Anyway, I think things were rough with Dustin Senior and him like they were with Dusty and his father."

"Maybe. In any case, don't let him know I spilled the beans. Please? I think that old coot could kick my ass."

Katie laughed. "I won't say a word, I promise. I'm just upset that he's getting in the middle of this."

"He didn't do anything wrong or try to do anything illegal. I promise you that. Don't tell Dusty either. Deal?"

"Oh, you'd better believe I won't tell Dusty. He'll lose it for sure."

Dean hugged her again. "Just go, Katie. Let me do my thing. I promise I'll update you often."

She ended the hug with a kiss to his cheek. "Thanks, Dean. I'm sorry I lost my shit."

"My wife is pregnant. That was nothing."

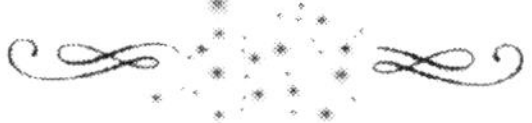

Before heading to the daycare to get Aiden, Vick returned to his cabin. He wanted to get the message to his crew about Xolo being in charge for the next two days right away. If it didn't come from him, the story would most likely get changed from crewmember to crewmember, much like the old "telephone"

game of earth's past. His simple two-day sabbatical would turn into stories of an emotional breakdown to being placed in lock up for a crime. Although his crew consisted of the brightest professionals, they were still human, so to speak. Nothing built rumors better than boredom, no matter what the species. There was no emotionless race that based their existence solely on logic. Sometimes Vick yearned for the Vulcan race of earth's old sci-fi channel stories.

As he was changing into a less formal jumpsuit, his screen came to life with an unwanted caller.

"Victor. You mind explaining yourself to me?"

"Dad?" Vick couldn't contain his shock. It was never a good thing when his dad called out of the blue. As a matter of fact, he was hoping for another two years of silence. The last time they'd spoken, the conversation hadn't ended well. It usually didn't. His father never could wrap his head around Vick's need to explore the unknown. It didn't matter that Space Command viewed him as the best of the best in his field, his father still turned up his nose, and his checkbook, at Vick and his achievements.

"To what do I owe the honor of the call, Dad? Another few days and you wouldn't have been able to reach me." *Of all the damn luck.*

"You're not still going in that nebula with my grandson on board, are you?"

"What? How in the hell do you…Fuck, Dad! I don't even want to know how you know. That means I have a traitor on my ship and I'll have to blow the whole crew up. How did you get under the skin of one of my people? What are you holding over some poor bastard?"

"Calm yourself down and watch that mouth, Victor."

"The hell I will. This is bullshit. This is my ship. You want nothing to do with me or anything about it. You couldn't care less if I fly us into an asteroid field. You'd find satisfaction in standing over my burial portal saying, 'I told you so.'"

His father sighed heavily. "I'll admit I never did understand your desire for space travel. Why you didn't go into the family business like your sister is beyond me."

"Maybe going to space was the way to find the furthest possible place to get away from the family business."

"Lawyers have had a rougher go of things than any profession since the age of the huge earth beasts."

"Dinosaurs, Dad. Dinosaurs. You could at least brush up on the history of home if you're going to use old expressions."

"I don't care about old stories, I care about right now. Why are you intentionally avoiding the conversation I called about? I want the details about my grandson. Why am I only hearing about this now? I hear the boy is three. Why is he even on that ship at a time like this?"

Holding his hand up, stopping the influx of more questions, Vick said, "Stop. Just stop. I know what you think of me, but even I wouldn't have brought him here – now – if it could have been avoided. I just took an earful from my first-in-command. I'm kinda done having my ass reamed today."

"You're the boss. You let your employee talk to you that way?"

"I'm in command, but it doesn't work quite like your office hierarchy. It's a little hard to fire someone, tell them to pack their desk, and walk out."

"If those under you don't have respect—"

"It's a mutual respect. I don't want a lesson in office politics from you. He happens to be right on all accounts. Unless Xolo is the one who called you. In that case, I'm going to go kill him with my bare hands."

"It wasn't him, not that I'll reveal my source. I'm ordering you to turn back immediately. Give me my grandson and you can go on your merry way, playing this Captain Kirk that you admired so much. I should have been more selective on the retro earth shows that I allowed you to watch."

"When were you ever around to monitor anything I did? All you did was work. How many half-siblings in how many races do I have out there who I don't know about?"

"Would you stop being ridiculous."

"Two, Dad. I've found two with no help from you. How many more are there?"

"So, that's what this last pout of yours has been about."

"Pout? Call it what you want. You were a sorry excuse of a husband when Mom was alive, and now you're making an ass of yourself in her absence. I don't need or want you in my life. Or my son's. You're not in any position to order me to do anything. This is *my* ship. Mine. You don't demand anything."

"I have a right to see my grandson. He does not belong on that ship. I can't believe his mother is okay with this."

"His mother is dead, Dad. She was murdered right on front of him. I only just found out about him myself. She was a former Athracki slave. My son bears the eyes of his planet's horrible history. He won't be accepted in many cultures as free. Certainly not in your circles. Now leave us alone." Vick waved his hand for the screen to shut off as his father shouted, "Wait!"

Vick stopped his hand mid-swing. "What? I'm really done here."

"Have you caught her killer?"

Sighing, he said, "No. I haven't even started to go there yet, Dad. Honestly, your timing stinks. I've had about two hours of sleep in three days. I really don't need this now."

"Give me her name."

Vick was confused more than ever. "Why?"

"I want to help. You know this is what I do. Despite what you think, I don't care what race the boy is. He's my blood. If you blow that ship up with you and him on it and die, I'll kill you."

Hiding the smile that wanted to surface was hard. He wasn't going to believe his father had any kind of heart after all this time. He wanted something…but what it could be was the question. Deciding it couldn't hurt; he gave his father her name.

"Deidre. Deidre Z694D1."

"And my grandson's name?"

The smile was completely extinguished now. "Aiden. She named him after you, Dad." He finished the wave, turning off the screen, ending the call. Now, feeling the exhaustion creep over him, Vick collapsed onto his couch and fell asleep instantly.

"Wow, hon."

"'Wow' what?"

"Vick was sure harsh on his dad. I know where it's coming from but still, wow."

"Come on, sweets. You know what Vick's been through with him."

"I'm surprised that you didn't have him tell his dad about almost sleeping with his Vanderheldi half-sister."

Dusty grinned. "I like to recap a little in the books, but not too much. I think readers will remember that one. I can't believe you thought my sister and I almost slept together before we knew who we were because of that scene."

Katie laughed. "You have to cut me some slack, Dusty. So much of your books are stolen from our lives. It's hard to separate what you've made up and what really happened sometimes."

"I told you we were around eight when we learned the truth. It wasn't likely we were about to bang and I caught a glimpse of her and my father on the nightstand."

Katie wrapped her arms around his neck. "Vick is kind of a man-whore. Maybe he is a Captain Kirk wannabe."

"You said it yourself. He's me. He's a stud."

Laughing, Katie stole a quick kiss. "Maybe here, but I bet on Forengi you couldn't even get a date. You could only grope half as well as those men."

Dusty laughed. "I love how much you pay attention to all the characters. Wouldn't you just love me with four arms instead of two?" He quickly moved his hands over her body, playfully.

She caught his arms somewhere between her ass and breasts and was suddenly serious again. "I hope your dad doesn't get sad when he reads this one."

"We're long over our squabbles. And honestly, I don't think he quite remembers things like I do. They are exaggerated in the book; he shouldn't see himself. Besides, I doubt he even reads them."

"Oh, you know he does. He may not be the most affectionate to your face, but you know he loves and is very proud of you."

"Only because I have you. If you weren't here, we'd still be on non-speaking terms over me dropping out of college."

"You don't know that, but don't you dare ever try to go to a different future again to find out."

"There is no way that is ever going to happen again. I swear I'll kill me the next time I see me."

That comment gave Katie a good belly laugh. "We have got to be the strangest couple on the planet."

"This one maybe," he said with a wink before he scooped her up. "Come on, honey buns. It's way past bedtime."

Chapter Fourteen

Vick was startled awake by Jody shaking his shoulder. He bolted upright and ran his hands down his face. "What's wrong? What time is it?"

"Nothing is wrong. I came looking for you when you weren't on the bridge."

"Did you talk to Xolo?"

"A little. He said he told you to take a couple days off. Is this the wisest way to use your time?"

"Cut me some slack. I collapsed. I haven't had any sleep lately." He scooted over and patted the spot next to him. Surprisingly, she took the seat.

"You look like feces."

He grinned. "It's shit, and thanks."

"That's not a compliment. Did I say it wrong?"

He laughed softly and placed a hand on her knee. "No, you said it right. I'm sure I do look like shit. I forgot you don't have a sarcasm meter." He removed his hand and leaned his head over the back of the couch. With an exhausted grunt he said, "I'm sorry."

She tilted her head. "You're sorry?"

He turned his head just enough to look at her. "Yes, I'm sorry. All I am lately is sorry. I know you hate when I use twisted English on you. Mostly I'm sorry about everything that has happened since we got back. I appreciate you coming to look for me, but I'm fine. I know you hate me right now. I'm sorry that I can't make it right. Maybe our timing will always stink and this will never be a good idea. I'm sorry about that, but I'm not sorry any of it happened." He stood. "I need to steam shower and get to my son. Thanks for waking me."

Vick was standing with his hands against the wall when he was startled by hands wrapping around his waist. He turned to face Jody, standing there naked.

"Are you trying to get rid of me with multiple heart attacks today?"

Jody's hands caressed down his chest. "You don't get to dismiss me so easily." She firmly grasped where he was most vulnerable. "I'm the one who's sorry. I overreacted yesterday. If you want me to go, I'll go. I know you're tired."

Leaning down to meet her lips, Vick kissed her as he pressed her against the wall. "I don't want you to go."

Jody slapped the button, causing the steam to thicken. "I've never been nailed in a steam shower."

Vick growled as he raised her onto his hips. "Made love."

As they toweled off, Vick couldn't keep his hands or lips off Jody. She squealed and turned away, only to be picked up and placed on the bathroom counter.

After a lingering kiss, Vick asked, "Not that I'm complaining, but why did you come looking for me? I thought you were pissed."

"I am pissed, but it doesn't mean I don't care. I went to visit Aiden before I came looking for you."

"You did?"

"Yes. I'm worried about him. You know, you're a real…yank sometimes."

"Yank?"

"Twitch?"

"Oh, jerk," he said with a chuckle. "Sorry. Yes, I am. Uh…but why in particular?"

"You made me angry in the way you talked to me about being there for Aiden. I like him. I would have wanted to be there for him. You didn't have to be a rectum and propose that I step in and act like his mother. I like having sex with you, Victor. I may not have liked all the games that were played that built up to this, but I do like it. This is a most unexpected twist so suddenly, but I am not afraid."

He stepped closer so their chests were touching. He was also aroused again. Jody put on her practiced smile. "It must be a rumor about you earth men not being able to go twice."

Vick grinned. "Baby, you have no idea. I shouldn't have put you up here. You're at a pretty good height."

"We shouldn't, Captain."

"You still won't call me Vick, sweetheart?"

"Vick is a word that translates to something unpleasant on my planet. I'd rather not."

"You call me all kinds of bad earth names. What could be worse than asshole and jerk?"

"Casherri sperm."

"That's your creature that's sort of like our horse but with six legs, right?"

"Correct."

"And its sperm is called Vick?"

"Yes. When not impregnating a female, it's quite deadly. You have no idea how revolting your language is to us. Your own name is a letter away from what you call that." She motioned to his erect penis.

He grinned. "Some guys actually go by Dick. It's the nickname for Richard."

"Ugh. You humans are disgusting."

He covered her mouth with his, lowered his hands to her behind and entered her. She wrapped her legs around him, keeping him there.

After a few moments, she broke the kiss. "This part of you may not be so disgusting."

"Happy to hear that," he said, burying his head into her neck.

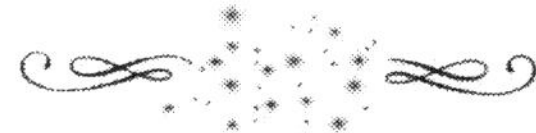

Vick didn't often have a wave of guilt after having sex. Actually, he'd never had guilt about sex before. This was the first time he felt like he should have said no, and gone to the nursery to pick up his son instead. The battle going on in his head was worse than the one previously waged over trying to decide whether or not to cancel the exploration.

Xolo had made an excellent point. Aiden would be safe in the nebula. They were safe from prying eyes in there, but that also meant he couldn't do any prying either. All of the ships systems would work, but there would be no contact with anyone outside of it. No reports could go out, no calls could come in. No investigating what happened to Deirdre. Maybe some time to let things settle down was what he needed, though.

Shaking his head clear, he opened the door to the daycare. He was immediately greeted by his son's shout.

"Daddy!"

Aiden ran toward him; Vick dropped to his knees with his arms open to accept him. Aiden clung to him tighter and longer than he would have expected. He was still a stranger to his son but right now, all he had. He supposed that counted for something. This was an emotion he never had before and was to date, the best sensation ever. Feeling guiltier than before, he returned the strong embrace.

"I told my first-in-command to take over for a few days, pal. I want to spend the time with you instead of my crew and ship. You're more important to me than anything."

Aiden was still clinging tight.

"Is that okay with you? Or does Miss Lenore not want to part with your handsome company?"

She let out a jolly chuckle. "He was a great helper today. Sure is as smart as a QR-6000 computer, too." She winked when Aiden finally looked up at her. "You'd probably be able to teach your dad a thing or two tonight. You certainly kept me on my toes."

Aiden finally smiled. "You're so silly. Do you mind if I stay with my dad tomorrow? Will you need my help with the babies?"

"My, you're a doll. I think I can manage, though, honey. Why don't you take one last peek and say goodbye."

After he ran off, Vick asked, "Was he really okay?"

"Perfect in every way. I didn't ask him any questions. I wanted him to know he could trust me."

"I appreciate that."

"I meant what I said; he is amazingly sharp for his age. He did show me that gadget of his and how he can change his eyes."

"He did?"

"He thinks it's…how did he say? Oh, cool."

Vick laughed. "I wish that's all it had to be. It's a shame to think he may have to use it for more than fun."

"Oh, he knows exactly what it's for. I said I didn't pry, that doesn't mean he didn't let little things out here and there."

"Like?"

"He said he had to use it when he traveled with Mommy to run from the bad men."

"The bad men? Did he say who?"

"No. But the way he talked about traveling made me think it wasn't on a shuttle." Vick opened his mouth but she held her hand up. "I don't want to know. Not now. He'll be safe when he's in my care. If I have to kill for him, know I will."

He smiled at her, trying to picture just that. Her build of a kindly grandmother was deceiving.

"I also have tracked-in on him. Until you tell me otherwise, there's nowhere the boy can go that I won't find him."

Not being able to help it, Vick hugged her. "I appreciate that more than you can know."

"Take care of him, Captain. Don't pull any funny business without keeping me in the loop. I hate being jostled into a track for no reason. I'll need to line up someone to watch these babies."

"I promise I'll tell you everything first."

Aiden ran over. "Zeerah is turning green, Aunt Lenore."

"Oh dear. You two best get going." She patted Aiden on the head and double-timed over to the cribs.

Safely out the door, Vick and Aiden strolled to his cabin hand in hand. "I'm glad you two hit it off so well."

"She's nice."

"I'm even happier you knew you could trust her and show her your Hawkeye."

"Mommy said I had to be careful, but I thought she may need to know what I could do. If she had to look for me, I wanted her to be able to know it was me with different eyes."

"You sure are very smart." Vick stopped and knelt down in front of Aiden. "This may sound really bad, and I'm sorry, but I need to know. Did your mommy steal your Hawkeye from some bad men?"

He shook his head. "No. It's mine. Uncle Frank gave it to me. I heard him talking to Mommy, though. They thought I was asleep. He said some bad men would always be after it."

"Do you know who?"

"No. We moved a lot. Mommy said we had to stay ahead of the bad men. We were supposed to be safe." He looked up at Vick with huge, questioning eyes. "Was it the bad men that killed Mommy?"

Vick pulled his son into a tight hug. "It was certainly bad men that killed your mommy, but I don't know who did it yet." He released the hug and met his eyes. "Do you know you have my dad's name?"

"Uh-huh. Mommy told me."

"Well, my dad is a pretty smart guy. He's trying to help us find those bad men so they will go to jail." Someone was walking toward them; Vick stood and took Aiden's hand in his again. "I have a lot to talk to you about, buddy. But I want to do it in my cabin." Vick nodded at the crew member as she passed them. As soon as she was gone, the familiar darkness surrounded them. It lasted for just a second. When things became light again, they were in his cabin.

"Aiden!" Vick bent down again. "You can't just do that, pal."

"But she didn't see us."

"That doesn't matter. Someone else could have. That's too dangerous to do here."

Aiden's lip began to quiver. Vick pulled him to his chest once again. "I didn't mean to scold you. I meant it to be more of a warning. You need to ask me before you do that, okay?"

A sniffle was the only response.

Vick sat him on the table. "You're the only person I've ever known who can do that. I trust my crew like I would my own family, but there's no telling what someone will do when they think they can have that kind of power."

With no words spoken, Aiden removed the Hawkeye and handed it to Vick. "You can take it if you're angry with me."

"No, son. I'm not angry and I don't want to take it from you. I just want a warning before you do that."

Aiden insisted. "But I don't need it to do that."

Vick didn't understand. As soon as he held the Hawkeye, Aiden disappeared. He panicked. "Aiden!"

As quickly as he disappeared, he reappeared. "I just went to the bedroom. I wanted to show you I don't need it."

"You teleport without your Hawkeye?"

He nodded. "Yes. Like Mommy, but only in today, not to tomorrow or yesterday."

"Without it."

"Uh-huh."

Vick sat down hard in the closest chair. "I thought…never mind." He realized Xolo was probably right about bringing in Jody. "Would you mind if I let my friend Jody look at this thing?"

"Of course she can. I like her. Can she come over now?"

"I'll see, pal. Go ahead and get yourself a snack."

While Jody did her scanning of the device, Vick found it hard to concentrate on anything but her. She was in his cabin, working off his computer. The system in his quarters was connected to the main servers by a secure line. Only the system at his captain's chair had this much access. The fewer eyes on this, the better.

He gave Jody's hand a gentle caress with the back of his. She pulled her hand away, motioning her eyes to Aiden.

Vick whispered, "He's not looking."

"Still. I…wait a second. I've never seen something like this." Placing the small probe on a tiny chip, the screen now came to life with a hologram of Deidre's face. The click it made caused Aiden to jump. Upon seeing her, he raced over.

"Mommy!"

Vick stood behind him as he held his gaze on the image.

"Play it!" Aiden begged.

"It's a video?" Vick asked.

"Uh-huh." He asked Jody for the device, swiped the front of it, which pulled up the same keyboard again, and he keyed some code in. The image began to move and speak.

"Vick, I hope it's you watching this. If you are, well, that means I'm no longer around. I hope you're taking care of Aiden. He's all that matters now." Her eyes lowered to where Aiden was standing. Vick was kind of freaked out at the accuracy of it. For a moment, he thought she'd time traveled here, and it wasn't just a video. It flickered, quickly dismissing that fear.

"If you're here, honey, I need you to step into another room for a moment. I love you very much and I have left videos for you, but I need to speak to Daddy for a moment."

The image stood there silently as Aiden said, "Okay, Mommy. I love and miss you." Without any further direction, he stepped into Vick's room and closed the door.

Deidre started to speak again. "I can't imagine when you've found this or if you've even found this. I'm recording this before I leave to come get you and tell you about your son. I'll apologize now for whatever happened this day." She paused to let a small smile show. "I recorded this in hopes you were smart enough to have someone from your ship examine the device, and not just make Aiden hide it. It's too sensitive to send to you over any other means."

"She's very pretty," Jody noted.

Vick replied with, "Shhh."

"I'm sure you've discovered what he can do; I hope you can come to terms with it and find a way to keep him safe from those that would do terrible things with his powers. You were too kind to ever exploit mine; I trust you would never do that with your son. You may not have exploited my abilities," she continued, "but there were others who did. The bad men Aiden has probably mentioned are men that want this device. It's the only one of its kind. It can do far more than change the color of his eyes and act like a mobile wrist computer."

"Not that I've found yet," Jody said.

Vick impatiently said, "Shhh," again.

"I went to the future, Vick. I stole the design for it. When I discovered what their plans were, how they intended to use it, I stole it back. I thought I could keep ahead of them but they were always one step behind of me. I knew the only way to keep Aiden safe while I took care of things was to send him to be with you. I was going to see to it that this device could never be created. I wish I managed this task before I'd been caught. I'm sorry that this has fallen into your hands."

"So you lied to me about knowing you were dying," Vick said to the hologram.

When she replied with, "I didn't lie about dying," it scared him. It took a moment to realize the hologram was still just automatically playing. "I knew I was playing a dangerous game and this was most likely how it was going to end. I deserved it for what I'd done. I hoped to never have to involve you, but I only had one ally and he was killed a few days ago."

"She must be talking about the Frank Aiden has mentioned a few times."

Jody paused the video.

"What did you do that for?"

"I think you need some time, Captain."

"Time for what?"

"Take a breath. You watched her murdered in front of you. This is her dying message to you. You're pale as bed linens. Please sit."

He wasn't about to correct her and say, "It's pale as a sheet." Doing as she asked was easier than fighting with her, so he took a seat.

"I wasn't in love with her, Jody."

"That doesn't matter. You were there when she took her last breath. It would be hard on anyone. I didn't even know her and I have a wrenching feeling in my stomach that I cannot explain." She moved closer so Vick's head was resting on her chest. "One more moment to take a breath, before you learn more about this device and the men after it, is not going to kill you."

He nodded. "Thanks for the help with this. You know I can't do this without you."

"I know," she said with a kiss the top of his head.

Aiden charged out of the room. "Daddy, there's a ship outside."

Jody quickly released her hold and stepped back. "There couldn't be another ship around. No ship is allowed near us. We've—"

A jostling shook the whole ship. The lights went out for a moment but came right back on.

"Were we hit?" Jody shouted.

The cabin speaker boomed with Xolo's voice. "Get your ass up here, Captain. Someone is firing on us."

Chapter Fifteen

Vick picked Aiden up and raced toward the door. Aiden shouted out and reached over Vick's shoulder.

"My Hawkeye!"

"It can wait, buddy."

"No!" Aiden forced himself out of Vick's grasp and raced over. "Mommy's in it!"

"Go," Jody insisted. "We'll be right behind you."

Vick sprinted out the door.

As Jody approached Aiden, he quickly disconnected his Hawkeye from the probes, but not before saying, "Bye, Mommy," to the hologram.

She extended her hand. "Come on, Aiden. We have to go to the bridge."

"Cool. I haven't been there yet."

"Not so 'cool,' as you say. I'm afraid we're in danger." She hustled down the hallway with him in tow. "How did you know there was a ship out there? There's no portal in your dad's sleeping quarters. There isn't one in any of the sleeping quarters, only in the living space," she added, as if he'd question her knowing that fact.

"I could tell it was there."

She stopped tugging him along. "How?"

Shrugging, he said, "They sent out a wave I felt."

"A wave?"

"Uh-huh. To determine our distance."

"You can feel that?"

"I need to. If I need to travel to it, I need to know how far."

She started hurrying again to the bridge and replied with, "I suppose so," even though she really wasn't even beginning to understand what he was capable of at all. They were still clueless to what he could do and what part of it involved the device he called his Hawkeye.

"Are the bad men who killed Mommy the ones who fired on the ship?"

"Most likely. There is no reason anyone would want to harm an exploration vessel."

"I heard Daddy say he thought about taking me and leaving the ship."

"He did think about that," she admitted.

"But he also said we'd be safe in the nebula."

"Yes, that's true." Still in a hustle, she glanced down at him. "We're you eavesdropping?"

"I know that's bad, but I was worried about him."

Indicating his device she said, "You did that with your Hawkeye?"

He nodded. "I'm sorry."

"I'm sure your father will talk with you about that later." She was grateful for this information, however. They'd have to be really carful around him.

Another blast jostled the ship.

"Are there shields?" Aiden asked.

"Not designed to take much more of a beating like this. We're an exploration vessel. We're not equipped with abundant defenses. It's illegal to be in our airspace as well as initiate an attack."

"I don't think these men are worried about rules."

"Fair enough."

They'd reached the control room by this point. Aiden walked over to the large viewing window as the crew hustled around. He stared out at the massive nebula. Not sure what she could do, Jody stayed with him.

Aiden spun around. "Dad?"

Vick lifted his head up from the center control desk. "Not now, son. I'm a little busy."

"But, Dad."

"In a minute."

Aiden looked up at Jody. "Are you way out here still studying it?"

"Yes. We have a few probes in there. We've plotted the safest course and have found a suitable place to dock, so to speak, safely, so we can study it some more and plan the next stage of the journey if your father thinks it's feasible."

The ship shook violently again. Jody called out. "Captain? What can I do?"

"Try to find another frequency to hail that ship. It hasn't been responding to me."

She grasped Aiden's hand again. "Come with me."

Once she was in her chair and working at her board, Aiden tugged at her jumpsuit. "Do you have the star coordinates for the safe probe?"

"Of course I do." She keyed away again before reaching for her earbud. Again Aiden tugged at her. "What? I'm sorry, but I need a minute here."

"Can I get them?"

"What? The coordinates?" She huffed as she scooted over and pulled it up on a screen. "I know you're a smart one, Aiden, but we're really busy here." She waved at the screen. "That's the position of Probe Delta four-niner-fourteen. Now please, I need a minute to do something for your dad." Earbud now secure, she returned to her task. She reached for her keyboard, but the bridge was suddenly engulfed in darkness.

"Captain?"

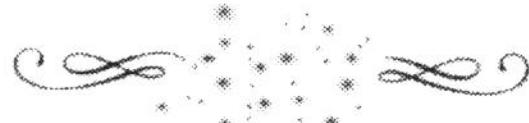

"Aiden! Jody!" Vick should have been concerned for the entire ship, and he was, but he frantically called out in the dark for the two people he cared for most. "Where are you?"

"Over here," Jody cried. "I have Aiden."

Within another few seconds, all the lights were restored. The computer screens came back up as well as the lighted control boards and cabin lighting.

"Did we take a hit to the main power source?" he called over to Xolo as he reached Aiden and Jody. "Are we on backup?"

"No, Captain. We're operating on full capaci—holy shit." He'd stolen a quick glance out the viewing window. His eyes lowered to Aiden, then back up to Vick. "Sorry, but you might want to turn around."

Vick and Jody whipped around to the viewing window. "Holy shit indeed." Vick knelt down, eye level with his son. "Son, did you do this?"

"I had to. They were going to hurt your ship. People would have died and they would have taken me away."

Vick didn't know what to respond to first. "Hang tight here for a second with Jody, buddy." He hurried to Jody's station, verified their coordinates, and turned to Xolo. "We're smack in the middle of what I plotted out as our first landing zone."

"How is that possible? We were weeks away!"

"Jody gave me—" Jody covered Aiden's mouth with her hand.

"Let's step out into the hall and wait for your dad, kid."

Xolo's eyes widened when the realization hit him. Vick shook his head, begging him to keep silent with the rest of the crew.

"Everyone listen up," Vick said. "We'll have to worry about explaining what just happened later. For now, double and triple check every reading. We appear to be where we were heading for in a few days, but there's just no telling what we're up against. We don't have the luxury of the calculated flight in here, through the path of our choosing. Due to our recent situation, I'll take this little hop as a gift."

"Yes, Captain," was all that was muttered by everyone. Xolo narrowed his eyes, but gave a simple nod in agreement.

Vick left to check on Aiden. Once he was at their side, he knelt down again. "You really did this? You moved the whole ship and everyone on it into the nebula?"

"Jody gave me the numbers of the safe place. She said you were going in soon anyway. Was that bad?"

"No, buddy. It wasn't bad, I'm just surprised. I knew you moved our pod, but this ship is a hundred times that size."

"It's all the same," he said flatly and held up his wrist. "It's the Hawkeye. I can travel in today without it, but I can move things with it. The size doesn't matter much."

"Hold on. That's what this thing is supposed to do?"

"They tried to use Mommy's power and time travel, but they couldn't. When I played with it, they found out I could move things besides just myself."

"Only you can work this thing?"

He nodded. "Yes. Only me. That's why the bad men want it and me. It's mine. They can't have it." Clutching the device on his wrist, he pulled it protectively to his chest.

"Aiden!" Vick reached for his son, whose nose has started to bleed. "Are you okay?" He scooped him up as Jody pinched it shut.

"Get him to the infirmary!" Jody shouted.

"I'm okay," Aiden said with his nose plugged. He was hard to understand, so Jody let go for a moment. "It happened before when I moved something big for the bad men."

"It's not okay, pal. If this is what happens to you, don't do that again. Understand?"

"But I needed to save everyone."

"And you did, but I can't risk *you*. Got it?"

He nodded. Vick was sure Aiden felt scolded but he was too worried to address that more. They burst through the door of the infirmary. The doctor was there and immediately hopped into action. Skinnard loved the idea of a Forengi for a doctor. Four arms can be quite useful in this profession. She and Xolo had been married by him after the first nebula exploration. Although he was worried he'd get some flak from his crew members about the "no sex rule," he knew a doctor would have access to great birth control.

She waved a hand to the exam table. "Place him there." Once he was settled she asked, "What happened?"

"His nose just started to bleed."

"Nothing preceded it?"

"Not that I'm aware," he lied.

After taking in their appearance, she said, "You two go wash up, I've got him."

Until he looked down, he didn't realize how much Aiden's nose had bled. "I'm not leaving him."

She gave a slight huff. "Then with all due respect, stay out of my way." Grabbing a few tissues from a cabinet above, she held it tight over Aiden's nose. "Hold this, little guy. Okay? Can you do that?"

He nodded.

As she reached to the side of the table for her scanner, she said, "What's your name?"

"Aiden."

"Aiden Skinnard," Vick added.

"I assumed the only boy on the ship was your son, Captain."

"He's half Athrackian, if that matters any with that contraption."

"There's no setting for that. It's never been documented before. It doesn't matter." She turned to Aiden. "I'll find whatever ails you, Aiden. You can trust me on that."

Although most rules and promises of secrets didn't apply to married couples, Vick was surprised Xolo hadn't told his wife about Aiden's abilities.

"Seriously, Dusty," Katie said after she greeted her husband with a kiss.

"Seriously, what?"

"The more I read, I'm beginning to think you can't write at all." Her arms were now crossed. "You're stealing everything from our lives."

"What now? The nosebleed thing?"

"Yes, the nosebleed. To quote you 'this shit hurts.' You put that poor kid through that?"

Dusty couldn't control his laugh. "Babe, he's a fictional character. Are you going to run to a toy store and buy him some earth toys next?"

She gave him a not so gentle shove. "It's like you're cheating."

"Cheating how? You ever heard the term 'write what you know' or 'fact is stranger than fiction?' Every writer pulls from things that happen in their lives. You never know what will trigger something. You know I'm always watching my surroundings, waiting for ideas to jump at me."

"I guess so. But now you're making me feel like there are other people out there like us. Maybe other fiction isn't so fiction after all."

"Quite possibly. Maybe I took myself into a ride through space and none of this story is fiction."

"You're a jackass. And of course I mean that with love."

"My favorite pet name from you yet. I'm getting a beer. You want one?" he asked as he headed toward the kitchen.

"I suppose. It's not like I can't because I'm trying to get pregnant or anything."

Dusty stopped in his tracks. His hand ran down his face. "Seriously?" He took her hands and pulled her to him, then cocooned her with all he had. "Don't do it, babe. You're getting awfully upset over something we only just decided. You weren't even sure you wanted another one a few days ago."

"I'm sorry. I'm trying to not get this way, but I can't help it. My mother said something to me years ago and it kind of stuck with me."

"What was that?"

"I was complaining about how every guy I ever dated was a walking erection. All they wanted was sex 24/7."

"You say that like it's a bad thing."

She got out of his embrace, tugged him along to the kitchen, and grabbed two beers.

"Anyway, my mother boldly said, 'look at what a woman is born with,' as she drew a circle over her stomach. 'We have the ability to give life and spend our lives feeding, protecting, loving, and so on. Now, look what man is born with,' and she wagged her finger at her crotch." Katie made the motion as she said it. "'And he spends his life trying to get that in here.'" She exchanged her waggling finger for a V shape, using both hands.

Dusty sent beer flying. "My sweet mother-in-law said that? Jesus, Katie. What do you tell her about us?"

"Please. Like I'm going to talk to my mom about us doing it on the kitchen counter for nooners, Dusty."

"I think I'm insulted. I do my share when it comes to taking care of the kids."

"I know. And I didn't share this to start a fight. I'm just sad. It's like Phoebe and the episode of *Friends* with the Christmas trees. I'm not fulfilling my destiny."

"That's bullshit and you know it." Dusty looked around. "Speaking of, where are our little Christmas trees?"

Katie smiled and hoped she didn't start a new onslaught of names for the kids. "Out with the puppy. Where else?"

"I'm going to start to feel neglected here. I usually get greeted at the door."

"Well, I hope she doesn't ever get to be old news to them. I picked up a book today on training her for the kids. This one specifically mentions how to train your deaf dog. We'll need to be diligent with them."

"You know I'll help, just give me the highlights and instructions. I'll be a little busy giving my manuscript some polishing up over the next couple weeks."

"I will." Her mood was still somber. "I can give you what I've read and marked up already. I've been pretty good on my notes. The stuff I yelled at you for I didn't bother marking."

Dusty closed the gap between them, kissed her forehead, and pulled her close. "Please be okay with this. I know I keep saying I want to kick the crap out of my older self, but I see why I came back. If you're this way so soon, I imagine you were really beating yourself up after trying for two years."

"I'm sorry." Her voice had begun to crack. "I just feel like I'm letting you down."

He squeezed tighter. "Don't ever say that. I'm so happy I don't know how I keep from exploding half the time."

She giggled softly. "You're such a sap."

"But I'm your sap, cupcake."

"Daddy!" Both kids came running into the kitchen. Ali was carrying the puppy. "I taught her how to sit!" she proudly proclaimed.

"You did? What's the hand signal for that?"

Ali put the puppy down and showed him. Once the puppy sat, Alex gave her a treat.

"What a great job, you two!" Dusty said.

"How many of those treats has she had, sweetie?"

Alex shrugged. "I didn't count. Half the bag maybe?"

"She's going to have an upset belly. Give that to me," she said with an outstretched hand. She turned to Dusty. "Coals should be ready when you are."

"Just let me get changed and I'll get right on it, my love."

Ali tugged on Katie's nightgown, waking her up with a start. "What is it, sweetie?"

"My tummy hurts."

Katie quickly got out of bed. "Did you throw up?"

"No, but I kina feel like I want to."

She picked her daughter up and hustled to the bathroom in the hall, hoping not to wake Dusty. Making it just in time, Katie held her daughter's blonde locks with one hand while she gently stroked her back with the other. "I'm sorry, honey." Now with an empty stomach, Alyson cried as she flushed the toilet. Katie brought her to her lap and rocked her. After a long kiss on her forehead, she determined it had to be just an upset tummy, not any kind of bug.

"What did you eat after dinner?"

"You'll get mad."

"No, I won't. Tell me."

"I found a bag of Easter candy."

"You did? Honey, that's old. Why didn't you give it to me?"

Fearing she was in trouble, she mumbled through her tears. "I wanted it." "It was my favorite." "Whole bag." And more sobs that Katie couldn't even make out. This final round brought Dusty into the bathroom.

"What's the matter, peanut?"

Ali immediately reached for her dad.

"She got into some Easter candy." Now free, Katie grabbed a washcloth and rinsed it with warm water. "I didn't even know we had any. Did you hide some?"

"Me? Hide chocolate from you? That's a laugh."

After washing her daughter's face, Katie rested her hand on her daughter's cheek. "Have you learned anything from this little experience?"

Alyson sniffed and nodded.

"Come on, baby doll." Katie took her from Dusty. "Let's go back to bed."

"Will you stay with me?" Ali begged on the way to her room.

"You know you're too big for that, but I will lie down with you for a few minutes, just to make sure you're okay. Only if you promise not to ever do this again."

"I promise."

Katie sighed as the bed groaned with her weight when she climbed onto the bottom bunk. She'd always hated the metal bunk beds they'd bought for Ali's room. Dusty promised to build a wood set but the task kept getting bumped. In all honesty, unless one of them crawled in it with her, they forgot about the racket it made. She hoped she could sneak away without waking Ali with all the creaking.

"I'll stay until you fall asleep; I'm not staying all night."

"Okay. I love you, Mommy." Ali contently snuggled on Katie's chest.

Chapter Sixteen

The sun shining through the window woke Katie up. She felt the familiar weight on her shoulder. *Dammit. I fell asleep in Ali's bed again.* She rolled to her side, but felt something was missing. There was no creak of the metal. *What the hell now?* Katie slowly made her way to the edge of the bed, trying to slip out.

"Good morning, Mom. Sorry I used your shoulder for a pillow. I guess old habits die hard. Remember the night I got into the Easter candy? I thought for sure you'd be pissed."

Her head whipped around. "Ali?"

Her nineteen or twenty-year-old daughter laughed. "Geez, Mom. You only had two glasses of wine. Did you forget where you were waking up?"

Putting on her best fake smile, she said, "You know I can't handle drinks like I used to, and no, I was a little thrown off at first. All's good, honey." *Her daughter's future? What's the reasoning behind this?* Katie tried to get familiar with where she was after climbing out of bed.

Ali's room was nicely furnished. They'd shared a Queen-sized bed and there was a good-sized bathroom to the left. This was no dorm room. Taking a peek out the window, it appeared to be a nice, rural neighborhood. Katie's guess was she was still in Minnesota, but she wasn't entirely sure.

A knock on the door caused her to jump. "Up and at 'em, Andrews! The BSU Beavers wait for no one!"

That made it easy for Katie. They were in Bemidji. It was an easy joke to make when the girls' volleyball team is named "The Beavers." Even a restaurant got in on the fun, adding Beaver to their name. Everyone across the state had heard about it. They prided themselves on the fact that they weren't having a grand opening, it was a "soft opening" instead.

BSU was a great college, but that meant her daughter had a change of heart about becoming a vet. Now was not the time to ask.

"You sure you're going to be able to occupy yourself until the game this afternoon? Sorry, but I can't skip a pre-game practice."

"Of course I'm sure. There are lots of things I can do around here."

"There's a gazillion coffee shops. I'll leave you the car and ride with Tina."

"Sounds great, honey. You need to shower or can I hop in?"

"I'm not showering only to get sweaty. Knock yourself out. And don't mind Dereck if you bump into him. He's just a harmless flirt."

"Alyson Marie Andrews. You have a guy for a roommate?"

Ali pulled a sweatshirt over her head. "Mother! I told you! He's sweet, handsome, loaded, and gay as the Queen Mary. Trust me, you have nothing to worry about. You said you and Dad were okay with it."

"I'm sorry. I guess I am still waking up. It just slipped my mind. He wasn't around last night." She hoped she was guessing correctly. With Ali's reaction, she couldn't have met him this trip.

"Boy, Mom." Ali walked over, giving her a tight hug. "You need to visit more often, but we're staying away from the local vineyard stuff. You can't handle it." She laughed before holding her mother's face in her hands. "But I do have to say, it agrees with you. Your skin looks great! I guess it's true what they say about red wine and antioxidants." Ali rushed out the door after kissing her mother goodbye.

Unsure what to do, she decided to give Dusty a call. Maybe she could get some kind of clue as to why the hop was happening.

"Hey, sugar bear. How's the visit with Ali going?"

She wasn't sure how to answer. This was obviously Dusty in the time he was supposed to be. "It's going great. We had a good time last night. I'm just bumming around until the game this afternoon. I wish you could have come."

"You know me and the kids do, too. Maybe next time."

Kids? As in more than just Alex? She knew they had adopted. Frank/Dusty told her so, but this made it more real. She was torn between dying to know more and not wanting to.

Dusty continued as her mind raced. "I hated letting Ali down, but her brother wasn't getting off that easy. Alex needs to mind his curfew. This is getting old. Now I'm the one being grounded."

"He's your son if no one's, Dustin Charles." She'd already known that Alex would be a handful from a very young age. She often teased Dusty about that. "I'm sorry I got to go and you didn't. If it happens again, I'll stay back."

"If it happens again, you'll be visiting me in jail. I'm gonna kill him, babe."

"Dusty! Stop that. It couldn't be all that bad." *Could it?* She was defending him and had no idea what had happened.

He sighed heavily. "You know I don't mean it, but damn. He's getting a mouth on him. I miss my little man. He hasn't been the same since Deidre died. Maybe you need to give in and let them get another dog."

Deidre died? Now Katie was upset. For not even wanting the puppy and only having had her for a few days, her heart broke in two. Now she remembered why she put off getting animals of her own. It was hard enough when clients brought in their pets to be put down. She did some quick math. The dog would have been fifteen or sixteen. That was actually about right. *Damn.*

"Do it, Dusty."

"But he's grounded. He was over an hour late. You're the one who was about to call the cops. He ignored his phone, or are you forgetting that?"

"I know. The last thing I want to do is reward the negative behavior, but I think you nailed it. It's not fair to him. His sister leaves and then the dog dies. He needs a buddy."

"His other siblings don't count?"

Wait! What? Plural? "Uh…" Katie had no words. She was certain now that she didn't want to know any more than he'd already given away. Dusty continued before she formed a proper sentence.

"You shouldn't have given in and let him sleep with the thing after having her for a couple days. I was the one against it."

This was good news to have, but Katie didn't think she'd be able to do anything differently. There was something about boys and puppies. Blue had always slept with Ali, it was only fair.

"You know we couldn't have stopped it if we wanted to. I'm sure you're the one who fought me."

"Details, Katie."

Her instincts were right. Dusty was a softie when it came to the kids if nothing else. Not knowing the specifics of the other children and their personalities yet, she knew her Alex was just like his father. "He's a different soul, hon. Please. I'll be the fall guy here if you want to play hard-ass. Go to the shelter. Let him pick something out. It's my fault for putting it off."

"Putting it off? It's only been a few days. You drove right up to tell your daughter face to face 'cause you couldn't take it over the phone. Are you okay? I knew you were more upset about it than you were letting on."

"Deidre was a member of the family. Of course I'm upset; I just tend to be more rational. I guess I was trying to put it off, thinking he's going to be off to college soon, too. I know whatever we get will be there long after he's gone."

"We already had this conversation. Babe…I'm not going to get a dog if you don't want one. I don't want an argument for the next fifteen years. You know I love you more than Captain Skinnard, but this is the last argument I thought I'd have when I married a gal in vet school."

This seemed like such a normal conversation to have. All she wanted was to shout, "It's not me! Help me figure this out!" Instead, she carried on as she would have if she was when and where she was supposed to be.

Her voice cracked. "You know she broke my heart, too, Dusty. You ever stop to think why I don't want animals? Maybe it's not because I don't like them but it's because I love them too much. How many times have I come home in tears when I lose a patient? You just can't separate yourself from that no matter how hard you try. You brought us Blue, and then you brought us Felicia. Court brought us Deidre. Don't tell me I'm the one keeping us from having animals. I've never said no."

"Whoa. You only bring up Blue when something is wrong. What gives?" His voice lowered. "Is this you-you?"

Shit. He figured it out, but she still felt she couldn't give in.

"Yes, it's me," she lied. "I'm begging you, Dusty. Take care of our son. Go today. Let him pick out a dog. I didn't think I wanted another, but the house will feel funny without one. Do it, Dusty. Please. You have my blessings."

"Why don't you do it? I don't know what I'm looking at."

"I want it to be his choice. I don't want him to think I'm influencing his decision. A nice mutt will be best, anyway."

"And your other kids? Are we going to adopt a whole litter?"

The mention of more kids again made her heart flutter. "It'll be the family dog. Just talk to Alex first. It's not a reward; I just want him to be okay. It obviously means more to him than we thought. Do you want me to talk to him?"

"I have him mowing the lawn."

"You big meanie."

"He scared my wife. It's the least he can do."

Katie smiled. "Teenagers, huh? Who knew?"

"We did. You're right, he's me. Might as well buy him a piece of shit Chevelle and get it over with."

She couldn't contain the pelt of laughter that escaped. At the top of Dusty's list for trying to piss off his very rich father, was driving the biggest junker around. No matter how bad things were, Dusty could always snap her out of it with a fun memory.

He continued. "I miss you. You still staying another night?"

"I guess we'll see how it goes. I kind of feel like coming home tonight now."

"Call and let me know either way."

"I will. I love you."

"Love you more, puddin'."

Katie hit end, leaned back on the bed, and closed her eyes. Within a few seconds, an arm was shaking her. The bed creaked. She opened her eyes and met Dusty's.

"Come to bed, babe." Confused as ever, she turned to her left and saw young Ali sleeping peacefully. Dusty grasped her hand to help her up. "Come on, sugar buns. I'll keep my hands to myself tonight."

She plodded along to bed, unsure what the hell just happened. Was it a dream or did she actually go forward?

"Did you let Deidre out?" she asked on the way to their room, having no idea how long she'd been in bed with Ali.

"I tried to beat her to the two a.m. whine, but she's in bed with Alex. He snuck her up there. Please just let him sleep with her. He's gotten so attached to her."

"Of course he can."

Dusty stopped dead in his tracks. "What? I expected a fight here."

"I don't want to fight, Dusty. Unless she starts keeping him up, she can stay."

"I think I may have lied about keeping my hands to myself."

"I know you did," she said with a kiss. "Counted on it, actually."

Katie woke up the next morning with Dusty snuggling next to her. Shrugging off what happened last night as a dream, she snuck away without waking him then picked up his manuscript, hoping to catch a few minutes before the kids woke up. As much as their latest revelation left her with a hundred questions as to how they ended up with at least two more children, she knew there was nothing she could do or change about it. It was meant to be. Right now, however, she could dive back into Skinnard's world and find out more about

Aiden, his powers, and who the "bad men" are that are after him.

Chapter Seventeen

Aiden had fallen asleep while Doc Aubrey gave him the body scan.

"The humming of the machine does that to just about everyone," she explained. She'd convinced Vick and Jody to step out to the waiting area while she ran his tiny body though the machine built for adults.

"Did it show anything?" Vick asked.

"I couldn't find a thing. Must have just been a fluke. He's normal as far as I can tell."

"As far as you can tell? What the hell does that mean?" Vick stepped forward.

She held her hand up. “Settle down. It means that the nosebleed has stopped and I couldn’t find a cause. All of his numbers seem normal for an Athrackian, a little high for a human. He’s resting peacefully, so he’s obviously not under any distress.”

“You sure he’s not passed out?”

She dropped her arms at her side in frustration before hitching her thumb at a framed certificate. “That degree on the wall tells me I might know what I’m talking about.”

Vick’s face softened. “I’m sorry. New parent here.”

“Since he’s just arrived on the ship, it could just be a shock to his system. I wouldn’t worry, but bring him to me immediately if it happens again. I don’t see a reason to keep him. Speaking of just arrived, I’d like that explained someday. We haven’t docked anywhere and I don’t remember a transport ship bringing anyone aboard, unless I slept through it.” When Vick offered no explanation, she continued. “You do realize I’d like to start a paper on him. I’m obligated to document him.”

That scared Vick. If she started poking and prodding, she might discover what he was capable of.

“Abso-fucking-lutely not.”

“It’s the law, captain. I’ve run his DNA. He is indeed what you say he is. A half-Human half-Athrackian and indeed your son. Having never been documented before, I have an obligation—”

“I swear I’ll throw you in the brig. I don’t care if you are my second in command’s wife. You have no idea who he is and what’s happening. Please…there’s more going on than I have time to explain right now.”

“Threatening me isn’t going to help matters, Captain.”

“Damnit, Aubrey. Did you notice the power go out?”

“Of course! I’m not blind.”

“The power didn’t just go out. We landed smack dab in the middle of the nebula.”

"What? How is that even possible?" She seemed to wobble where she stood. Vick was worried she needed to sit. He took her by the arm. Jody joined them just then and went to her other side.

"What's going on?" Jody asked.

"Nothing! I'm fine. Let me go," Aubrey demanded.

"I just told her where we were."

"Wait." Aubrey pulled herself out of his grip and turned around. "Has anyone else reported this? Do you think you could have started with that fact? For crying out loud, Skinnard. That's probably what's wrong with him."

"Pardon?" Could she have figured it out already?

"He just got here, and I have no idea where from, or how for that matter. The poor dear goes from one unstable atmosphere to inside a nebula? How in the world is that even possible?" She reached inside a cabinet and pulled out a black bag.

"Where are you going?" Vick asked.

"I need to go to the nursery and check on those babies. Their little systems can't take a trip like that. They're not conditioned like we are." She paused. "Not that we're truly prepared, either. You've brought me two very troubling facts today, Captain. Our discussion is not done regarding Aiden."

"Trust me. We'll be talking later. There's not a heck of a lot you can do right now, anyway. There's no telling what brought us into the nebula and how long we'll be here. You can keep what you've documented for now, but it stays with you. Am I clear?"

"Yes," she growled as she brushed past Jody.

"Wow. What did I miss when I went to get changed?" Jody asked.

"She wants to document Aiden."

"It's the law, Captain. You can't threaten her for doing her duty."

"You know what this could mean. What if her tests reveal his ability? My son will not become a lab rat!"

"I didn't say we'd allow it, I just meant I understand where she's coming from."

He grinned. "We?"

She gave him a shove. "Don't be an asshat. Wait. Asshole."

He held her hands in his and gave each palm a gentle kiss. "They are both correct."

"Humans have hats for their bottoms? I've never seen this."

Knowing it would upset her, Vick couldn't help his laugh. "No, but the phrase is correct. You should know by now, you can pretty much mash up anything with a swear word and make it an instant insult. I'd be guilty of being any of them. Fire away, my sweet. I won't correct you. And you can stop correcting yourself."

"Dad?"

Vick dropped Jody's hands and rushed over to his son. "Hey, buddy." He ran his fingers through Aiden's thick hair. "Doc Aubrey said you're just fine."

"Am I in trouble?"

"Of course not. You have to promise me that you won't do anything like that again, though. We're safe for now, thanks to you. But I want you to relax and let me and Jody worry about the men after you. Okay?"

He nodded and mumbled a soft, "Okay."

Xolo's voice boomed over the ship's system. "Captain, we need you on the bridge immediately."

Vick turned to Jody. She took Aiden's hand and said, "Go. I'll stay with him."

"You sure?"

"Of course we are. Aren't we, Aiden? How about we go get something to eat? You feel up to it?"

"I am kind of hungry."

She faced Vick once again. "Go. We'll go back to your cabin when we're done. I know there are a lot of questions that need answering. They need you up there."

"This is one question I know the answer to, but can't risk sharing it. I've never lied to my crew before, Jody."

"You have to. At least for now. The time will come when you can address this."

He gave her a quick kiss, and then bet down to Aiden. "It seems like all I do is leave you somewhere, buddy. I'm really sorry."

He shrugged. "I know. It's okay. This is my fault, but I had to."

"We're done with the blame, pal. I'll be back as soon as I can. You take care of Jody for me."

Aiden smiled wide. "I will."

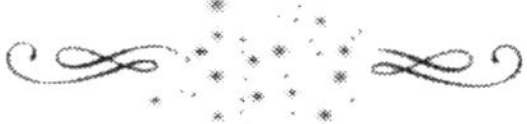

When Vick reached the bridge, everyone was still scrambling, confused as ever.

Xolo got to his side in a few long strides. "How long are you going to let me run around, searching for answers you already have?"

"I don't have the answers. I know who put us here, but I have no idea how."

He shouted, "You—" then lowered his voice again. "You do know how. It's that device."

Vick grabbed Xolo by an arm and took him to a corner for more privacy. He asked the man at his station to leave them for a moment.

"Aiden is the only one who can operate that thing."

"What do you mean?"

"It works because of what he can do. If you got a hold of it, you couldn't do jack with it."

"Have you tried?" Xolo asked, eyebrows furrowed.

"When the hell have I had time to do anything? He just told me this. He said Deidre's powers didn't do anything to it, but they discovered he could make it move objects other than just himself. Who the hell knows what mixing my human genes did to mess him up."

"Maybe there's a reason Athrackians don't breed with humans."

"Breed? That's the best you can do?"

"Whatever, Vick. Now's not the time for biology class."

"Deidre being Athrackian has nothing to do with it. As far as we know, there isn't another time-traveling anything. She got these powers mysteriously when she was well into her teens. The fact that Aiden does something like this at his age…Hell, Xolo. I'm at a loss for what to think about any of it."

"For starters, you need to put your crew at peace."

The words were barely out of Xolo's mouth when his chief helmsman called out, "Captain, I'd like to show you these numbers."

"Be right there, White." He faced Xolo. "We'll finish this over a Terian ale later. Let's put out a few fires first." With a slap on Xolo's shoulder, he headed to the helmsman's station.

"What do you have, White?"

"Everything is perfect, down to the last coordinate, Captain. We are smack in the middle of what we plotted out. Exactly where we wanted to be. Readings are as we'd hoped; no debris in sight."

"Great." He faced the engineer next to White. "What do we have for a damage report, Schooner?"

"Nothing a little paint won't fix, Captain. They barely grazed the loading dock panel. The ship shook like hell, but we must have been hit with more shockwave than anything. Either they can't aim or they weren't trying too hard. The ship's engine functions are perfect as well, and everything down to the last bolt is sound. I can't explain how we got in the nebula, but the ship is in top shape from the trip."

Vick turned to the officer on his right. "Every member of the crew accounted for and okay, Officer Yuri?"

"Yes, Captain. Everyone has checked in. Doc called in from the nursery. The two babies are in perfect shape as well."

"That's all I can ask for." He clapped his hands together then turned around.

"All right, everyone. I know we've had quite a scare. We can't explain it and we can't compromise our safety any longer, wasting time on anything but how to go forward from here."

"Captain." Officer White called out. "We didn't get our last transmissions out before we entered the nebula. I'm concerned Space Command will worry something has happened to us. I don't want the families of the crew worried."

"I'll have Jody working on a probe. She was able to navigate some in here for readings; she'll be able to navigate one out to send a transmission. I'll have her get started on that immediately."

"All due respect, Captain, but she is needed here."

"And she'll be here. You have a point, White?"

"I think you chose a hell of a time to start playing house."

Skinnard closed the gap between them. "Don't lecture me on timing. Having my son's mother murdered in front of me as well as him wasn't in my plans, either."

"I…I…I'm sorry, Captain. I guess I'm with the majority of the crew that just doesn't understand how or when he even got here. *And* what suddenly makes our communications officer his nanny."

"When that's your business, you'll be the first to know. Am I clear?"

White turned away as he spoke. "Yes, Captain."

"Everyone, as you were. You all have the reports on what our plans were going to be a few days from today. The time table has been bumped up. You've got an hour to compose any message you want sent out. Get them into your private accounts; I'll see to it that they get to your families. Understood?"

A collective, "Yes, Captain," echoed on the bridge.

"Then I want everyone back on track. No more looking back. We're doing the job we came to do."

One hand was raised.

"Jorgensen. What it is?"

"Do we know what that ship firing on us was after? Will they be following us?"

"I can't answer the question of their determination. No one in their right mind would follow us in here. But one thing for certain, they shouldn't be able to see us at all. Lieutenant Opex's readings have taught us that this particular nebula is the next best thing to a black hole. You already know we can't transmit out. Any scanning they do searching for us will come up empty. You have my word on that."

"That answers the second half. So…you do know why they were firing on us?"

Vick glanced at Xolo for a brief second before answering. "I'm sorry. I don't know who the men were." *Not totally a lie.* He hoped he wouldn't be called out on avoiding the question again. "I'm being pulled in fifty different directions here, people. Nothing like this has happened to me before, let alone ever been documented. A few of you have been here through my other excursions to past nebulas. Each one is unique and we've learned a shit-ton, if you don't mind the non-technical term. This voyage is no exception."

He scanned the room, their expressions screaming that they needed more. He continued.

"Did it just suck us through its vacuum? Do these short-lived stars have tiny, conflicting atmospheres that pulled us through? Despite what all our readings showed, is one about to go supernova? We need to look ahead and do what we came here to do. The answer to what happened may very well present itself if we continue looking forward. I don't think any good will come of it if we try to look behind us. What-ifs and guessing aren't going to do us any favors."

Jorgensen raised his hand again.

"Yes?"

"You made excellent points. Permission to send out the probes for gas readings."

Vick nodded. "Granted. Don't bother asking me from here forward, unless it's going to put anyone or this ship in harm's way. I'm giving all of you free rein here. Get creative. This nebula is a doozie and we're smack in her center."

"Reports every hour?" White asked.

"Report if you have something to report. I'm not going to make you stop what you're doing for nothing. Call me any time, day or night, if you don't find me right here in this chair. I'll apologize one last time for the twist that I've thrown in the mix, but that's it. I'll try to keep the distractions down to a minimum. I know I try to make it seem otherwise, but I'm only human."

"You got that, right," Xolo said with a laugh. The rest of the crew joined in.

"I need to hit my personal computer for some past charts and get Jody working on that probe. Get busy. It's show time."

Vick heard murmuring as he left the bridge, but at least for now he'd stopped the questions.

Chapter Eighteen

When Vick reached his cabin, Aiden was occupied on a computer. Jody had the Hawkeye hooked up again. He couldn't help himself; he bent down and gave her a lingering kiss.

"How come with all the crazy that is going on, you can make me forget it with just a kiss."

"I haven't been able to make that message play again."

"I love you, too."

"Stop it, Captain. This isn't the time for that." She motioned over her shoulder to Aiden as she returned her attention to the Hawkeye.

"I needed a second of downtime. Sue me." He kissed her again, this one on the forehead. "I need you to get a probe ready to launch. The crew is worried about getting messages to their families. Anyone who needs one outgoing will have it ready within the hour. Can you do that for me?"

"It's already been set up. I got the message from you with everyone else. I'm just waiting to download them."

"How do you have it ready? We didn't foresee this."

She stared hard at him. "Maybe your name does fit. You are thinking with as much brains as Casherri sperm." When he said nothing, she continued. "I had probes sent in, taking readings for the trip inside. It will be the same thing to bounce them out. It just took a moment to reprogram it to go the other way. Do you think I'm new here?"

With a slap to his own forehead, Vick said, "Shit. Now I know I'm operating on less than half of my mind. Aiden could have probably figured that one out."

"Actually—"

He cut her off. "Are you sure the first probe will be positioned far enough out to transmit?"

"It'll get to Castelli 12's satellite."

"And you can encode it to keep it from the ship that was firing on us?"

"Please." She shook her head. "My grandmother could do that much."

Now grinning, he strode over to Aiden and picked him up. "You still doing okay, pal?"

"Yup."

"Think we can talk some more?"

"About the bad men?"

"About anything you can tell me. I think you know we can't search anything other than what our databases already have while we're in this nebula. We're safe for now, but we'll have to come out of it eventually."

"But it's stable. You wouldn't have been planning on going in if you were worried."

"Of course not, but it's not like this is going to be home. We had two months of exploration and lab work planned, unless there's a drastic discovery, and then we have provisions for another month as emergency backup. We need to leave sooner or later."

"Then where will we go?"

Vick sat down with Aiden on his lap. "I haven't called any planet home since I was a young boy on Earth. This ship and others like it are all I've had. Would you like to go back to your home?"

He shook his head. "I'll miss Mommy even more. Besides, the bad men will look there."

"You have another place you want to call home?"

"We'll find somewhere for the three of us," Aiden said as he wrapped his arms around Vick's neck. Vick caught Jody looking at them. She'd heard Aiden, and he didn't care. He stood and placed him back down. Not wanting to push for information that wouldn't help him right now anyway, Vick decided to drop it.

"If you can think of anything about these men, let me know. A name, a uniform, anything. Okay?"

"I'll try hard to remember."

"That's all I can ask, buddy." He scruffed his son's hair. "I need to get to work. You okay entertaining yourself?"

"Uh-huh. I'm reading your pervious papers on the nebulas you visited before."

"Reading my…uh…okay. Knock yourself out." He walked away, shaking his head. He couldn't comprehend the level of his son's genius. Those papers put most college kids through their paces. Returning to Jody, he said, "I need to stay here for a bit. You want to go set up that probe?"

She placed the Hawkeye on the table. "Might as well. I'm not getting anywhere with this thing." She stood. "Did I hear him correctly? He's reading your papers?"

"That's what he said."

"Incredible. I'll come back after I launch the messages and you can go back to the bridge."

"Actually, you'd better go. I was getting flak about you being needed. I can hide here with charts and readings for a while. I'll get Lenore to watch him when I need to go."

Aiden shot up when Jody opened the door. "Where are you going?"

"I have to launch a probe and some messages for the crew."

"Can I go with you?" he asked, stopping at his father's side.

"You should stay here, son. I don't think Jody needs you underfoot in the bay."

"Pleeeeeeeeease? I won't be in the way, I swear. I want to watch her launch the probe."

For seeming like a genius one minute, he sure could show his toddler side as well. "You'd rather go with her than stay with me?"

"You're going to just look at your computer. She's doing cool stuff."

Jody grinned. "It'll be okay, Captain. He can come with me."

"All right, but you be sure to stay out of her way. No funny business, either. Promise me."

"I promise." Aiden swiped his device from the table and ran to Jody, taking her hand.

"I'm going to put in some bridge time if you have him."

"Do that. We'll switch when I'm done. I shouldn't be long once the messages come in."

Aiden waved until the door slid closed.

Jody reached for the small screwdriver for the fourth time. For the fourth time, it disappeared and showed up on the opposite side of the desk. Aiden giggled as she crossed her arms and spun around.

"Your father said no funny business, Aiden."

"I bet he didn't even think I could do something like this, huh?"

"I'm certain he didn't think that you would do something like this. I'm sure he meant for you to not whine or complain and touch things you shouldn't. Now, will you please stop? If I take you back with another nosebleed, your father will be very upset with me."

"Moving small stuff never makes my nose bleed."

"Please stop, anyway."

"Okay," he said, kicking the ground. He stood by her, tiptoeing to see on top of the counter.

Jody put the screwdriver down then retrieved a high stool for him to sit on. "Better?"

"Thanks." He rested his chin on the back of his hands on the countertop. "You have all the messages on there now?"

"Yes, I do."

"What happens now?"

"I have to launch the probe and get it lined up with the next closest one, so it can transmit the messages to the next one, and so on. The last probe will be just outside the nebula enough to reach a satellite that will get them all the way to Space Command. They'll get the messages to their intended recipients."

"What if the bad men get the message, too?"

"I've encrypted it. On the off chance they get the message and break the code, the likelihood of them finding us in here, flying blind, are next to zero. You're such a smart boy. You know how big this thing is."

"Yeah…but still."

"Come on," she said, picking him off the stool and placing him down. "I'll let you key the code to release the probe."

She placed the probe in the small bay and sealed the door.

"Is that for torpedoes?" Aiden asked.

She laughed. "No. We have only a few weapons on board. This is its sole purpose. We launch a lot of probes. Mostly they collect dust and gas samples."

"Oh." His tone was as if he thought he sounded foolish. It wasn't lost on Jody.

"That was far from a silly question, Aiden. You're a very bright and amazing boy."

He shrugged. "I didn't have many friends."

"Really?" She knelt down by him. "Kids are stupid. Come to think of it, most adults are stupid, too. Too much time is spent judging others for not being like us." She took his hand. "Don't ever change, Aiden. Always be yourself. She stared into his eyes. "Starting with those. Don't change who you are for anyone. I think you're perfect." She tapped him on the nose and went to stand, but he stopped her. He hugged her neck so hard; he didn't even budge as Jody stood. She laughed. "I can't breathe, Aiden."

"Thanks for bringing me with you."

"My pleasure. Now let's launch that probe." She carried him to the computer and keyed away at coordinates with her free hand. "That's what we need right there," she said, as she pointed at the screen.

"There?" he repeated.

"Yes." Jody turned around. "Now we just need to—" The bay was empty. She put him down and crossed her arms. "Aiden Skinnard!"

"It was easier."

"You can't do things like that."

"Yes, I can. It's very easy." He didn't grin. She didn't think he meant to be sarcastic.

"You know what I mean. I asked you not to do that anymore." Running her hands over the keypad, she franticly keyed away to make sure it was indeed where it should be. A degree off one direction or another would make it totally useless.

"It's where you wanted it. I promise. If I could, I'd send the messages straight to Space Command."

"You can't send things that far?"

"It needs to be an item. I can't forward data."

Again her arms were crossed. "Then I'm grateful I didn't simplify the information onto a chip for you."

"I can't be as precise as placing in a computer, anyway. At best it would show up on the floor in the bathroom or something." He giggled as a three year-old boy should then became serious. "Are you going to tell my dad?"

"I'm not sure. I don't know if he'll be angrier at me or you."

"I won't do it anymore. Don't tell."

"It'll be our secret, honey bee," she said as she took his hand and headed for Vick's cabin. She was beginning to understand the pleasure in using nicknames.

It was well past two a.m. when Vick arrived back to his cabin. He'd gotten so involved with his crew while they searched for reasons for the teleporting; he'd forgotten he already knew the answer. Even though he'd asked them not to, the scenarios they came up with intrigued him so much and led to new ideas, he let them run with it. He couldn't believe when he looked at the time and realized Jody hadn't come back at all. After Xolo had said the probe was sent and all was going well so far, he'd carried on with the crew running numbers, codes, and equations. He couldn't believe he'd forgotten about her altogether, but forgetting Aiden was inexcusable.

He opened the door carefully, hoping not to wake anyone. She was asleep in his bed with Aiden. After shaking her gently, she turned and faced him with a sleepy Terian smile.

"I'm so sorry," he whispered.

"We had a good day," she said softly. "I called Xolo. I got done what I could. I didn't need to be on the bridge. White can go lay himself."

Vick chuckled. "You want to go back to your cabin?"

She motioned to Aiden. "I'm okay here. I'd hate to wake him."

"I want nothing more than to crawl in with you two, but I'm afraid how that'll look to him. I'll ride the couch."

"You sure? You could go to my place."

"Nah. I'll be all right. I just need a couple hours to recharge."

"Goodnight, Captain." Jody turned back to Aiden and wrapped her arm around him.

"Goodnight, Lieutenant." Vick kissed her forehead, then Aiden's.

Vick awoke to Aiden tugging on his arm. "Dad. Someone is outside the door."

"Huh? No one is—" He was interrupted by banging.

"How did you—" More banging kept Vick from finishing his thought. He hurried to the door and placed his hand on the pad. As soon as it slid open, White was there and obviously furious.

"What the hell is up your—" Looking down at Aiden, he changed his words. "What's wrong so early in the morning?" Vick could tell it wasn't something with the ship with the way the anger in White's eyes bore through him.

"Jody promised that probe would go out. That our messages would get through."

"She assured me it did."

Aiden jumped in as well. "It did! I was with her!"

White held his hand up to Aiden. "Sorry, kid, but this is between me and your dad. Beat it."

Vick took him by the collar of his jumpsuit. "Don't you dare talk to him like that. He was with her and she did get it out. She said there should be no issues. The messages will take time to bounce through."

"Her system is going crazy. They're not going out, they're bouncing back. Those messages need to go out, Captain! My fiancée probably has me written off as dead!"

"Hold on. I'm sure she can take care of this easily."

"I'm sure she can. You need to get her out of your bed first?"

He was right, but Vick hated the way he said it. Especially in front of his son. He landed a solid punch on his helmsman's chin, sending him against the wall. White slid to the floor.

Jody came running to the door from the hall. Vick was surprised to see her. He thought she was in his bed. Her face showed great confusion before her eyes even fell on her crew mate. "What happened to him?"

"He just needs to learn some manners, is all."

"Daddy punched him!"

"You punched him?" Jody helped White to his feet. "What's the matter with you two? There's not enough going on right now?"

White hissed as he wiped blood from his mouth. "I'm not the boss around here, but I'd really like to see you do what you promised. Not all of us have…" he looked down at Aiden, "illegal companions on the ship. My Gail would like to know I'm alive. Get on those messages." Then he added, "Please," before harshly spinning away.

Vick pulled her in and closed the door. "When did you leave?"

"I didn't." She looked down at Aiden. "Did you send me to my room?"

He nodded. "That man seemed mad to think you were here, so I made him wrong."

She knelt down. "That man is wrong. It's not his business where I sleep. I was with you; there is nothing wrong with that."

"But—" Aiden's lip quivered.

"No buts, pal," Vick interrupted. "You teleported Jody?"

"I knew where her cabin was. We went there yesterday."

"That's not the point. You know you're not supposed to do that."

Aiden's eyes went to Jody. Vick watched as her eyes looked away, then her mouth quirked. He was intrigued that she was learning human facial expressions, but more importantly he wondered what it was for.

"What exactly are you two up to?"

"Nothing," Jody said. "What was White carrying on about?"

He sighed, hating that the two of them were keeping a secret. He'd have to work on Jody later. "Your messages are getting bounced back. He's pissed."

"What?" Her eyes went to Aiden again. "That probe is exactly where it should be. There has to be a problem on the last one. Maybe it's too far in the nebula to reach the satellite."

"Damn. I was afraid of that. No way to redirect the last one out a little further?"

"You know I can't control it through this space muck. I have a chance at programming a new one but it would take days to get in position."

"No, it wouldn't," Aiden said.

"Son, I'd have to say I trust Jody on this. She's the best at this stuff."

"But I can put it anywhere you want it."

Vick closed his eyes and let his head fall slightly back as he took in what his son just said.

"Yes, I suppose you could, but I don't want you to. You'll get hurt."

"No, I won't. I did it yesterday."

"Way to get me in trouble, kid," Jody said under her breath.

"What? He did that yesterday?" Vick's voice raised a few octaves.

"It's not like I let him, he just did it."

Aiden tugged on Vick's leg. "Let me, Dad. I don't want that man to be angry at you again. I only put it where Jody said, but I can make it go way further."

"Aiden..."

Unaffected by his father's unrest, he asked, "Why did you call him white when he was green?"

Vick gave a soft laugh. "That's his name, Aiden. Corponius White. Deltorians have adapted earth names to make it easier on us. We're not capable of pronouncing some of their sounds."

His child-like expression told Vick that he felt silly. Once again, Vick was happy to see the three year-old boy come out. He adored the fact that his son could read college level papers, yet still question the simplest details. "Don't feel bad, son. No question is a dumb one."

"I know," he said in a way that made Vick feel he hadn't hurt his feelings after all. "Can I help Jody? Please?"

"He can come with me if it's okay with you," Jody offered. "He says it won't hurt him and I want to believe him. It needs to get done. Once I get that probe in place, it'll be a piece of dessert to reprogram the relay."

Not correcting her with "piece of cake," Vick said, "Okay. When you're done, get him to Lenore. I have a few things to wrap up then I'll get him from her." He turned to face Aiden. "I promise this time. I'm really sorry about last night."

"It's okay, I know you're busy. I don't mind."

"No more transporting Jody. Got it? I'll deal with the crew."

Aiden gave his dad's leg a quick hug before he went to Jody's side. "See you later."

Vick had his hand on Aiden's head as he kissed Jody goodbye. "I see how I rate around here."

She smiled and shrugged before opening the door. "I'll see you on the bridge soon."

Vick caught her by the arm, leaned in, and whispered in her ear, "Not if I catch you in the shower first."

Chapter Nineteen

Katie had read what she could between patients. On one hand she wanted nothing more than to take a day off and read the whole thing, but on the other, she wanted to drag the book out as long as she could. One the drive home, she grinned thinking she and Dusty must be overdue for sex in the shower.

Dropping her purse on the counter by the door, Katie walked over and kissed her husband.

"You made me laugh several times today."

He gave that slight grin that revealed the dimple she loved. "What did I do now?"

"You making Aiden move that screwdriver. Was that because of what Alex always did to you?"

Dusty laughed. "You know, I guess so. That little shit always ran away with my pen when he wanted my attention. I didn't think about it, but yeah, I guess he's my inspiration for that."

"See."

"What?"

"You can't write, you just steal from our lives."

Quickly grabbing her by the waist, he dipped her back. "You're right. I can't. I need to work through the details of the shower sex. You want to have a go at it?"

She pushed him back with a laugh. "Where are the kids?"

"Where else. Outside with the puppy. Alex was relentless from the time I picked him up about letting her sleep in bed with him again."

"You might as well let him, Dusty. You know you give in, anyway."

"No, I don't know that. Do you know something I don't?"

"I talked to you when I…when we…" Shit, no she didn't. "Uh, I must have dreamed it."

"You okay, babe?" Dusty asked, rubbing her arms. "You need to give the book a break and get some sleep."

"No, I'm fine. I'm almost done."

"I'm going to hide your reader when I go to bed."

Katie crossed her arms. "And the dog? Are you going to hide her, too?"

He shook his head. "I don't care if Alex sleeps with the dog. I just don't want any fights with Ali about it."

"She already told me it was okay. You know Blue curls up on her head when she sleeps. She doesn't want to disturb her."

"Right, because the cat only gets twenty-three hours of sleep. I'd hate to interrupt that."

Katie laughed hard, and then got serious. "Did May call you?"

"May? No, why? She call you?"

"Over lunch. She wants us to come out on Saturday for dinner."

"As in tomorrow?"

"Sorry. Yes, tomorrow."

"Did she mention why?"

"I don't think she needs to give us a reason, other than your parents want to see the kids, Dusty. It's been a few weeks since we've gone to see them."

"Mom and Dad don't hold back when they nag to see the kids. It just seems odd they felt the need to sick May on you."

"Maybe it's her that wants to see them. She's just as much their aunt as Dana or Alyson."

"You're probably right," Dusty said as he reached for a beer. "She's probably ready to quit again and needs her fix to change her mind. You want a beer?"

"No, thanks. I need a shower first. You got the coals started?"

"Just about to get them going."

"I sure love summer when you take over cooking duties. I'm not looking forward to the early winter they're predicting."

"Don't start worrying about that already. We're barely done with summer, puddin'."

"We're not true Minnesotans if we're not bitching about the weather, Dusty." Katie removed the e-reader from her purse.

"You little liar." Dusty smirked.

"What?"

"You're not taking a shower; you're going to read in the tub."

"Damn straight. Stall dinner, will you?"

"Sure. You going to say hello to your children? You know they'll barge in on you if you don't."

"They'll barge in on me no matter what."

"I'll keep 'em busy. You have half an hour, oh love of my life."

She turned away, but then stopped. "Dammit. You know I can't not say hello to them first."

"Go. They're plenty entertained."

She said, "Thanks," as she blew him a kiss then took the stairs two at a time.

Once Katie was out of earshot, Dusty called his parents' housekeeper, May. She'd been in the family longer than he had. She could never keep a secret from the kids.

"Hey, May. Katie said you called today."

"Hey, yourself. You've been neglecting us. I found an excellent roast at the market and thought of you. Katie said it was okay. Is it a bad time?"

"No, we can come. I'm just wondering what it's really about. You ready to kill Dad again?"

"When don't I want to kill your father?"

"True. But I sense there's more."

She sighed and hesitated for just a moment. "Your father knows you and Katie are looking to adopt a baby."

"How does he know? It's not like we're keeping it a secret, we just decided to do this a few days ago."

"How does your father ever learn anything?"

"Is he flipping a gasket? Going on about the Andrews name or something? I'm not coming if it's just going to be a shit storm. I won't do that in front of the kids. We haven't even talked to them about it yet."

"No, I'm sorry. He's not upset at all. He actually seemed kind of excited."

That took Dusty by surprise. "Really?"

"I don't know what it is with him lately, honey. It's like he's feeling his mortality or something. He lives for those kids of yours. I guess the thought of more makes him happy."

"Even if we adopt overseas?"

"You father is a pretentious ass of epic proportions, but a racist bigot he is not, Dustin Charles."

Dusty smiled. The fact that she used up breath to defend his dad was a nice change.

"Yeah, I suppose you're right. Hey…we just got a puppy. She's too little to leave home alone, and I'm not sure the kids would even do it. How bad will Dad crap if we bring her along?"

"I'll tell him you're bringing her. It's not like Princess Sophia is around to care. Maybe it'll get your mom out of her funk and make her go get another."

"I guess I wasn't thinking about that. That damn dog lived forever. She's still moping about it?"

"It comes and goes. I have to run. See you Saturday about four? Give us some time to mingle and have a cocktail before supper."

"Sounds good. See you then, May." Dusty hung up with a, "Shit," then quickly looked around, making sure there were no kids in earshot. He took a long swig of beer. "Bullshit he's that happy about it."

That night in bed, Dusty told Katie about his conversation with May. He didn't want to talk about it in front of the kids.

"Honestly, Dusty. You're so paranoid when it comes to your dad. May wouldn't make anything up. He's happy. Let him be happy."

"Well, explain to me how he found out? We haven't told anyone but Court and Dean."

"And Dean's a lawyer, dumbass. He had to make calls. Does anyone in a legal office in Minnesota not know your dad?"

His furrowed eyebrows softened. "Well, shit. That has to be it." He got out of bed.

"What are you going to do? Go beat up Dean now? He's only doing what we asked him to do."

"It's not his fault. For once I'd like to be the one to tell my dad something and not have someone beat me to the punch."

Katie joined him by the window. "You're getting upset over nothing."

"He'll stick his nose in, Katie. You know that."

"So."

"So?"

"Yes. So what? Let him help."

"I believe we've already had this conversation."

"Dusty…for fuck's sake. If he wants to help, he can help. You know how long this kind of thing takes. Of course he has connections or knows how to cut a little red tape. I'll take it. Why are you being so stubborn about this?"

"Damnit, Katie. Not to compare kids to dogs, but you know how you felt when I picked up a puppy without asking you."

"You got an Irish Setter."

"And that meant nothing to me. You have a personal experience or knowledge that I didn't and you lost it."

"You're seriously comparing your father picking out a child to a breed of dog?"

"No! I mean…I don't mean to. We've already said we don't care where it comes from, or if it's a boy or a girl, as long as he or she needs a home. But that's *our* decision to make together. Not his."

"You said May commented that he didn't mind an overseas adoption."

"I just find it hard to buy coming from him."

Katie crossed her arms. "I'm so angry with you right now, I can't even see straight." She spun away, but he caught her shoulder.

"Don't let us get in a fight because of my dad."

"It's not because of your dad, it's because of you. You're making the man happy and you're still upset with him."

"I've had a lot more years of dealing with him than you."

Katie walked over and grabbed a notebook and pen, then slammed it at his chest. "You'd better get busy writing, Dusty. The only sex you're getting tonight is if you write it." She grabbed her reader off the bedside table and headed out the door.

She was two chapters in before Dusty came down and joined her on the couch. She was sprawled out across the whole thing with her head on the armrest.

Dusty said, "I'm sorry."

She flopped the reader on her thighs. "For what exactly? I don't want to just hear the words, Dusty. I want you to really think about it."

"I'm sorry I'm not getting sex."

She laughed and smacked him gently with her reader.

"That hurts a little less than when you used to smack me with a ream of paper. I'm glad I mail you a PDF now instead of printing it out."

"I hate that I can be so pissed off at you one second and you make me laugh the next. Nice attempt, funny man. Try again."

"I'm sorry I can't let go of the bad history with my dad. You know what I went through. For God's sake, Katie. We both literally traveled through time to fix it."

"And now we have each other, our lives together, and the kids. You think he'd do anything to hurt that?"

"Not hurt it, but I still feel like he's going to try to make it about him."

"It's not about him. As much as we want to control it, there's only so much we can do. We need to be happy with what we're doing or it'll be for nothing. I need to know something, Dusty. And I want the truth."

Taking her hand he said, "Anything, babe."

"Are you really okay with this?"

"Of course I am. Why would you even say that?"

"Because of this. I don't understand why you're getting so freaked out over your dad. Are you the one who isn't happy with the decision to adopt? Will you feel like something is missing if it's not your DNA in our child?"

"No, babe. Don't even go there."

"I know invitro is out because of what the older you told us, but I don't know about finding a surrogate. Do you need this baby to be really yours?"

Both of her hands now in his, he took his time and planted a long kiss to each palm. "No. If he or she isn't a part of both of us, then no. I want our baby or one we share because of love, Kaitlyn Elizabeth Barrow Andrews. I don't want a part of anyone else." He leaned down and kissed her gently on the lips. "I'm sorry I was an ass. If you want my dad to help, he can help." He removed her reader and placed it on the carpet. He lay flat on top of her and began kissing over her neck then down her chest.

"Dusty…the kids. We're not having sex on the couch."

"A bomb wouldn't wake those two up. Come on…" He leaned up on one elbow. "You hear about the lawyer's wife in the kitchen preparing to boil eggs for breakfast?"

She grinned. "Enlighten me."

"When he walked in, she turned and said, 'You've got to make love to me this very moment.' His eyes lit up and he thought, 'This is my lucky day.' Not wanting to lose the moment, he embraced her and then gave it his all, right there on the kitchen table. Afterward she said, 'Thanks,' and returned to the stove."

"I'm intrigued, really," Katie said after a yawn escaped.

Dusty continued. "More than a little puzzled, he asked, 'What was that all about?' She explained, 'The egg timer's broken.'"

Katie had a good belly laugh at that one. "That's not really a lawyer joke."

"I had to improvise. My stash is getting thin after years of living next to Dean."

"Are you telling me I should set the timer? That's so romantic."

"I promise my eggs won't be done before yours."

"My eggs are already cooked, dear husband."

"You know what I mean." He growled and a gently bit her neck.

"Okay. No couch. Let's go work on that shower scene."

Dusty's eyebrows rose. "Really?"

She nodded and scooted him off her. "Race you."

Chapter Twenty

It had been two days since Jody and Aiden got the last probe in place. All messages were sent and the crew was happy with the results. Most of the crew had given up on figuring the equation for how they got there and moved on as originally planned, taking samples and readings of this unique nebula.

Vick was managing the juggling game between running the ship and caring for Aiden pretty well so far. He felt bad his son spent so much time in daycare, but he seemed to really like it and Lenore really enjoyed having him.

Doctor Aubrey had insisted that she needed him for a few hours of follow up and some tests, but he couldn't allow that; not yet.

"Where are we going to run off to? You'll get him when I can spare the time to be with him," he'd reprimanded her.

Having taken time for everyone but himself, he was now lying in bed, spooning Jody. He gently caressed her arm as he gave her shoulder a kiss. "I feel guilty as hell, but I needed that."

Jody leaned back and met his lips with hers. "I'm very pleased to learn what the Athracki women say about human men is untrue."

He sat up. "What do they say?"

She held up a pinky and wiggled it.

Vick raised an eyebrow. "Seriously?"

"Yes. Actually, they say it's even worse than that. They say you do nothing to try to please your women." She grinned. "I'm quite fond of that trick you do with your tongue. They could not be more wrong."

"Hmm. Deidre didn't mention those rumors. Although—" He suddenly felt bad for mentioning her.

"What did she say?"

"Nothing. I don't want to ruin this moment."

"You were broken up with her for years, and now she's dead. How upset do you think I'm going to get if you tell me she thought you were an incredible lover?"

He caressed her arm some more. "I wasn't going to say anything like that. She just made comments, wondering why it had always been the way of her people to hate humans so much. She was so afraid when she first found her way on my ship. She initiated things with me, not the other way around. You'd think if I repulsed her, I would have had to woo her."

"Woo?" she asked.

"You know. Sweet talk and do nice things to win her over."

"You did not do those things with me."

"Sure I did. You hated me, so it made it that much harder." He gave her a tight squeeze before he kissed the back of her head. "I'd stay like this for a week, but we have to get to the bridge. I've stalled long enough. Thanks for agreeing to be with me. I'm sorry the start of our relationship is this way."

"What way?" she asked, as she climbed out of bed and reached for her clothes.

"All the sneaking around. Hiding what we're doing." He stood in front of her and wrapped his arms around her again. "I want nothing more than to shout to everyone that you're mine. I see the way White looks at you. It takes all I have not to punch his lights out."

She leaned back with a grin. "Captain Victor Skinnard. You're jealous?"

"Hell, yeah, I am."

"He says he's engaged."

"It doesn't stop his stares. As soon as we're on our way back, I'm announcing it over the com that you're mine."

She ran her finger down his chest. "I agree. I think this needs to wait."

"You know the rules we try to keep on this ship. Sex complicates everything."

"I already said I agree with you. Sex complicated things no matter what rules you try to instill, Captain. Is it not running through your head all day anyway? It seems to me that the more you try not to think about something, the worse it becomes."

He let out a soft laugh. "Well…yeah. Kinda worse when we're not." Reaching down, he grasped her ass and pulled her close again. "How come you're so smart?"

"You earth men think you corner the market on what you call horny. You don't even compare to Terian men. Why do you think they have more than one wife?"

"I guess I didn't think about it. Even some earth cultures allow multiple wives. I'll admit to not knowing a lot about your planet. Is it a religious thing?"

She shook her head. "It is a female's choice. Our day and night are not the same as yours. Sex every quadrant of our day to keep our men happy would be impossible. Especially after we have children. It is usually then that a husband will take on another wife, with the female's blessings."

"Uh…you don't ever just say no?" He let out a chuff. "Earth women tend to play what we call the 'headache card.'"

Again she shook her head. "We do not play card games with sex."

Vick laughed. "Don't the women get…you know…jealous or something?"

"It is how it has always been, Captain. It is simply expected of Terian women. They know they are loved and time is shared."

He swayed with her. "I'd kill before I'd share you with someone else."

"It is not in our culture for the women to have more than one mate."

He still felt like she was merely answering matter-of-factly, and not getting how much he cared for her. "You certainly wouldn't expect me to get others, would you?"

"Seeing as how we have to sneak around and only get to hammer every few days, I would prefer not."

Vick chuckled. "How many times do I need to tell you we're 'making love?'"

"The difference is still new to me. I wish to adapt your earth ways."

"I feel like hell for not knowing much about your culture. I don't want all the giving to be on your end."

"You don't want to live our way." She kissed him. "You should get going."

"But this is important. I need to know everything about you, Jody. I want you to be mine. I don't want you to return home. I don't want to share you with anyone else or have anyone else that you have to share me with."

"This has been covered."

He could tell he was just confusing her. "Tell me you don't have to return home when this is over."

"My life is mine to do with as I choose. Not many leave my planet. And no, I do not have to go back. As a matter of fact, it is forbidden that I go back."

He took her hands and sat her on the couch. "Does this make you sad?"

"No. It was my choice. I did not wish to live as my mother and sisters have. I craved science and wanted more for myself. It's new to my people, but things are changing. Unfortunately not enough that I'm welcome back. My father is very traditional."

"It sounds like a few cultures on Earth as well."

"You know the ways in which I'm different and you have told me not to change, but I cannot help it. You stir things in me that I never knew existed. Have patience with me…Vick."

He smiled that she used his name. "That tasted terrible, didn't it?"

"Yes. But if it's what you want, I'll try."

Holding her chin he said, "Don't do anything you don't want. I don't care what you call me."

"I'll find something. You need to go. I wanted to say hello to Aiden before I returned to the lab as well. He said he'd let me look at his Hawkeye again."

He stood and kissed the top of her head. "You know where to find me if you need me."

"You want to do what?" Xolo practically shouted.

Despite what he and Jody had discussed, Vick wanted to change the rules and had decided to enforce it immediately on his walk to the bridge.

"Lift the ban. What's the point in having a rule no one follows? It was dumb to even try. Maybe if they didn't have to try to sneak sex, we wouldn't have two infants on board right now."

Xolo ran his hands down his face. All four of them. Vick knew he was going to get an earful. "You're a jackass. Just because you want to bone Jody doesn't mean it should be open season on fornicating."

Vick smiled.

Xolo frowned. "What's that for?"

"That's one expression I hadn't used yet. So far, it's been pretty much tools." Xolo wasn't humored. "Xolo, this doesn't affect you. You're the only crew member whose spouse is on board. You take some sort of pride in thinking you're the only one having sex on this ship?"

"I'm not so stupid as to think that. It's not that I'm against it; it's just that if you make an announcement like that, everyone is going to wonder what the hell is up. They know they're doing it and you know they're doing it. What difference is it going to be if you make an announcement? They'll figure *you* want the okay for yourself. You don't need permission from your crew. You're the captain, in case you've forgotten."

"Right. And as the captain, I hold myself to a higher standard. How can I expect anyone to respect me or my rules if I don't follow them? I don't want the fact that Jody and I are together to be a secret. I know how it'll sound and I understand the flak I'll take, but I'm doing this. Write it up and get the message out to everyone."

"Do I include an engagement announcement with that?" Xolo replied, obviously upset.

"No, asshole." He paused and grinned. "Assholes. Just do it. This time tomorrow, this ship will be filled with more smiles than your grumpy ass will be able to stand."

Xolo spun his chair around and started typing away. "If you think I was bad, wait until Aubrey gets hold of you."

"She'll have to catch me first." Although the men tried to keep the conversation between them, they were on the bridge. The handful of crew members there had heard everything. Grins were ear to ear and several messages were being sent from their personal devices, no doubt already securing their dates for the evening.

Vick's intercom squealed to life with Jody's voice. "Captain, can you come down to the lab? I need to show you something."

White chuckled from his desk. "I'll bet she does. Can it wait till she's off duty?"

Vick rushed him, but Xolo got between them.

"This is what I was expecting," Xolo said.

"Not that I'm explaining anything to you, White, but your pea-brain can't even comprehend what she's working on. It's vital to our discovery here. One more outburst like that and you'll finish the duration of this exploration in the brig."

Xolo turned around and shoved White, sending him against his control board. "I'm not sure when it became okay to disrespect your Captain. I'm second in command and have every right to remove you from your station."

White stood up and pretended to adjust his uniform. "I was just having a little fun."

"Have it on your own time." He addressed everyone. "I allowed your ears on our conversation for a reason. We're a team. Vick and I banter and call each other names, but it's to keep it light. I have nothing but respect for him and his decisions. It's called playing devil's advocate, people. If you're not familiar with the earth term, look it up. If anyone disagrees, speak up. Say it to us directly, not in hushed tones, passing us in the hallway." No one said a word. Xolo faced Vick again. "Go. I got it covered here. If Jody hailed you, she's got something."

"Thanks." Vick nodded to him, squinted his eyes at White, and left the bridge.

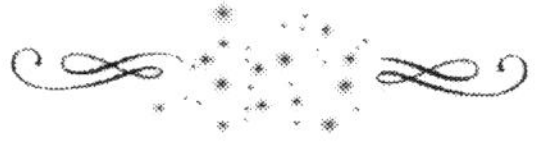

"What is it?" Vick asked as he hustled through the lab door. "Were you able to open up that message from Deidre?"

Jody held up Aiden's Hawkeye. "No, but I'm receiving a message from your father."

"What? How are you doing that? Nothing can get in or out from here. I thought that probe you sent would only transmit, that there was no chance of a signal being bounced back to us."

"I did set it up that way. The message isn't finding us through our probes." She placed the device down and stood to meet Vick's eyes. "You said Deidre didn't contact you over the last three years. Not until she took you back to Einnoc to meet Aiden."

"That's correct."

"This device is linked to your secured lines. Your encrypted servers. All of your personal data, your message board…everything."

"How did you get into that?"

She grinned. "Did you not hire me because I was the best?" Crossing her arms she said, "Afraid I'll find something?"

He held her hands. "No little black book, sweetheart." Her blank expression told him she didn't get the reference. "No. No personal secrets to find, just private crew files, banking, everything else." Vick snapped his fingers. "Xolo told me a few days ago that she had popped into my quarters a few months back. Maybe she set something up."

"Whatever she did, your father has been hailing you on your private line. It appears as if you can answer him."

"In here?"

"This device moved an entire ship. I imagine it's capable of opening up a communications line. Even in a nebula."

He let out a long breath. "Open it. I'll talk to him. I can't imagine it'll lead the men after us in here. Not unless they have this same device. If they did, I don't think they'd be so dead set on getting their hands on this one."

"Nothing says they don't…Vick. Ugh. Can you give me one of those terms you like? Any that are for a man?"

"It's not usually the choice of the person that gets the nickname. It's supposed to be natural. Don't you call a loved one something? Nickname your friends even?"

"No, I've never done that. What did your mother call your father?"

"An asshole."

"Obviously not a name like that," she said with the smile she was still practicing. "Those I know. At one point they were in love. What did she call him?"

"Hon."

"Hon? What is that?"

"Short for honey, I'm pretty sure."

"Okay. Then I will call you 'hon' if you'd like."

He smiled. "Only if you like it."

"I have tried your earth honey. I like it very much. This works for me. So, hon, there is nothing that says these men don't have another Hawkeye. I don't see this device connected to another, but that doesn't mean it isn't. There is still so much unknown. The men are after Aiden as well, not just the device. If you talk to your father, there is a risk they will know what you're doing."

"He may have information we need. I'll have to take the chance. In the meantime, find us a new place to park this thing. After I transmit, we'll move."

"This area is getting us excellent readings. Are you sure?"

"I trust you. If you think it isn't safe to move, we won't. But if you think it's feasible, this may be an excellent chance to study this thing further."

"I'll do my best."

"That's all I ask. Now, how do I get my dad?"

Jody connected three tiny clips to the exposed back of Aiden's Hawkeye. She had it clamped to a small stand. "There's a built-in mic and camera. He'll show up in a screen here when he answers," she said, waving above it. "It'll keep hailing him until he does. Do you want me to stay?"

"No. It'll be best if you start plotting a new course right away. The sooner we move, the safer I'll feel."

"Feeling safe or not, I think it's a good move. There's so much to this nebula, the thought of going in deeper make good exploration sense. No one will question you." Just then, her personal device went off at the same time as his. Knowing it was his message about lifting the ban, he ignored his. She took a moment to read the message. Her head whipped up. "Already? We talked about this."

"I didn't see the point in waiting."

"So the crew knows about us?"

"Bridge crew, yes. As far as the rest, word will spread, I'm sure. I wanted it to come straight from me, not from someone who may have seen you leave my cabin." He was dumbfounded by her light orange shade. "Is that on your way to being really mad color? Tell me you're not angry, Jody. I had to do it."

"I'm confused. I guess I just didn't think you'd do it so quickly."

"Like I said, no point putting it off."

She motioned to the device. "And your father? Will you tell him?"

Jody had been halfway to the door; Vick waved his hand, calling her back. She leaned into him as he sat at the stool by the Hawkeye. "My father and I haven't gotten along for years. I've never actually brought a girl home before."

"You're afraid because I'm Terian?"

"No. I swear that's not it. He's not one to freak out about that, not that I'd care if he did. Don't ever let me hear you say anything about that again. Okay?"

"It's new to me. I know many people don't take a liking to humans and other—"

He placed his hand over her mouth. "Anyone who doesn't accept other people's love is just an idiot. It's none of their business. We're all that matters."

"And Aiden."

"Of course and Aiden. My dad and I have business or we wouldn't be talking. I know he doesn't care if I'm happy or not."

"Of course he cares for you, hon. Wait. That's nice. I mean you schmuck."

Vick laughed. "You don't know him."

"Well, I'd like to."

"I'll never get to know your father. That's not fair."

"No, that's doing you a favor. My father most certainly would not take to me being with a human. Let alone anything I do from now on."

"I hope I can make you happy enough so you'll never regret leaving your home." Vick held her face and lingered over a kiss.

A cough interrupted them. "I see you're really distraught over your situation."

Vick broke the kiss and turned to face the image that had appeared above the Hawkeye. "Hey, Dad."

"Who's this?" he asked.

"Jody. Lieutenant Jodessa Opex. My chief communications officer. She's the one who busted the code so we can be having this conversation. It should be impossible to talk to you right now from inside this nebula."

"*Inside* the nebula?"

"Yes."

Jody pushed herself away. "You two need to talk and I need to get to work."

"I'll see you soon." Vick kissed her goodbye, despite being in his father's sight. He hadn't planned on announcing anything to him, but there was no point in denying it now.

After the door closed, Aiden Skinnard asked, "She Terian?"

"Yes. I hope there's no negative comment coming from you."

"Don't be asinine, son. Unless you shack up with a rebel drug lord, you have my blessings."

"I honestly don't care what you think. I wouldn't have even brought her up, you just caught us—"

His father cut him off. "I have some information for you."

"You found Deidre's killers?"

"I think I just may have, son."

Chapter Twenty-One

Dusty let out a heavy sigh as he turned off the car in his parents' driveway. Katie gave his leg a squeeze.

"Don't start anything, okay? We've had nothing but great visits with them for years. Why do you still get your hackles up?"

He shrugged. "Years of practice."

"Grandpa!" Ali hollered from the backseat. "Unbuckle me, Mommy!"

Katie climbed out of the car to free her daughter. Dusty took care of Alex who promptly ran for May, who had joined his father at the door. Returning to her husband with the puppy in hand, Katie said, "Lay off the Captain Morgan 100 proof."

Dusty said, "No promises," as he kicked at the ground and headed to the house.

"Did you seriously just kick the ground like a seven-year-old boy?" Katie whispered when she caught up to him.

"Put a sock in it, Andrews. I need someone on my side today."

Katie gave him a nudge before hugging her father-in-law. "Great to see you, Dad."

"Glad you kids could come on short notice. I was hoping grandparents didn't need to schedule an appointment." To Dusty's surprise, he gave the puppy several pats. "She sure is cute. She's really deaf, huh?"

"As a doornail," Katie replied. "You sure you don't mind that she comes in?"

"Not at all. I think it'll do Norma some good. Can't say that I miss that old dog, but she sure is moping."

"I was glad she went on her own. It would have been too hard on me to have to put her down," Katie said.

"There you are!" Dusty's mom said as she came out the door. After tight hugs to everyone, she took the puppy from Katie. "What a sweetie." She bent down and received kisses on the chin from Deidre.

Dusty reached for her. "She's pretty good with the house training, but I should walk her before we come in, Mom."

"Nonsense. I'll take her. Meet me at the pool. May has refreshments set up."

Dusty grinned as his mother walked away, talking to the dog. "She does realize she's deaf, right?" he said to his father.

"Don't think it matters, son," he said with a pat to his back. "Come on out back. I have a new craft beer I want you to try. I like it so much, I'm buying the brewery."

"Really? That's a twist for you. Is it a buyout? They in trouble?"

"Just the opposite, actually. It's a new start up. Your sister's husband turned me onto them. I'm going to have him run it."

"Jim? A brew master? That's hell of a switch from accounting."

"He's bored. So is Dana with analytical talk. She's actually encouraging him."

They'd reached the patio by this point. Katie took the kids to the pool house to change into their suits. Dusty was reaching for a chilled glass when May got behind him.

"Sit. I'll get it. I'm kinda having a kick with this thing," she said, motioning to the beer taps. "All these years of pouring whiskey over ice, this is kinda fun."

Dusty chuckled. "We can get you a part-time job at a bar in Dinkytown if you want."

"Brat. Go sit. I'll fill up a flight. Your dad will want you to try them all."

"Flight glass sizes are great. I don't want to get trashed."

"Need to stay at the top of your game, do ya?" She winked.

"You know me too well, May."

Dusty joined his father under an umbrella. "Someone from Dean's firm talk to you about our situation?"

"You don't waste any time with small talk do you, son?"

"If there's a reason behind this invitation, I'd like it out there."

"The reason is it's a beautiful day. We won't have many more of these. Your mother wanted to see the kids and the dog. If I waited for you to come over on your own, we'd never see you."

"I'm sorry, it's just been a crazy month at work."

"How's that book coming? Rumor has it you're done with number three."

"You're done with the third one?" May asked as she dropped off the two flights with five glasses in each one, filled with samples ranging from light to dark beers.

"Katie's still reading it," he answered. "When she's done, I can use another set of eyes if you want to give it a go. I don't need to get it to the editor for another month."

"I'd love to. I'm going to check on lunch. I'll be back in a few."

Norma joined them with the puppy in her lap. "She's a doll, Dusty." Again she accepted kisses to her chin from Deidre. "She did a number two, if you're keeping track."

He laughed. "No, but thanks."

The kids went running by, heading to the pool. "You two walk," Katie called out before joining everyone at the table.

"Oooh," Katie reached for a light colored beer. "Do they have fun names?"

"They are on the taps. You'll have to ask May," Dustin Senior said. "Silly ass names if you ask me. Jim will have to come up with something more professional once it gets going." He turned to Dusty. "You see on the news that there are lawyers that make a living off lawsuits over those beer names? It's insane."

"I did see that. Kinda crazy."

"Did you tell him who's coming?" Norma asked.

Dusty face lost its smile. He knew there had to be more to the visit. "Who's coming?"

"Ariel. She's back in town and wanted to say hello. Isn't that sweet?"

Dusty felt the color leave his cheeks. "Yeah, that's sweet. I'm going to get my suit on and cool off." He picked up a dark beer and drank the whole thing in one gulp. "That one's good," he said as he walked away.

Katie caught up with him in the pool house, her eyes filled with concern. "Who's Ariel? An old girlfriend?"

"No. Not really. Uh, babe…you don't want to know. Really."

"Oh, I think I do." Katie folded her arms over her chest. "If it's gotten you to look like you've seen a ghost, I most certainly do."

He ran his hands down his face. "You'll get pissed. Please don't get pissed. I can guarantee they don't know."

"They don't know what?"

"Remember the maid I told you about?"

"*That* maid?" Katie broke into a laugh. "The one who took your virginity? The one who taught you how to please a woman after your Becky Swenson disaster?"

"I'm glad you're humored by it." He tied his swim trunks with a little more force than necessary.

"I'm sorry, Dusty, but it's funny." She wrapped her arms around his waist. "We both have skeletons in our closets and people from our past. I'm not going to get angry with you for something you did when you were sixteen. If she wants to change your sheets with you in them this afternoon, then I'd get pissed at you."

He smiled. "Fair enough. You going to join us in the pool?"

"Maybe later. I'll chat with your parents. You have fun with the kids."

After lunch, May escorted a tall blonde woman out to the porch. A very attractive tall woman. Dusty recognized her right away. He held up his small glass of beer, as if in a toast.

"Hi, Ariel. Nice to see you again."

Norma squealed and hopped up. "So good to see you, dear. Sit."

Dusty tried to gage Katie's reaction. She didn't give him anything to go on.

"Did you eat, dear?" Norma asked. "We just finished lunch, but May could get you something."

"No, I'm fine. I had lunch with an old friend." She turned to Katie. "You must be Katie. May has told me so much about you." Now smiling at Dusty, she said, "You got lucky,

Andrews. I was afraid we'd never get you settled down." Again to Katie, "He never dated much. Always wanted to hang out with that Alyson and be best friends."

"They still are," Katie replied. "We've named our daughter after her."

"That's fantastic," she said with a flip of her hair.

Katie gave a slight smirk, obviously amused by the show. She pushed back her chair. "I think I'll go check on the kids."

"I'll go, babe," Dusty said, scooting back.

"No. Don't be silly. You catch up with your friend."

"I'll join you," Norma said to Katie.

Dusty now felt cornered. Alone with his dad and Ariel, he waited for the bomb to drop.

"I'm going to run for a cigar. You two catch up, I'll be right back."

Dusty downed another glass. Of course it went down the wrong pipe, sending him into a coughing fit. Ariel stood and gave his back a few pats.

"Are you okay?"

After a few more coughs he said, "Yeah." She returned to her seat. "What brings you back here, Ariel?"

"Just passing through, really. May and I still talk, so she invited me over. I was thrilled to be able to see you again."

Dusty felt his cheeks flush. He hated that she could still do that him. "It's more than a little embarrassing, Ariel."

She flipped her hair again and placed her hand on his knee. "Don't be silly. You were a wonderful student."

For a lack of a better way to remove her hand, Dusty stood and went over to the beer taps. "You want a beer?"

"Sure."

"Light or dark?"

She shrugged. "You pick."

After pouring one, he sat again and handed her the beer.

"I promise, no head jokes," she said with a devilish grin.

Dusty looked over to Katie, grateful she was well out of earshot. "You need to stop."

She laughed. Man that hair flipping was annoying. Dusty was feeling more comfortable as he realized she had no power over him. He was happily married and she wasn't even an old girlfriend. Why the hell was he so nervous?

"Your father told me about your situation."

"There it is. I knew there was a reason for this visit and you showing up."

"He only wants to help."

"Yeah, I've heard that before. What do you do now? Work with an adoption agency?"

"Oh no. Nothing like that. I don't work, Dusty. I'm quite well off. I left here and married my next employer. Go figure, huh?"

"Employer? You worked for an old fart, married him, and then left with his fortune?"

"You say that like it's a bad thing."

"Jesus, Ariel."

"Don't judge me, mister born with a silver spoon in your mouth."

He held his hand up. "Exactly what did my dad hail you for then?"

"I want to be your surrogate."

"My what?"

"Your surrogate. I wouldn't even mind…you know. We don't have to do the lab thing."

"You want me to sleep with you, get you pregnant, and you'll give me the baby?"

"I don't want children, but I wouldn't mind doing this to help you out."

"I can't believe what I'm hearing. Are you all mad?"

"I didn't tell your father the sex part, obviously."

"Does he know about us?"

"No. Not that he's said, anyway."

Dusty took a deep breath before he spoke. This was too much. "If you're so set for money, why would you want to do this to your body?" He motioned over her size three frame and double D breasts that weren't there in his youth.

"Your dad can offer other things, Dusty. A favor in his direction goes a long way. It's not that big of a deal."

"The fact that you even said that makes me believe you have no idea what you're agreeing to. You have no idea what being pregnant does to you. The restrictions you'll have to make to your diet, the hormones, The weight you'll put on—"

"So, I'll read books."

He couldn't help but almost feel sorry for her. "I don't know what my dad has over you, but the answer is no. I'm flattered, really, but Katie and I have already ruled this out."

"Don't be pissed at your Dad. It came up in conversation and I offered." She licked her lips a little too flirty for Dusty's taste.

"Are you sleeping with him?"

"No, Dusty. I knew about your father's reputation. Word has it he's off the market. Has been for years."

"So he's been keeping his promise. That's something." Dusty relaxed into the chair. His father was on his way back. He needed to take a few deep breaths and clear his head. This was too insane to be happening.

"You two have a nice chat?" he asked.

"Yup. And I've decided I'm not going to rip your head off and shit down your neck. I appreciate that you think you're helping, but we've got things covered, Dad. Dean will find us a baby. If you'd bothered to ask me, I would have told you we're not looking for a surrogate. Whatever you have on Ariel, let it go."

"I have nothing over this girl. I thought it was a generous offer."

"If I didn't want to upset the kids, I'd leave right now."

"Why does everything have to be a battle with you? I thought you'd jump at the chance to have your own blood in your child."

"Mine or yours?"

"Don't be ridiculous. I'll love whoever you adopt. I just wanted to help."

"I see I'm not needed for this." Ariel stood with some force behind her motions.

"Don't go," Dustin Senior said. "May and Norma will be disappointed."

She sat back down.

"Did Mom know what you were trying to do?"

"No. I didn't want her to get excited. You know how fond she was of Ariel." He faced her. "Why did you leave us, dear? I don't remember the reason."

She grinned and faced Dusty before turning back to his father. "I had a better offer. Higher position."

Dusty stood. "Meaning I stopped sleeping with her and she found an employer who would pay her for the privilege."

"Come again?" Dustin senior said.

"I'm going to play with the kids in the game room. You guys have a nice visit." Dusty walked toward the house with his head held high. He was furious with his dad, but he knew he'd never understand. Somewhere in his father's brain, he thought he was really trying to help. He wasn't looking forward to telling the story to Katie.

Chapter Twenty-Two

Vick listened as his father explained what he'd found.

"They're Rhenharts, son."

"Rhenharts? I guess that makes sense. They aren't known for their diplomacy."

"I found out that they were the ones who kidnapped Deidre in a roundabout way. I'd heard rumors of them trying to develop a device for time traveling. I'm not sure what they wanted with her, but she was into them pretty deep. I won't sugarcoat it, Vick. She ran with some bad news."

Vick wasn't sure how much he should tell his father. He decided he'd keep him on a need-to-know basis. "Well, like you said, she was kidnapped. She was forced to do their bidding. From what little I understand so far, she was trying to get away. That's why she was killed."

Aiden leaned into the camera. "Did she give you something? Are the men who killed her after you now?"

As Vick hesitated, his expression must have given him away.

"Son, I'm trying to help you. If you hold information back, that isn't going to help matters."

Taking a minute to gather himself, Vick finally spoke. He had no choice but to trust his father.

"There is a device, Dad. But that's not all."

"What else is there?"

"Aiden."

"Aiden?" he roared. "What could they possibly want with him?"

"He can make the device do things that they haven't been able to make it do without him."

"I know Athrackians are highly intelligent. Is he an off-the-charts genius?"

"He's a genius all right, but…there's more to him." Vick stood and stepped out of sight of the video screen.

"Vick," his father called out. "Come back and explain this to me. This is my grandson we're talking about. I'm going to do everything in my power to protect him, but I have to know what I'm dealing with."

He stepped back into sight. "I can't, Dad. I've unknowingly placed my whole crew at risk by bringing him on board. We're safe in this nebula for now, but I don't know for how long. Aiden can make this device do things, but I don't know for sure that there isn't another. I've taken a chance opening up this communication with you. We should probably kill the feed."

"I'll respect that for now, but I'll want answers. And soon. Space Command is following leads on the Rhenharts' whereabouts. They're in your neighborhood."

"I guessed that much by the blast we took before we entered the nebula."

"Was anyone hurt?"

"No. The ship and crew are fine. We're trying to carry on, business as usual, while I sort this out. It's not easy juggling this and worrying about Aiden."

"Welcome to fatherhood."

Vick refrained from saying, "Like you were ever much of a father." As much as he hated it, his father was his only link to the outside right now. He needed him, and it tasted terrible.

"I'm going to have Jody tinker with this device some more. Maybe it has some back door that will lead us to its creator."

"Good thinking. I'll keep up with updates on the Rhenharts. The ones that pulled the trigger on your ship aren't necessarily the ones who held her captive, but it's a start."

"It's a hell of a start. Can you call the same time tomorrow? I assume Jody can work her magic again."

"I'll be available and keep the line open for an hour. If I don't hear from you, we'll try again in six hour intervals. We'll keep that up until we talk. Deal?"

"That'll work."

"Make sure it does. I'll go insane with worry if you leave me hanging. On the bright side, your mother will be thrilled to know you've finally found someone."

"Your wife, who is younger than me, is not my mother."

"Let's not end this on that note, son."

With a huff, he held his hand over the button to end the call. "No, but we need to end it. Bye, Dad. Thanks."

"Bye, Son. I lo—" Vick hit end.

"That wasn't very nice."

Vick spun around to find Jody standing in the doorway with her arms crossed.

"Were you listening to the whole thing?"

"Not the whole thing. I was concerned about leaving the line open. I wanted to be sure to shut it down properly and warn you to keep it short."

"Done and done."

She walked over and disconnected a couple small clips. "Now it's done." She faced him. "Why do you dislike his wife so?"

"Because she chased away my mother and destroyed their marriage."

"Maybe your mother was unhappy and she wanted out."

"That's not the way I remember it."

Pinching her lips tight, she held up a hand. "I'm not going to fight with you. I don't have what I need for this argument."

"The facts?"

"No. You told me to never argue with an idiot."

Vick grinned. "Babe, I think you're finally getting the hang of this sarcasm thing."

"No, I'm not. I'm serious. Your father wants to help us. He's the only one helping us right now. You be nice, or no hammering for you."

He wrapped his arms around her waist and dipped her slightly, certain by now she had to know that he wanted her to call it "making love," but she was teasing him. "Threatening to hold back sex. You're learning earth ways. I'm not so sure I like it." Giving her a hard kiss, he returned her upright. "I'm going to go spend some time with Aiden, then get on the bridge. Come up when you have the new coordinates, would you please?"

"Sure. I won't be long."

Within the hour, Jody gave White the new set of coordinates. He was less than happy to be told what to do by her. Vick walked in as they were arguing. He promptly stepped between them.

"What the hell is going on?"

"Since when do I take orders from your sweetheart?"

Vick grabbed him by his shirt, but Jody clasped her hand on his. "Let him go. If that's the way he feels, I can't help that." Once Vick let go, she continued. "I wasn't giving you orders. I was giving you the coordinates so you could prepare them. I'd call you an ass name that you people seem so fond of, but that wouldn't get us anywhere."

"Give it your best shot, sister," he growled.

"I refuse to satisfy you with one."

White smirked. "You mean give me the satisfaction?"

Vick gently pushed Jody aside then pulled White out of his chair. "You're relieved of your duties."

"What? You can't do that!"

"Really? Last time I checked, I was Captain of this ship. You've shown nothing but disrespect to me, Jody, and anyone else you've come in contact with. Before we entered the nebula, someone was feeding information to my father. I can't prove it was you, but you're at the top of my list."

"I know nothing about that!" he shouted with spittle flying.

"You think I'm some kind of idiot? You claim to have a fiancée that you are desperate to get a message to and yet you continually hit on Jody."

"I told you he does not," Jody said angrily.

"Yes, he does," came from at least three crew members.

Jody arms dropped in frustration.

"Sorry, Jody. This isn't about you." Vick turned back to White. "You seem a little too preoccupied with my love life. I came clean and kept it no secret, out of respect to my crew. That's more than you offered me when you added to the count of members on this ship."

"What's that supposed to mean?"

"I know you're the father of little Montreux. The only other Deltorian on the ship is a woman. Last I checked, the people of your planet couldn't change their sex or spontaneously reproduce. I've avoided disciplinary action because Rhodan was determined to keep your identity a secret. And as you can tell, I think that rule was a little off base and did my best to remedy it. No matter what I do, you're determined to make everyone's life hell. You leave this bridge now and I won't have you jailed for insubordination. Make me remove you, and you can kiss your freedom for the next two months goodbye."

He squared off with Vick. "You think someone else can fly this ship the way I do?"

"Sure do. I can name a few, actually. Take the day to chill out. See Deborah tomorrow morning about your reassignment."

"This is unheard of, you know. I gave up a position with Space Command for a chance at working with you."

Vick wasn't being swayed by his words. "Then you should have acted like it was a position you wanted. Leave. Now."

Corponius White stormed away, leaving Vick a little uneasy about what he would do. He'd realized the Deltorian was a hot-head after just a few days at space. It wasn't anything he hadn't dealt with before, but White certainly proved to be the most difficult crewmember Vick had ever worked with. Vick was known for taking a lot of flak from his crew. He encouraged open discussions on big decisions, but things had gotten out of hand lately and he blamed himself.

Vick turned to Jody. "I lied. I have no idea who to put in charge of steering this beast."

"I'm more than capable, Captain," Jody stated firmly.

"I second that," Xolo said.

"You have enough on your plate with communications."

"I can do both. Let me, at least while you find a replacement for either position. I'll do a quick search of personnel files and send you the records of the four most qualified to your personal device."

"I really wanted to move the ship now." He held his expression, not wanting to actually say, "Since I took that call from my father," in front of Xolo.

"I understand, Captain. I came up with the new coordinates; I assure you I am more than capable of carrying them out."

Xolo stepped forward. "Not that I want to question you and lose my position as well, Vick, but this is something you've never done before. Do I want to know why we're moving?"

As much as it pained Vick to keep his second in command in the dark, he couldn't share that information yet.

"You've gone over the readings as well as I have. This thing is amazing. Even for us, we're in a unique situation. We have the opportunity to gather more samples and I think we need to take it."

"I understand, but you usually consult with me before you do something this drastic."

"I'm sorry. I stopped to check on Aiden and Jody beat me here." He motioned to the corner of the bridge again. Xolo followed.

"I knew there was more," Xolo said with a sigh.

"I just want to move around since we can. I don't know what the men who were firing on us are capable of. If there's a chance they can follow us back through the signal we sent out, I'd like to stay a step ahead."

"Well, that's all you had to say, Captain."

"Again, I apologize. You know how many directions I'm getting pulled in."

"And that's exactly why you should give me some more duties. Send me the records. I'll find us a new helmsman."

"Or someone for communications. I want whoever is best at what they do. I trust Jody for backup on either position. You can't deny her ear. If it's communications you find, be sure it's someone who won't mind having their toes stepped on. She may not give it over as eagerly as she sounds."

"Will do, Captain. I have to say thanks for getting rid of White. I never would have suggested it, but I'm glad he's gone."

"He's not out of our hair yet. I don't think he'll sit back and take this."

Lowering his voice even further, Xolo said, "I'll get someone from security to tail him for a while. See to it that he calms down."

"Find a friend if he has one. Get him drunk or something. Let him sleep it off."

"I'll see what I can do."

Chapter Twenty-Three

Katie opened the door to Alyson's smiling face. Alyson was unofficially her sister-in-law since she and Dusty shared a father, but it had never been officially accepted in the Andrews household. Dusty's mother knew the truth, though, and had helped her out years ago with a business loan. Dusty's father was never the wiser. Katie admired Norma's pride and large heart. Right now, she was extremely happy for the unannounced visit.

"Alyson!" Katie squealed as she leaned in and hugged her with all she had. "What brings you here?"

"I had a hankering for a deep-fried Twinkie and a mini-doughnut-flavored beer."

"You're going to the State Fair?"

"Yes, and I want to take the kids. Please don't say no. I'd love for you to come, but I know you hate the crowds. I can't deny my niece and nephew the bellyache that only comes once a year." Katie turned to see where her eyes wandered to; Dusty was coming down the stairs. "Please?"

"Hey, Alyson!" Dusty hurried over and leaned in for a hug and kiss. He was still in just his boxers. They had a late start after such a long day with his parents. "Please what?"

"She wants to take the kids to the State Fair."

"Gonna be busy as hell on Sunday. I thought about taking them on Wednesday. Getting them out of preschool and daycare for a day is tradition."

"So take them on Wednesday. I want to go today."

Dusty crossed his arms. "You and Robby fighting?"

"No. Actually, he has a friend who lives across the street. He promised to only charge us fifteen dollars to park instead of twenty."

"Sounds all heart."

"I'm teasing. He's not charging us. They have this whole party thing going on. I didn't want to waste the drive in that mess for just us. It's more fun to buy a bunch of useless crap for kids."

"And this just came to you at," Dusty looked at the clock above the TV. It was almost eight. "Seven o'clock this morning?"

"They called late last night." She laced her fingers together and bounced her body up and down. "You guys go to Taylors Falls or someplace quiet. I'll get them home by bedtime."

Turning to Katie, he said, "I don't see why not. I'd love to spend a day with my beautiful wife and have her all to myself."

Katie and Alyson said, "Sap," at the same time.

Dusty swept his arm toward the kitchen. "Come in and have a cup of coffee. I'll drag them out of bed."

"Thanks!" Alyson gave Katie another tight hug.

"I'll get them up, Dusty. You fill your sister in on the visit with your parents yesterday."

"Was it bad?" she asked.

"Oh yeah. Poor thing had to turn down an offer of sex with Ariel."

"Whaaaat?" Alyson shouted. "Ariel? The hot maid you—" Her hand quickly covered her mouth.

Dusty grasped her by the arm. "Come on, sis. I'll fill you in over coffee." He turned to Katie, "Thanks, doll face."

"Oh, if you think I'm anywhere near done with this, you're mistaken, Mr. Andrews." Katie laughed as she headed upstairs to get the kids.

After a wonderful day in Taylors Falls, wandering around the park, they decided to take their time getting home. They found themselves in the tiny town of Harris at a quaint little bar called Big Daddy's. They bellied up to the bar at the tail end of the local happy hour.

A young bartender with long pink hair welcomed them. "You guys are just in time to get in your votes for our chili contest."

"Chili contest?" Dusty asked.

"First annual," she said with a smile. "Fifteen entries are set up on one of the pool tables – not a bad turnout for our first year. Help yourself and bring me your vote. What can I get you in the meantime?"

Katie spotted a display card for a new item – a hard root beer – and ordered it. She frowned as Dusty took off for some chili after he ordered his Lineys. He came back with five disposable small, black cups on a paper plate.

He grinned. "Round one."

"You are so sleeping on the couch tonight."

"I just may have to." He lifted a spoonful to his mouth. "This one is named Satan's Diarrhea."

That almost sent beer flying out of Katie's nose. As Dusty fanned at his tongue, she slid his beer closer.

He said, "Thanks," with tears in his eyes. He pushed the plate of bowls away.

"Chicken. You quit at just one?"

"I need a break. I shouldn't have led with that."

Eying the plate, she pointed to a white one. "That doesn't look too bad."

"Don't let it fool you. It was labeled Widow Maker." Needing to take a break, Dusty stood and read some wooden signs on the wall. Katie grabbed her beer and joined him. The two had several laughs over the sayings. Dusty took one off the wall.

"I'm so buying this for Dean." The sign read:

Ditcher, Quick, & Hyde
Divorce Lawyers

Katie laughed. "You sure they're for sale?"

He pointed above.

"Morning Wood? Gotta love small town humor."

"A subsidiary of Skidmarks Engraving, no less," Dusty added. His taste buds already giving in, he returned to the bar with his purchase and picked up another cup. "Next up is titled The Clap, I'm not really sure I should try that."

"The Clap?"

"Yup. Dude back there guaranteed it would hurt coming out."

Katie shook her head. "That's terrible."

"That was nothing. I wandered away as they were teasing about the art contest in the bathroom in a few hours."

Luckily, Katie had paused the beer on the way to her mouth this time. She pelted a laugh before taking another swallow. She frowned as Dusty hailed the bartender back over and gave her a twenty for pull tabs along with the sign money.

"That's such a waste of money," Katie scolded him.

"Right. And four bucks for a beer not on happy hour isn't," he said, motioning to her bottle.

Katie held it up for him to try. "It's really good. I'm going to buy some when we get home."

When the bartender brought the pull tabs over, Dusty asked, "What does your pull tab money go to?"

Pink Hair answered with, "A local youth baseball team."

He thanked her then turned to Katie. "See. I'm doing a community service here." After opening a few, Dusty hollered "BAM!" as he slapped a ticket on the bar. There was a red line down a bunch of fruit pictures. He'd won a hundred and thirty-three dollars.

"You suck, Andrews." Katie glanced around. The bar had temporarily gone silent. "It doesn't look like the regulars are too happy that you won."

"The unspoken rule is that you tip ten percent, so the bartender will be happy."

He was going to call her over, but a woman who appeared to be the owner stepped behind the bar. Apparently she was clever with a crochet hook. She was showing off her latest creations to the regulars. The boob pillow complete with baby nipples would have any man sleeping well, and the enormous pink "junk" was a great conversation piece, if nothing else.

Katie glanced up at the television. "Oh my God, Dusty. That's horrible."

"What is?" He spun to the set behind them. They were showing an image of a boy who looked around three. He was dead and washed up on a beach.

"Holy shit. Is that the Syrian refugees?"

The bartender muted the jukebox and turned up the news. The group watched in horror as the news story showed more dead bodies. There was even a story recapped of people who had suffocated in a truck.

The day had lost its good mood.

When the bartender returned with Dusty's winnings, he gave her a twenty with, "This is for you," then added, "buy the bar a round and cash us out." Hoots, hollers, and raised glasses greeted him but he wasn't up for his normal starting up conversations with strangers. He could feel how upset Katie was and wanted out of there. They'd only managed to finish half their drinks before he got up. "Let's go, babe."

Katie was unusually quiet for the drive back to the cities. She brightened up for just a moment when Alyson texted a picture of them in front of a Ferris wheel.

"I'm glad they're having a good time."

"We had a good time, too. The world sucks right now, my sweet. Don't let it ruin our day. This is why we cancelled TV. Nothing but bad news. I get enough of it at the paper."

"But all those children…"

Dusty knew it was best just to keep quiet. He gave her knee a gentle squeeze. "Want to keep going and meet Alyson at the fair?"

"It'd be crazy to pay the entrance fee for the little time we have left."

"So what. I have more than fifty bucks left from the pull tab earnings. I don't know how that place stays open with drinks so cheap. That's nothing like Minneapolis bar prices. Come on, let's go. Send her a text."

"I'd really rather go when we have more time. Let's stick to your Wednesday plan. We should probably rescue Court from Deidre."

"Dean loves that thing. It won't be long before they get a puppy, too." He gave her knee another squeeze. "Expand your practice by one more family member."

She still wouldn't respond.

"How many lawyers does it take to screw in a lightbulb?" he asked.

"None. They can only screw over the lightbulb."

"I need new stuff, huh?"

"Yes, my love, you do. 'E' for effort though. Now let's just go home. I'm fine. Sad, but fine. I'll have a glass of wine and dive into your book again until the kids come home. If it wasn't Sunday, I'd go grab some more of that beer. It'll be nice after the new year when you can buy alcohol on freaking Sunday."

"It will be. I'll get you some tomorrow. I bet it would go great with some ice cream." He laced his fingers with hers. "Thanks for the day. I'm surprised you didn't insist on staying home to read."

"I thought about it."

Dusty kissed the back of her hand. "I love you."

It had taken a good portion of the night but they were repositioned in the nebula, safe and sound. Aiden was curled up under Jody's now-empty communications station. He hadn't wanted to stay with Lenore in Vick's cabin; Vick could hardly force him. He didn't feel right leaving the bridge at such a crucial time. No one complained. In fact, they seemed to enjoy him being there.

Vick loved seeing how his small command crew came to life, answering the toddler's questions. He was grateful Aiden knew to not mention his device or what he could do. A few had commented. "What a nifty watch you have." Aiden just smiled and said, "Thanks."

Stretching, Vick said to Jody, "Why don't you go get some sleep? The dirty work is done. I appreciate you stepping up. Xolo will be here any moment, and can take over for a while."

"What about you? You're as dead on your feet as I am."

"I'll leave when Xolo takes over. I promise. Now get."

She bent down and watched Aiden sleeping. "Do you want me to take him?"

"Thanks, but he'll be fine there. I shouldn't be long. I'll get him tucked in his own bed."

Jody stood. "All right. I'll be back after a few hours." She nodded to Vick, then the rest of the crew, and left. Vick longed to give her a kiss goodbye, it killed him that he felt like he couldn't.

Now sitting in his chair, he stared out the viewing window. The nebula was even more breathtaking from this position than it was before. He didn't think that was possible. Every time he did this, he couldn't believe it wasn't a dream. The fact that he was able to travel into a nebula still made his head spin. His ship alone could do this. The newness and the discoveries they'd made were ones that people told stories about. Others will follow, but he did it first. He did what he set out to do – leave his mark.

Their first nebula had brought four new metals and eight unknown gasses to the universal elements charts. The second was less fruitful, only adding a crystal that, although new, was less exciting for Vick. He hoped to find something extraordinary with this one. He had a feeling he wasn't going to find anything more extraordinary than his son. He looked down at Aiden and thought if he had to give it up, he could. For Aiden, he could leave this.

He returned to his chair, taking in the view through the massive window again. He'd been so deep in thought that he hadn't heard Aiden walk over. He felt him climbing up onto his lap. Vick reached down and helped him up.

"Hey, buddy. Something wake you?"

He shook his head and nestled into his dad; gently breathing again in seconds. Vick doubted he'd actually fully woken up. He kissed the top of his head, then stood, cradling Aiden.

Facing his navigator, Vick said, "I'm going to turn in. Xolo is due back any minute. You take off when he arrives and go get some shut eye."

"Aye, Captain."

As Vick left, he ran into Xolo. "Everything go okay?"

"For all the rest I got, I should have stayed on the bridge."

"Sorry, we did fine though. It's an even more amazing sight than the last spot. No debris worries here that we can find."

"That's what worries me. It's a nebula, Vick. It shouldn't be predicable and stable."

"Jody thinks we're clear for days. Go ahead and run the numbers."

"Oh, I will." Xolo glanced down at Aiden as Vick shifted his grip. "How was he?"

"More behaved than you'd expect."

"I don't expect anything." Xolo studied Aiden's sleeping face for a moment before he spoke again. "Aubrey rode me pretty damn hard about doing her tests on him."

"He's my son, not a lab rat."

"She has a job to do same as us, Vick." Xolo glanced around, making sure they were truly alone. They should have been at this hour, but he was noticeably nervous. "Blood tests aren't going to reveal what he can do."

"Did you tell her?"

The way Xolo moved his tongue from cheek to cheek, stalling, Vick was worried he was concocting a lie.

"No, I haven't. Do you have any idea how hard it is for me to lie to her? Psych was part of her schooling, you know."

"You're not lying, you're just not telling the whole truth."

"Oh, that'll hold up in the divorce."

Vick laughed. "Just give me some time with him. Before we go, I'll let her do what she needs to fulfil her oath. I just don't get the big deal. Just because Athrackian females have hated human men for centuries, it doesn't mean Aiden is alone in this racial mix."

"You have small wieners and you don't please your women. I'd stay away from you, too."

Vick laughed. "Yeah, I heard the rumors. Just keep her away from him. When I'm ready, she'll be the first to know."

He turned and headed toward his cabin. "I'll be back in a few hours. Oh!" He took a few steps back to Xolo. "How's our buddy White doing?"

"Sleeping it off like you wanted. I have a man not so obviously watching his door in case he comes to and decides to get ugly. I know he had it coming, but you've been rough with him. He'll more than likely have it in for you."

"Hopefully he'll have the balls to deal with me in private, and not in front of my son."

"You can hope." Xolo did a slight mock salute and headed for the bridge.

Within minutes, Vick was back in his cabin. He placed Aiden in bed, and then collapsed beside him, fully clothed.

Three hours later, Vick was startled awake. A chair had been kicked, sending it sliding across the floor. When he bolted upright, he was greeted with a gun pointed at his head.

"Stand up, you fucking coward."

Worried more for his son than himself, Vick quickly turned to his left. Aiden was already awake, leaning against the wall, terrified.

"Stay put, buddy. It'll be okay," Vick said, offering what little comfort he could.

"You're an idiot for thinking so, Skinnard. The Rhenharts have a hell of a lot more resources than your father. You think it'll take long to find you in here?"

"You're the one that's in cahoots with them?" He wanted to use better language but even in a crisis like this, he was worried about what Aiden would hear him say. "You acted like a jerk, complaining about your fiancée and the messages, but the whole time it was really to try to send them a message."

"You're not as dumb as you look. I'm taking the kid and the pod. We're out of here."

"You can't go out in the pod! You're insane!"

"He can get us out of here, can't you, kid?"

Aiden disappeared. White shot the empty spot where Aiden once sat. "Get him back here!" White shouted.

With Aiden safely gone, Vick took the chance to tackle White. The struggle that ensued as both men tried to get control of the gun destroyed Vick's cabin. Mirror doors shattered, glass tables smashed into pieces, leaving both men cut and bleeding. A shot fired. It took Vick a few seconds to register the burning pain in his side. He'd been hit. As White pushed himself off Vick, another shot fired. Vick braced for the pain, but it didn't come. White landed on him – dead weight. He could see Jody just over White's head, gun in hand. Aiden had gone for help. "Good kid" is the last thing he remembered thinking.

Vick came to in the medical ward. His head hurt like a sonofabitch, and his side burned. In trying to lift his arm, he discovered he had an IV in him. The oxygen tube in his nose pissed him off, so he yanked it out.

"Doctor Aubrey will have your ass."

He glanced over to the doorway. Jody was leaning against the door's opening with her arms crossed. "You stubborn Casherri."

"Huh. On earth we say mule."

She walked over and replaced the oxygen line before giving him a gentle kiss. "You feel like feces?"

He groaned. "Yes. Is White dead?"

"Most certainly. Was he just upset about losing his position, or was there more?"

"Definitely more." He tried to sit up, crying out, "Aiden!" but Jody pushed him back down.

"He's fine. He teleported out and got me, then brought us back together. He's worried about you. Can I go get him? He's just outside."

"Is he asleep?"

"Yes."

"Then don't wake him. Poor thing has been through enough."

Giving his hand a squeeze she said, "Talk to me. What did he want?"

"He's been getting messages to the Rhenharts. He was trying to take Aiden and get out on a pod. He knew Aiden would be able to teleport it out of here to them. He'd have to do it over my dead body."

"And he almost succeeded." Still holding his hand, she leaned in. "I'd miss you. Don't do that anymore."

He grinned. "I'll try. How bad am I?"

"In and out wound. Pretty small beam. He either wasn't trying to kill you, or forgot to change his setting. Missed all your organs, but you'll be sore for a while. I know you. You won't want to stay in bed, but I'm begging you to for one day at least."

"We need to pull the satellites, Jody."

"Already done."

"Do I want to know how?"

"Not unless you want to be really mad at me and Aiden."

Vick closed his eyes. "You let him bring them in."

"Let him, my ass. Once you were in surgery, he ran for my lab and began doing it. He had two in before I managed to get the door open."

"He lock you out?"

She grinned. "Fried my board."

Vick shook his head. "Not sure if I should beat him or send him to college."

She ran her fingers through his short hair. "He loves you. It's been such a short time, but I can see it. He was amazing when he teleported into my room. I was asleep in my bed. He shouted to wake me, grabbed my gun from the nightstand, and took my hand. All he said was 'Dad needs you' then we were in your room."

"Smart kid to go for you. You do have the best range record on the ship."

"No, Victor Skinnard, he knows I'd kill for you."

"And you did. Kiss me."

She complied.

"Dad?"

They broke their kiss to find Aiden standing by the bed. Jody picked him up. He promptly leaned into Vick.

"Hey, buddy. Thanks for saving my life."

Aiden wouldn't say anything nor would he let go of the grip he had on his dad's neck. He pulled himself out of Jody's grasp and landed hard on Vick's side. Jody gasped, but Vick held his hand up.

"It's okay. He's on my good side." Despite the IV, Vick held Aiden tight. "I'm fine, buddy. Thanks to you, I'm going to be okay."

Jody turned a hue he'd never seen. Vick could only imagine that was some shade of worry.

"Should I get Doc Aubrey?" she asked.

"I'm thinking Doc Duiz may be more who we need for this," he said at a whisper, although he knew Aiden could hear them fine.

"Duiz." Jody nodded then left in a hurry. He was a Terian as well, and a hell of a shrink. Vick knew things had been moving along too fast. He felt responsible for Aiden not having the proper time or way to grieve for his mother. No doubt, the choke hold on his neck was a sure sign that Aiden had feared the worst – that he was left an orphan. Vick could only stroke his back and repeat, "It's okay, son. I'm going to be okay."

Twenty minutes after Dr. Duiz arrived at Vick's room, he was able to convince Aiden to go for a walk with him. Jody sat on the bed.

"Poor, kid. He's more worried for you than he's been letting on."

"I don't know if he'd been hiding it well, or if it just didn't hit him until now. He has to be a hundred times worse after watching me get shot, just like with his mother. I'm kicking myself for not bringing him to Duiz sooner."

She took his hand in hers and gave it a firm squeeze. "I won't have you feeling guilty about this, Captain."

Vick grinned. "Hon."

Jody continued with her scolding. "I'd like to know a time when he wasn't on your mind. You've been worried about nothing but his safety and the safety of this crew. You couldn't foresee White doing what he did. He was an asscrack, but he was doing a heck of a job."

"Asshole," he corrected.

"You said I could mix things up."

"I did. I'm sorry; it does work just as well. I need to learn to stop that."

She shook her head. "It doesn't matter. I was actually surprised White had been mouthing to you the way he was. If your mind wasn't racing in so many directions and we were on a more normal mission and not inside the nebula, I'd think his actions would have had him arrested sooner. You'd think he wouldn't risk that."

"I don't know what to say, babe. I guess I cut the crew a lot of slack when it comes to having an active part of the everyday ins and outs. I encourage ideas. I may be the captain, but I don't want to be a dictator."

Jody leaned forward and gave him a kiss on the forehead.

"You missed." Vick pointed to his lips.

She kissed where he wanted; he held her there for a few seconds longer than she'd intended. Pushing away she said, "I need to go update Xolo. He's worried as the Underworld."

Vick grinned. "We say hell, but you're on the right track. I told you reading old Earth Greek mythology wasn't a way to get a good idea for Earth history."

"I like the idea of these gods. Terians don't have this higher power that most other planets do."

"No religion?"

"No. We're supposed to be kind to others, respect our parents, and not kill each other because it's what's right, not because we're afraid of what's in the clouds."

He gave her hand a squeeze. "We got a little off track here."

"Sorry. Xolo is worried. He's asked me to set us a course out of here if you didn't pull through."

Vick felt his blood pressure rising. He wasn't mad at Xolo for thinking that was necessary, but he was still frustrated over it. "Go tell him I'm fine and I want no such thing. I'm not going to stay in here tonight. I refuse to put Aiden through that."

"I won't even bother telling you no, but I insist on at least staying with you. You'll have to stay at my place, yours is still trashed. I'll sleep on the couch."

"I won't bother fighting with you, either. I'll leave as soon as they let me."

"You'll stay until I come get you," she insisted.

He said, "Okay," as his eyelids closed. He was more tired than he realized.

Chapter Twenty-Four

When Vick woke up, Jody was asleep in a chair next to him. Aiden was curled up in her lap, also sound asleep. He was only mildly upset at her for not waking him and helping him back to her cabin. Logic told him that he needed to rest to heal, he just hated being helpless.

The clock indicated it would be time to check on a call from his Dad in half an hour. He didn't want to miss that chance – he'd already missed one window – he had to go. When he sat up, the bed creaked enough to startle Jody awake. She stood, with Aiden still asleep on her shoulder.

"What do you think you're doing?"

"I can't miss my dad's call again. He'll worry if I'm not there."

She raised an eyebrow. "What's the matter? You think he'll be afraid you've been shot?"

Vick grinned. "I thought Terians didn't do sarcasm."

"You're a great teacher."

Feeling himself flush, Vick leaned back in bed. "Ah, Christ on a crutch."

"Do I even want to translate that?"

He shook his head. "I can't go."

"I didn't think so. Scoot over."

Vick scooted closer to the wall; Jody carefully placed Aiden next to him. "I'll go talk to your father. We had such a great introduction."

He barely squeaked out "Thanks" before his eyes closed again.

When Jody returned, Vick was sitting up with Aiden at his side. His IV was gone and they were both eating. He was starting to feel better, but seeing Jody did wonders for his spirit.

"You look better," she said with a smile. "That constant pale shade of your skin is dreadfully unappealing as it is. When you go pasty-white, it's a terrible turn off."

Aiden laughed hard. "I think it's cool the way you can change colors."

She sat on the bed with them. "It's a funny thing indeed, Aiden. Did you know I can't make it do anything? You always know where you stand with a Terian."

"Hear that, buddy? If you make her mad, you'll sure know it."

Aiden giggled again.

Without prompting, Jody said, "Nothing new to share on the home front, Captain."

"Oh, that's good, I guess. Did you…uh…did you tell him…" his motioned his eyes to his wound.

"No. That was not my news to share."

Vick mouthed, "Thank you," then asked, "Has Rhodan been told about White?"

"Xolo broke the news to her."

"And?"

"She's not going to come after me for revenge, if that's what you're worried about. According to her, things had turned bad in their relationship ever since the baby was born. Male Deltorians aren't there for their children the way humans are, not to mention…she, uh…said I wasn't the only one he…tried to 'woo' as you put it."

Vick gave a soft laugh.

Jody continued. "She didn't seem upset at all, actually. She was surprised he had been conspiring against you. Officer Rhodan promised if she knew, she'd have told you."

"We have to prepare for the fact that he probably wasn't the only one."

"Later." Her eyes motioned to Aiden.

"Wasn't the only what, Dad?"

"Nothing for you to worry about, son. There's always a member of a crew who thinks they know more than the captain and lashes out. In all honesty, that was me many years ago. That's why I'm captain of my own ship now."

"You tried to kill your captain?"

Vick gave him a comforting squeeze. "No, it didn't get that far. I just knew it was time to go when I didn't agree with his decisions. My crew teases that I take risks, but I don't do anything that I believe will put people in harm's way."

"Your dad is fibbing only slightly, Aiden. You know an exploration vessel takes risks that normal ships don't, but I've never seen someone double and triple check things before following through like your father."

"Stop trying to flatter me, Lieutenant. You're not on my list for anything." He winked.

Aiden slid down. "Do you want me to stay? I'm pretty sure Lenore needs my help today."

Jody was surprised. She was sure he'd insist on staying with Vick after what had happened.

"Son, if you want to go help Lenore, that's fine by me. I'm great, there's no need for you to just sit here and babysit me. I'm sure the real babies need you more." He held his hand on Aiden's head for a moment. "You're such a big boy."

"Can I go by myself?"

Jody bolted to her feet. "No! I'll take you, Aiden. I know you can do it yourself but I actually have to go that way anyway. I'd love the company."

Vick was grateful that she'd recovered from her outburst. He didn't want Aiden to wander on the ship alone, but he didn't want him to be afraid, either.

"Okay." He tiptoed up and gave Vick a kiss on the cheek. "See you later, Dad."

"See you soon, son."

Jody covered Aiden's kiss with her own and whispered. "I'll come right back."

"I'll get dressed. I need to get moving."

"You can wait fifteen minutes. I'll help." She turned, took Aiden's hand, and left the room.

Not heeding her wishes, Vick stood after just a few moments. The ship jostled hard. He was thrown to the wall, almost sending him to the floor. Grasping his side, he took a deep breath, willing the pain to pass. After a brief moment, he punched the code for the bridge on the com on the wall and hailed Xolo.

"What the hell was that? Were we fired on?"

"No, Captain. A large chunk of debris exploded a little too close to the ship."

"Exploded?"

"Well…you know. Clouds filled with gasses and interstellar dust tend to do that from time to time."

"Nothing we've been monitoring has marked this area as unstable."

"Didn't we just go over this? It's a nebula, Captain. The whole beast is unstable. Much more so than you'd like to admit. We can take all the readings we want, but you know as well as I do, surprises happen. What do you want me to do?"

"Just hold the fort. I'm on my way up."

"Are you sure that's a good idea?"

"I'm sure it's a terrible idea, but I can't just sit here. Especially not now. Hail Jody up there. She was on her way here but the bridge will be faster for her from the nursery." The ship shook again. This time Vick did hit the floor.

He was trying to stand again when Jody burst into the room. "Captain!"

"I'm fine," he said as he refused her help to stand. "I need to get dressed. Get on the bridge. I'll be right behind you."

"I'll help you there. You're not going to make it on your own."

He leaned against the wall, defeated. "You may have a point."

Jody gathered his clothes. As he dressed, she found a wheelchair.

"You think I'm going to ride in that?" Vick frowned.

"I'm not giving you a choice. We need to go. You'll take command a little better if you're actually conscious."

They reached the bridge in record speed. Even crew members, frantic for answers, stepped out of the way at Jody's insistence and shouts of "Get out of the way!"

Xolo rushed over. "I didn't realize you were still so bad."

"I'm not. She's just a brute." He hitched a thumb at Jody.

Jody gave his head a slight shove forward and rushed to the helm.

"Give me something, Xolo," Vick said. "Is this nebula starting to form a star?"

"You know this thing has been unique from the beginning. Why don't you ask me if it's going to go Super

Nova? I've got nothing. The readings over the last hour have been off the charts. You want another batch?"

"We don't have time for that. I'm not going to sit here and wait for more. We're getting out."

"Seriously?"

"Discovering new gasses and elements isn't worth anyone's life." He wheeled over to Jody. "I know you're going to kill me for this, but there's no time to start plotting us a course out of here. Get moving."

"Fly blind? Are you insane?"

"It's not blind. It's what we call 'old school.' Use the viewing window and your eyes. I'll help look ahead with the radar. It'll be slower, but we'll be on our way."

"But, Captain…"

"Now, dammit, Jody. Now is not the time to decide to argue with me!"

Letting out a heavy breath, she said, "Aye, Captain, grasped both handles, and eased them forward.

"Xolo, get me another set of eyes. I want someone top deck with infrared."

"Done." He took his device off his belt and began keying away.

Vick wheeled himself to the communications station, grabbed a headset, and then tossed it to Jody after shouting, "Heads up."

"What's this for?" she asked.

"I'm going to bounce a wave out there. It should work as sonar to help you. What pitch do you want it?"

She rushed over. "That's a great idea, but it'll be faster if I do it myself." She keyed away.

"You're needed at the helm, Lieutenant."

"I know what time I have!" Not facing him, she frantically keyed away. In just a few seconds she said, "Done." Another hard jostle sent her and all the crew members to the floor. Vick was stable in his wheel chair.

"Everyone okay?" he asked.

A few grunts and a "Yes, Captain," or two was all that was said before everyone returned to their stations.

"I'm afraid you're old school isn't going to do the trick, Captain," Jody said, halting the ship. "Whatever those explosions were, they've completely surrounded us."

The door slid open and Aiden came running in. "What's happening, Dad?"

"You shouldn't be up here right now, son."

Lenore barged in after him before the door slid shut. "I'm sorry, Captain. He got away from me."

"What about the babies?"

"Their mothers had already come for them in a panic. What's happening?"

"It doesn't look good."

Vick was surprised when Aiden crawled up on Jody's lap instead of his. He grasped her necklace. Vick shouted, "No!" as darkness consumed the ship.

Chapter Twenty-Five

Having read herself to sleep earlier than she'd expected, Katie was the first to awake again. She got Deidre from Alex's room and went out to the backyard. To her surprise, Courtney was in her yard as well. They met at the five foot chain link fence.

"I've wanted to take this thing down for years," Courtney said through a yawn.

"I know; me too. I guess it's nice now that we have the puppy. You won't end up with landmines in your yard."

"Fat chance of that. You have Dean wanting a dog now."

"Hey…who brought her home?"

Courtney laughed.

"What are you doing up so early, Court?"

"'He who snores a lot' had a few too many last night. That makes it worse. Once I'm up, I have to pee. You know the drill. I just didn't see the point in going back." Courtney grasped Katie's hand. "I'm sorry. I shouldn't bitch about being pregnant. I'm a jackass."

Katie shook her head. "Don't feel bad. You shouldn't think you have to walk on eggshells for me. It is what it is. I'm okay with it. I can't get upset over every pregnant woman I see."

"You seem down, though, hon. What's up?"

"It'll sound stupid."

"Try me." Courtney walked over to the gate and into Katie's yard. The puppy caught sight of her and ran over for her greeting. After some loving, she ran off again; the girls headed to the porch and sat in the swing.

"Dusty and I had a great day yesterday."

"So what happened? Why so blue?"

"What's going on in Syria is so damn depressing."

"Oh. I saw that clip about the young boy, too. I just don't understand how a leader could drive everyone out of their country. What is going to be left for him to rule? I'll never get it."

"It's such a horrible waste of lives."

Courtney grasped Katie's hand. "You know the first thing I thought when I saw that?"

Katie shook her head.

"What a wonderful mother you would have been to that little boy."

Katie let a tear fall as she leaned into her best friend. "He had parents, Court. Probably wonderful ones. These aren't poor, homeless people. At least, they weren't. They could be you or me. I saw a teen with braces interviewed. That's gotta be big bucks, even there. He spoke excellent English. They're educated human beings for fuck's sake."

"The president is calling for ten-thousand refugees to be brought here."

"Court. I'm not swooping in on their misfortune. People aren't going to give up their children."

"Hon…babies aren't the only people dying. I can't imagine there aren't a slew of orphans in one of those camps. Of course a community is going to take care of them, but don't you think if one doesn't have a family that they would want a better life for him or her?"

"It makes sense, but I'd still feel like a vulture."

"Bullshit. With all the people who need to find new homes? You think parentless children would be better off in orphanages than with you? You know I'm right. You're not the one killing the parents and stealing their babies. I'm surprised Dusty's mom hasn't already started some kind of fundraiser for them."

Katie sat up, feeling like smiling for the first time since she got up. "It would only take a call to get her going."

"Do it. I'll talk to Dean. Maybe whoever he's dealing with is already going this route. You two said you wanted whoever needed you most."

"We do. I guess it was in the back of my mind, it just didn't feel right thinking that way."

"You want to be the good guy, not the vulture. Point taken. You're not, now get over it."

Dean called out from their deck, standing there in his boxers. "Girl time?" he said as he scratched his bare chest.

"I'll be right over, you big stud."

"Pregnant hornies kick in yet?" Dean asked, as he approached the fence.

"Take me to a nice breakfast and I'll let you know."

Without another word, Dean hustled back to the house.

Katie laughed. "I so love having you next door."

Courtney stood. "Gimme a hug."

Katie was more than happy to do as she was asked.

"How about we barbeque tonight? I'll grab stuff while I'm out," Courtney offered.

"Sounds great to me. Anytime the guys have to do the work is okay in my book. You want us to watch Jacob so you can have a nice breakfast?"

"Nah. He's actually pretty good at breakfast. You know pancakes are his favorite. Thanks though. I may take you up on watching him if Dean holds me to my comment."

Grinning, Katie said, "Of course. I think we're a few ahead of you on the kid watching for sex time."

Courtney waved it off as nothing. "Who can keep track? See ya later, hon."

When the control room brightened again, Vick gazed out the viewing window in shock. He was now looking at Teria – Jody's home planet. What he'd feared when things went black had come true. Aiden had teleported them there.

"Aiden!"

Jody's blood curdling scream got him in gear. Hustling to her side, the sight that greeted him caused his heart to sink. Sliding out of the wheelchair, he dropped to Aiden's side.

"No, no, no, no! Dammit! No!" He took his son from Jody's lap and pulled him to his chest. He was as limp as a wet rag, and had blood coming from his nose and ears. "Come on, buddy," Vick gave Aiden a hard shake. "Come on! Don't you dare leave me!"

Vick could hear a faint heartbeat when he put his ear to Aiden's chest. Now with his cheek to Aiden's nose, he could feel only weak breaths.

"He's hanging on, but not by much. Dammit, son! You didn't have to do this!" Pulling him tighter to his chest, he let out a gut-wrenching howl.

"Get in the chair with him, Vick. Let's get him to Doc Aubrey. I'll take you. Hurry!"

He was frozen in fear; capable of nothing but holding his son tight.

"Vick!" Jody shouted again, finally snapping him out of it.

He stood with Aiden then got into the wheelchair. Jody raced them to the infirmary at lightning speed. Doc Aubrey was there waiting, Xolo must have called her.

Not waiting for Vick to stand, she reached for Aiden and placed him on the table. As she checked him over, she reprimanded Vick. "You lied to me."

"Not now, Aubrey."

She didn't stop her hustling to set up an IV as she continued. "I don't know how, but he's responsible for this. Isn't he?"

Vick remained silent. She pulled a syringe out of a drawer, drew a clear liquid, and injected it into the port in the line. He was amazed, watching her do this simultaneously. Having four arms sure scored points during a trauma. Checking his pulse again, she allowed her top shoulders to drop a little. "That's better little guy. Come on."

She placed her hand on his forehead, she said, "He's a little cool." She turned to Jody. "Get me a blanket out of the warmer there."

Jody quickly retrieved it and draped it over Aiden. She stayed there, holding his hand. Feeling like an idiot for not knowing what to do or how to help, Vick stood beside Jody, out of Aubrey's way.

She was now checking both ears and cleaning up the blood.

"I don't like this, Captain."

"What do you see?"

"I can't see anything. I won't be able to get a decent temperature through this mess." She looked up and gave him a harsh stare. After digging through a drawer, she held a thermometer under his tongue. "I hate going old school with this but the forehead scanner is in the nursery." It gave her a reading in just a few seconds with a soft beep. "Hmmm," was all she said at the reading. Now shining a light in Aiden's eyes, she let out a huff. "His pupils don't dilate."

"Is that bad?"

"It's not good or bad. They just don't. Apparently the half that is you doesn't include ocular genes."

She pulled her personal device off her belt. "If you had let me do more tests on him like I'd asked, I'd have more to go on." After scrolling for a minute, she put it away and checked his heart rate again. "There you go, buddy. Keep fighting." She took a moment staring at him. "You're too little to play hero, big guy." She smoothed the hair away from his face. "Your Dad always has our backs." Looking up at Jody, she said, "Bring me the portable scanner." Jody wheeled the device over. The screen wasn't much larger than an IV bag. Attached to the cord was a handheld unit, much like as ultrasound wand.

"I don't see any hemorrhaging or swelling in his brain. The bleeding appears to have stopped. I'll run a full scan when I have his temp stabilized." After giving his shoulder a gentle squeeze, she crossed her arms and squared off on Vick.

"Xolo told me about Deidre."

"I figured as much. That's why I didn't want you near my son. He's not a lab rat. I won't have you probing his brain, trying to see what makes him tick."

Doc Aubrey shoved at him hard with all four arms. "Just now, you idiot! He called to tell me you were on your way. He said you'd kill me but I'd need to know. You mind telling me what the hell just happened? And for crying out loud, sit down. You look like you're about to faint."

Not arguing, he sat down in the wheelchair. "The nebula became unstable. I've never seen anything like it before. It was millions of years away from becoming a star."

"I don't give a hot damn about the nebula. I want to know what happened to Aiden."

Xolo burst into the room just then, buying Vick a moment to gather his thoughts. "How is he, Mo tok?"

Vick had learned, after the two started dating, that "Mo tok" was the Forengi equivalent of a small Earth dark chocolate bar. Apparently giving your loved ones nicknames with sweet treats was universal.

"He's stable, but it's taken a lot of out him. He'll be out for quite some time. What did you say to the crew?"

"I didn't. I told everyone to hold their stations until the Captain returned."

Returning her attention to Vick, Aubrey continued. "Well?"

Vick wheeled over and removed the Hawkeye from Aiden's wrist. "Deidre time traveled. Past, future…whatever she wanted. Aiden can travel within today. He teleports, Aubrey. He moves himself, someone else with him, even small object with no problems. With this," he said, holding it up, "he can move large objects as well."

"Right." Jody jumped in. "He was playing games with me in my lab. Moving my pen and such around. He also placed probes and brought them back with nothing more than a blink." She knelt down in front of Vick. "When he moved the pod, he was fine."

"That was just two of us and the pod is barely the size of this room. Maybe the men testing him were building up his resistance. Maybe their goal was for him to do things like this without these side effects."

"What men?" Aubrey asked.

Vick placed his hand on Aiden's head and gave his cheek a kiss. Jody answered for him.

"The men who murdered his mother are after him. She traveled to the future to get the plans for this device, then stole it and tried to run. They've been trying to track Aiden ever since."

"They're the ones who fired on the ship?"

"Yes."

"And why we switched positions in the nebula?"

"Yes. I found a way to talk to Vick's father with it, even within the nebula. Vick was worried they may be able to track us. We don't know that there isn't another device."

"May I see it?"

Vick scooted back and offered it to her. After only briefly examining it, she handed it back. "I don't see more than a knock-off of an old watch. I assume if you're digging into it, Jody, there's nothing more I can do." She retuned her attention to Aiden, once again going over his vitals.

"Is he going to be okay?" Vick asked.

"I'm not going to lie to you. He's stable, but far from good in my book. He's a toddler, Captain. I don't know what kind of stress this is really doing to his body. I can give you his vitals and have an idea of where I'd like him to be, but it's as if he's gotten crushed in a trash compactor without the broken bones to show for it."

"Is he in a coma?"

"As far as his brain activity goes, yes. It's something like that, but I don't think it's that dramatic. I see him waking up soon, just weak."

"Will there be permanent damage?"

"That's really hard to say. If it were you or me, then absolutely. You have to realize, Captain, he's wired for this. Somewhere in his genetic makeup, this is what he does. I could chart out his DNA, but it probably won't make sense – even for me. If you'll let me, I'll run it. It wouldn't hurt to compare a sample of his with yours. If he ever needed blood, you'd likely be the only suitable donor." She placed a hand on his shoulder. "All parents like to believe their kids are one-of-a-kind. Yours actually is."

"Then take his blood. Run the DNA. What else can I do to help?"

"Nothing. All we can do is wait. He doesn't appear to be in any pain, there's that."

Once again Vick stood. He held Aiden's hand for a brief moment then took the Hawkeye from Jody's hand. He promptly threw it to the ground, smashing it under the heel of his boot.

"Captain!" Jody shouted as she grabbed at his hands. "What have you done?"

"That thing shouldn't be here. His mother stole the plans from the future and he's been paying the price ever since. We're idiots to think there isn't some kind of GPS in there. They could have been tracking us since day one."

Xolo's device went off. "Lieutenant Gatron, we're being hailed from Teria. They want to know what our intentions are."

Jody placed her hand on Vick's chest. "Let me go. I'll ask for permission to land."

"But the Rhenharts are still out there after us. I won't put your people in danger."

"You are my people. This crew is my people, Captain. Teria can hide us safely. We're half-way across the Galaxy. The Rhenharts won't be onto us. Not for days, if ever." She eyed the device. "Maybe that was a smart move. Maybe it did hold some sort of tracker that I couldn't find. Let me go. I'll talk to my father."

Once again Vick felt the need to sit back down. "Is he some kind of big wig?"

"Wig? He has his own hair. What does that have to do with anything?"

Vick pinched his lips together, holding back a laugh. "Sorry. Is he in charge or up there in rank or something? A king?"

Her eyes lowered for a brief second. "We don't have a monarchy. He's what you would call a President."

"Your Father is president and you fled your planet?"

"I didn't flee, I left. There's a difference. His life is not one I wanted."

"You said you couldn't go back."

She shook her head. "I said I wasn't welcome back. I'm in no danger. Teria is neutral, Captain. We're peaceful people.

If we are in danger, they will assist us." She squatted down in front of him. "Let me go make the call."

Vick placed his hand behind her neck and pulled her in for a kiss. "Go. I need to stay with Aiden. Come back and let me know how it goes. Give my father a call as well. Let him know how he can contact us. Set up a secure line. The Rhenharts could be watching him."

"I will, Captain."

He grinned. "I assume it's because we're in mixed company you dropped the hon?"

She kissed him. "Yes. I'll be back as soon as I've made arrangements…hon."

Jody stood and turned to Doc Aubrey. "Is there anything you need on my planet to help Aiden? I can get the medical station on alert."

"My supplies on this ship are superior. He can't get better care than he's getting right now. We really shouldn't try to move him just yet."

"Some crew remaining on ship won't be a problem. We'll be guests, not prisoners. I'll be back soon."

As Jody left, Vick felt all his energy leave him. "I need to lie down," he said to Xolo. "You're in charge. Go make the necessary arrangements with Jody."

"What do I tell the crew?"

"That whatever force took us in the nebula brought us here and we're looking into it. Whoever wants off at Teria is welcome to leave. Either for a brief leave or to leave the ship for good. I'm not forcing anyone back on. Under no circumstances do you bring Aiden into this."

"I'm not an idiot, Vick. I've got your back on this; I have from the start." Xolo kissed his wife goodbye.

Aubrey stopped him. "Help me get him in a bed before you leave. I won't be able to pick him up off the floor after you've gone."

"I look that bad?"

They both replied, "Yes."

Chapter Twenty-Six

Dusty scared Katie as he stepped outside. She'd been curled up on the porch swing reading with Deidre sleeping on her lap.

"Sorry, cupcake." Dusty wrapped his arms around her from behind and gave her cheek a kiss.

The puppy woke up and promptly hopped down to greet Dusty. After a few pats, he sat next to Katie.

"Am I still keeping your attention?"

"Of course. I know you value your life, so you won't kill off Aiden, but I'm worried about him."

"Good," he said giving her leg a squeeze. "If you don't hate the writer at some point, they aren't doing their job."

Katie let out a soft laugh. "I keep waiting for Doc Aubrey to say, 'Dammit, Vick, I'm a doctor not a…' whatever."

Dusty laughed hard. "The backspace button is a wonderful thing."

"You didn't!"

"Twice actually. I wasn't sure if it would bring chuckles or groans, so I left it out."

Katie rested her head on Dusty's shoulder. "Court already came and went this morning. They want to barbeque tonight."

"That's a given. Is that what brought her over before breakfast? I know she wasn't worried about us having plans."

"She could tell I was mopey."

Dusty pulled her onto his lap and rested his forehead to hers. "Still, babe? This kind of crap has been going on for centuries. You can't let it get to you. With all the talk of how much Cuba is changing, there are still people flocking here on rafts as well. Didn't you like my little dig about Teria and no religion? I'm sick of religious wars. I edited it quite a bit. I didn't want to get preachy."

"I appreciated that, but you can't ignore what's happening because we don't like it. Not when it's thrown in our faces that children are suffering that way."

"Take it from a newspaper guy, that's the power of the media."

"Well it works. Court thought we should add them to our search."

"Already being done."

She lifted her head up. "Really?"

"Dean and I talked about it. When I said we wanted to help a family in need, not that we were dead-set on a baby, he brought up this type of scenario."

With her arms now wrapped around his neck, Katie gave Dusty a lingering kiss. "You're so smart."

"That's a nice change from smart-ass."

"Oh, you're that, too."

Katie heard thundering footsteps racing down the steps. "The troops are up. Quiet time is over."

"I got breakfast. You keep reading."

"Don't need to tell me twice."

Vick was happy to see Jody enter sick bay. It had been a little over two hours and he was feeling much better. He got out of the bed Xolo and Aubrey put him in and had crawled in with Aiden.

Jody held a gentle kiss to Vick's lips for a long moment before she said, "You look better."

"I feel better, but there's been no change to Aiden."

"The best thing for his little body is rest. If it's what he does, he has to have a way to heal from it."

Vick stroked his son's cheek. "But that had to push the limits. You saw what just moving us into the nebula did to him. This was clear across the galaxy."

"I'm aware of that. Don't you think I feel a little responsible for his choice of where to go?"

He reached up and grabbed her hand before she could spin away. "Don't. You can't go blaming yourself. If it wasn't here it would have been someone else probably equally as damaging or worse. He could have asked Xolo for his planet's coordinates."

"I should have known what he was going to do. I could have stopped him."

"How could you possibly have guessed this?"

"We know what he's capable of and how big his heart is. I just feel like I should have seen it coming."

"Bullshit, Jody. There's no way—"

"That's a bad word, Daddy."

Vick shouted, "Aiden!" as he gave his son a tight hug. "You really scared me, buddy. Again."

"But the nebula was going to 'splode."

"It looked that way, but I would have known if it was going to do that, son."

"This one did."

Vick looked up at Jody. She bolted to the computer terminal and began keying away. After a minute of what appeared to Vick like frantic typing in confusion, she looked up. "It's gone."

"What do you mean it's gone?"

"I can't get readings on any of the masses that we logged."

"It imploded?"

"It appears that way. There's no black hole that I can get a reading on from here or anything of that sort. If you want to know for certain, we'll need to go back."

"This is unheard of." Shaking off this interesting discovery, he turned back to Aiden. He's all that mattered right now.

"How did you know, son?"

"I just do." He turned his head to the right and spotted the shattered device on the small surgical steel table. "What happened to my Hawkeye?"

The heartrate monitor started to beep faster.

"Don't get excited. I'm sorry, that was my fault. I was angry at it. You were hurt and I didn't like you using it."

"That's not fair!" His heart raced so much that an alarm went off. "It was mine!" Vick was surprised. He'd never seen Aiden react this way.

Doc Aubrey came charging into the room. "What's going on?"

"He's upset over that device."

"It was mine!" Aiden shouted again with a little screech behind his words.

She stood next to him. "You'll need to calm down, Aiden. Your body has been through a lot. That device can be repaired. If you get too damaged, I don't know that you can be. Got it?"

Aiden sniffled and wiped away his tears. His heartrate slowed down, but tears still fell.

"You can fix it?"

"Not me, but I bet Jodessa could do wonders. Now, I need to you to be still for a moment."

Everyone was quiet as Aubrey re-examined him.

She turned to Vick after several moments. "He's not a hundred percent, but he's close. If you're up to it, the two of you can leave the ship when we dock on Teria. The change of scenery will do everyone some good. I'd prefer you stayed in the wheelchair, Vick, but I know I can't make you."

"How long till we dock?" Vick asked Jody.

"Because of where Aiden brought us, it'll be about six hours to properly navigate into the atmosphere, then another two before we can leave the ship once it's situated."

"Why is that?"

"It's just standard procedure. They'll do a complete scan of the ship before we're allowed to open any doors. They check everything from cargo to air quality and of course do a background check on the crew. Until they are assured there are no toxins and no criminals, we won't be permitted to leave. We've only been granted permission to dock because…"

"Because you're on board," Vick finished.

"Don't get any of this wrong, Captain. My father is no happier to see me than I am to see him. I think we need them right now and I accepted their hospitality in hopes that it doesn't come with an ulterior motive."

Not wanting to do this in front of Aiden, Vick looked down at his son. He was out cold again.

"Is he just asleep?" he asked Doc Aubrey.

Returning the scanner to her holster she said, "Yes. The worst of it has passed, now he needs his rest. You two take this outside. I have some work I can do."

Although he was more than a little uneasy by the tests she wanted to do, Vick knew he had to let her. He took Jody by the arm and led her out of the room. They sat on a couch in the tiny waiting area.

"What do you mean by that, Jody? Your father isn't going to make you stay or anything, is he?"

She shook her head. "He wouldn't want that. Even if he begged me, the council would never permit it."

"But you're not in any danger, are you? I mean…you won't get locked up for returning, will you?"

"No. I've been given permission. I left of my own free will. I'm not a criminal who was banished. My…I guess you would call it influence, is not wanted."

"Influence? Like you'll start a revolution with the other women?"

She laughed. "Not that dramatic, but yes, something along those lines. I've read your earth history. We do have some things in common. Millions of miles, thousands of years, galaxies away with hundreds of species and races, most females are still expected to live as males desire."

"I'm amazed that you came out of that situation and do the things you do, babe. I've never had a communications officer with your ear, a technician with your skills, and I bet you could fly the pants off White."

"White flew without pants?"

Vick chuckled and pulled her close. "I sure hope you never get the knack of slang. You are too damn cute for your own good." He gave her a deep kiss and sat back again.

Jody took his hand. "Do you want me to look at the Hawkeye and see if I can repair it? Aiden was really upset."

Vick stood with a bit of a huff. "No. I don't want that goddamn thing fixed. It almost killed him."

"It wasn't the device, it was his big heart. We'd all be dead if he didn't do what he did."

Not being able to face her, he turned and watched Doc work on his son.

"I can't even think about that right now. That would make me the worst captain in all of history. I have to have faith that you would have gotten us out of that mess."

"If we're being honest here, I have to say, no, I wouldn't have."

He rounded on her. "So you repair that thing and what? Let him have it so he can kill himself next time?"

Jody stood, and closed the gap between them. "I just don't like seeing him upset. I haven't studied it enough to know what makes it tick. I don't know that I could ever understand it. It's just like Doc Aubrey examining Aiden. She can study his DNA, but I can't imagine she'll discover the secret to teleportation."

Vick's teeth were gritting together as he spoke. "My son is not a device."

"You know…I'd say some expletive here, but I don't want you to think it's cute!"

Jody brushed past Vick and went into Aiden's room. Vick watched as she kissed his forehead. She bent down and whispered something to him, then kissed his cheek.

Zolo bumped his shoulder from behind to get his attention. "If I don't produce answers about how we ended up here, I'll be lynched, Vick. You need to come up with a statement for the crew."

Jody stormed past them and continued down the hall.

"What's got her panties in a bunch?" Xolo asked.

"She's sleeping with the biggest asshole in the galaxy. That's upsetting enough in itself."

"Aiden's okay, isn't he? I talked to Aubrey not ten minutes ago. Has anything changed?"

"No, he's fine. The three of us just have a difference of opinion on his device, that's all."

"I can't blame you for destroying it. I'd have done the same thing." Two hands reached up and grasped a shoulder. "Come on. I need you for a few briefings."

"I can't leave him."

"Yes, you can," Aubrey said as she walked up behind them. "I can't imagine he'll be awake before you get back. If he does, I'll call for you."

Vick looked through the window again. He shouted, “Sonofabicth!” as he slapped it.

“What it is?” Xolo asked.

“Jody swiped that fucking device.”

Xolo grasped him by the forearm, using his two right arms. “Later. Your crew needs you more right now. You don’t have time for a domestic.”

Jody had successfully avoided Vick for the remainder of the trip to her home planet. She wasn’t at any of the mandatory sessions he had called in order to explain the situation to the crew. With the number of people on board, he had to schedule three sessions to accommodate each shift. When she wasn’t at the last one, he was pissed but not surprised. She didn’t need to be filled in since she knew the situation first hand, but she still should have attended.

He’d fibbed through a partial explanation regarding the teleportation. Since most of the crew consisted of science majors, it wasn’t an easy bluff. With the speculation of the nebula imploding, which was in itself unheard of, that helped leave all sorts of scenarios open as to how their arrival outside Teria came about. There were the few who continued to run tests and scenarios, stretching their theories even further than they had after their first encounter. The hardest ones to convince were dead set on finding out the real “math” behind it. That would keep them busy until the truth could come out. If it ever could.

After the three one-hour sessions, Vick was ready to collapse. He returned to Aiden’s room to find out he hadn’t woken up. He barely managed to stay awake as he was updated by Doc Aubrey. After wheeling a bed by Aiden’s, he fell sound asleep. Hours had passed before he began to stir.

He found Aiden still sound asleep next to him when he did finally open his eyes. Next to Aiden was Jody. He sat up.

“Nice of you to make an appearance.”

"I thought you'd want to shower before we meet the president of Teria."

"You mean dear ol' dad, don't you?"

Ignoring him, she gently shook Aiden. "Sweetheart, are you ready to get up?"

"He should have his rest," Vick said, hurrying out of bed and to Aiden's side.

"Doc had him up once already."

"She did?"

"She wanted him to move around and go to the bathroom on his own. You slept through it."

"I did? Holy shit. Father of the year, huh?"

"Why is the feces so filled with holes on earth?" When Vick laughed, she turned dark pink. "Stop doing that!"

"I'm sorry. I can't help it. Just because I'm pissed at you doesn't mean I don't love you."

Aiden stretched, putting the argument on hold. He smiled at Jody and reached up for a hug. Vick wasn't sure how he felt about being in second place right now.

"Good morning, sweetheart," Jody said with a long embrace. "Doc said you are perfect, but I already knew that." She gave his nose a tap. Her dark pink was fading back into the olive shade which was her normal color.

"Were you mad at Daddy?" Aiden finally looked over at his father.

Not waiting to be asked, Vick leaned down and gave his son a tight embrace. "I'm so glad you're back, buddy. You'll never know how scared I was."

"But you do all kinds of dangerous stuff all the time. You really got scared?"

"Of course I did. I don't worry about anything, really. But you – you're worth worrying about. I'm the dad, Aiden. I'm supposed to protect you, not the other way around. If we're going to be a team, you need to trust me and stop putting yourself in danger."

His face became sad again. “You broke my Hawkeye, anyway.”

Jody held it up, causing a huge smile to spread over Aiden’s face.

“You fixed it!”

Vick quickly grabbed it from her. “I didn’t give you permission to do this, Lieutenant.”

It disappeared from Vick’s hand. “What the hell…” Turning to Aiden, he saw he now had it.

“Buddy, that’s not funny.”

As he reached for it, Jody picked Aiden off the bed. “Give me a minute to explain, Captain.”

“Explain what?” he said with a huff. “How you disobeyed a direct order and now are trying to win my son’s love with it?”

He took a step toward them, but they both disappeared. “Sonofabitch!” Vick shouted. Slapping his hands on the bed caused a not so mild pain in his side. He stayed leaning against it, trying to recover, when his personal device went off. It was Jody.

“You need to calm down, Captain.”

“You two are conspiring against me and I’m supposed to remain calm?”

“That was not my intention. If you bothered to let me explain, I could have told you I found out what makes the device boost Aiden’s teleporting ability. I’ve disabled and removed it. There was no tracking device or GPS. What’s left is his personal computer, camera, watch, eye changing system, and whatever else it does that I haven’t tapped into yet.”

“You found what did that?”

“You had doubts?”

He let out a heavy sigh. “You stole it, Jody. How the hell was I supposed to know what your intentions were?”

“This is not what I signed up for, Vick. I was hired to be communications officer, now I’m bedding the captain and care deeply for his son who neither of us knew existed. And before

I continue, yes, I used your name. The way you've been behaving, the disgusting taste that word leaves in my mouth is a good fit for you lately. You think I would let any harm come to this boy and do something like that against your wishes?"

"Where are you? Where'd he take you?"

"We're in my cabin. I asked him to shower so he could be his best when he met the president of Teria."

"Can I come there so we can talk?"

"I don't think that's wise right now. I told him I'd talk to you, but he's upset."

"This isn't fair, Jody. You know why I hate that device."

"I know, and so does he, but he's still upset."

"Did you tell him what you did to it?"

"In the five seconds since we were teleported away from you? No. I'll tell him when he gets out of the shower. I suggest you do the same. Aubrey was up with you both most of the night. She went to bed when I showed up. You're both cleared to leave. She wants to go over Aiden's numbers with you in a day or so, after we're settled in on Teria."

"So what's the plan? You act like you don't even know me?"

"Please, Captain. This is not your earth high school days." She ended the call, leaving him confused as ever about how to act with her in front of her father. On his planet. The one he was in charge of and could probably have him killed with a snap of his fingers. Shit.

Chapter Twenty-Seven

Vick was already at the ship's main door waiting with his bridge crew when Jody showed up with Aiden. She had changed into her dress whites like the rest of them. He gave her a nod of approval and bent down to Aiden.

"Are we okay, pal?"

Tiny arms wrapping tightly around his neck gave him his answer.

"I'm sorry I ran away."

"I'm sorry I gave you reason to think you had to. You know I love you and just want you to be safe."

"I know."

A loud bang caused Aiden to jump back.

"It's okay, son. It's just the airlock being released. We're allowed to go out onto their planet now."

Aiden tugged Jody's hand. "Is your planet pretty?"

"It's beautiful, Aiden. From what I hear, it's a lot like earth's surface. It's far greener than Athracki's mostly rocky surface. You'll love getting some fresh air here. I'm overdue to be off this ship, aren't you?"

"I sure am." He smiled wide as he took her hand.

Vick was about to be put out by it, but Aiden reached up, wanting his as well. The door clanked and slowly began to swing open.

Jody stepped forward, tugging Aiden along with her down the tube. Vick released his hold and walked closely behind. He thought as Captain that he should be in the lead, but Jody obviously felt no danger was awaiting them. She was the obvious choice for a liaison to whoever was there to greet them, since it was her home planet.

A row of five men stood as they reached the end of the tube. They were in uniforms very much like the ones Vick and his crew wore. Theirs had a little more flair to the shoulders and round medals went down each sleeve instead of on the chest, like earth and most other space command uniforms.

The man at the end bowed slightly at the waist to Jody. She returned the gesture.

"Father."

"Who is the boy?"

"This is the captain's son Aiden."

He gave Aiden a stern look before turning to Vick. "You bring your son on dangerous exploration missions?"

"That actually wasn't part of the plan." Vick stepped forward and extended his hand. Jody's father looked down at it with disgust.

"I know of this custom. I do not wish to touch your extremities."

"Father!" Jody said with a little force behind her voice. "When I left, you weren't so rude to guests."

"I've never had to greet an earth mate of one of my children. I can't say I'm happy with your choice." He took a second, scrutinizing the six crew members behind them. "Are you bedding them all out of wedlock?"

Jody covered Aiden's ears. "Father!" She continued in what sounded like a scolding in her native tongue. Vick wasn't sure he even wanted to know what she was saying.

Her father held up his hand, stopping her rant. "Enough. We'll talk more on the matter privately later."

She took a step closer to Vick. "You will not say anything to me that you will not say to him. We're a family. I won't have your prejudices over their race even attempt to belittle our relationship."

Again his hand went up. "We do not need to do this now. Do you not have two hundred crew members who would like some fresh Terian air and a ship that needs attending?"

Vick stepped forward. "We do, sir. I appreciate your hospitality. I understand it's not normally your way."

"No, it is not. Especially had I known my daughter would be so disrespectful before a full minute had passed."

A loud cry was heard from across the room. "Jodessa?"

Jody took off at a full run. "Menawhen!"

Assuming it was her mother, Vick stayed back with Aiden. The silence from her father was uncomfortable. He wasn't sure how her father knew that they were together, but now that the news was out, he needed to man up.

"I'm not as up on your customs as I should be, sir. Should I be asking your permission to be seeing Jody?"

"Isn't it a little late for that?"

"I'm sorry. It just sort of happened."

"You mean your…" He glanced down at Aiden before he finished, speaking softer. "Your parts just ended up in her, did they?"

Vick wasn't sure why he'd expected this to be easier. "No, sir. I mean...I wouldn't normally have started a relationship with a member of my crew. I'm not sure if you understand earth ways, but I do love her."

"Yet you have a child with another woman. An Athrackian slave at that."

"My mom is dead, Mister Jody's dad," Aiden interrupted. As much as Vick wanted his ears not to be in on this conversation, there was no avoiding it. "My dad is trying to find out who killed her. They're after us. I brought us here, hoping you could help. I didn't think you'd want any harm to come to Jody. Please tell me I'm right. I love her, too."

For the first time, Opex's face showed the briefest of what could be called a smile. He bent down to Aiden's level. "Well, son. We have that in common. Of course I'll help keep all of you safe. But first, I think Jodessa's mother has some treats for you and the rest of the crew. Do you like earth chocolate?"

"I do!" he exclaimed. "Very much!"

"Then you'll love our version even more."

After clapping his hands, at least two dozen people came out of six archways that surrounded the room. He turned to Vick. "Tell your crew to disembark. Food and drink are waiting."

Vick nodded to Xolo, who made the call to the awaiting teams.

Jody called Aiden over, he ran to her and her mother. They led him directly to a table loaded with sweets of all kinds. It reminded Vick of a Sunday buffet dessert table at a fancy Earth hotel. All they needed was the champagne. Terian ale would do nicely, however. He was beyond ready for a drink.

Opex continued. "There will be no restrictions placed on your crew, Captain. We only ask that each one registers as they leave the ship. They'll each be given a two week pass. If this little dilemma takes longer than that, we'll need to come up with a plan 'B'."

"Sounds fair to me. I really appreciate this."

"Is everyone okay with staying here or do I make arrangements for a ship to return some of them to one of your ports?"

"No. Everyone is staying. My crew is committed to me and what we do."

"And what about what your son does?"

That took Vick aback. "Pardon?"

"Don't look so frightened, Captain. We're a peaceful people. We farm, we mine. I have no need for a teleporting child. I'm here to help, not steal him for observation."

"How did you know? Did Jody tell you?"

"She put me in touch with your father. He's due to arrive tomorrow."

Vick swallowed hard. He was regretting his decision to not take the wheelchair. Beads of sweat formed on his forehead.

"Are you all right, Captain?"

Vick cleared his throat and straightened up as best he could. "I'm fine. I just wasn't expecting him."

"He wanted to see you and the boy. He had reason to believe you would be found by the men after you, even here, and is bringing an entire regiment to protect you."

"You're allowing that here?"

"No, not here. There will be no fighting here. Boundaries will be set and fighter planes will be in place. Smaller fighter ships may be easier to maneuver through our atmosphere, but we will be able to maintain a safe distance with them. Only your father's will be allowed to land. All other incoming ships will be diverted to our third moon until everyone is safe."

"Wait a second. Regiments? Fighter planes? My dad's a lawyer, not a general. Where is this coming from?"

"He's an excellent lawyer with favors owed to him is my guess. He filled me in on these Rhenharts who are after you. They won't be easy to stop."

"I'm really sorry we brought this to your front step. Aiden thought he was saving us, he didn't think about any harm it would be doing to you."

"No harm will come to us." He grasped Vick's shoulder gently. "If I do say so myself, you look terrible. Do you need one of our physicians to look at you?"

"Thank you, but no. I'm fine."

"Maybe some good Terian food and drink is all you need. Now, come join me and my wives in the banquet room. You'll be my guest at the head table."

They headed to the banquet room and continued. "I can't tell you how much I appreciate this," Vick said.

"Of course we're going to do what we can. You seem very surprised of our willingness to help. I'm sure my daughter has painted a terrible picture of me."

"In all honesty, she hasn't said too much. She feels unwelcome here, that's about all I got."

"I'm afraid that's true. Anyone not willing to live as we do…well…it's better that they move on."

"I imagine it was hard for you, given your position and all."

"All the more reason she had to go. I can't have someone the whole planet is looking up to 'stir the pot,' as you would say on earth."

Vick chuckled softly. "You are better with our slang than your daughter is."

"Oh? That surprises me. She's a smart one. Always the head of her class and taking on far more than she should have at any given time." He turned to Vick. "Perhaps she enjoys…" he paused as if searching for just the right phrase. "Jerking your chain?"

Vick laughed. "There is that possibility."

"Between you, me, and the wall, I can't say I was surprised when she asked to leave."

"She asked to leave?"

Opex nodded. "There was no changing her mind. She broke her mother's heart, but I had to let her go."

"I'm sorry if this sounds like an insult, but it seems to me that someone like her is an incredible asset, not a threat."

Opex didn't respond, he continued to the table. "I'm grateful she has found her place with you and your ship. She would not have thrived here." Opex motioned to an open seat at the head table. "You really do look terrible. Sit, Captain. Someone will be along to start serving you. I need to go talk with my daughter."

Vick didn't argue and took a seat. Xolo joined him a moment later, offering him an ale as he sat. "This shit is even better straight out of the tap. Heck of a talent your son has, Captain."

After a long drink Vick replied, "When you're right, you're right. He knows about Aiden, Xolo."

"Opex?"

"Yeah. Apparently he's been in touch with my father."

"Ouch. How is the old boss of Dewey, Cheatum, and Howe?"

Vick choked on his ale. "Nice, dickhead."

"Sorry, but you're the one who's painted that picture of your father."

"Well, it's true. Now it appears he has military backing him."

"Military? Why? What's up?"

"He has back up coming to protect us."

"Here? Opex is okay with that?"

"Apparently so. My father has him schmoozed."

"Does he know you're banging his daughter?"

Vick nodded through another sip. "And I'm still alive. He doesn't want her back here, so I guess that makes home planet shopping that much easier."

"No in-laws next door, aren't you the lucky one."

"Damn straight." A plate was dropped off between them. Battered something or other. Vick hoped whatever it was, it tasted like chicken. Xolo dove right in; Vick followed his lead.

"Not that you've said anything, but I figured you'd be tying the knot with her pregnant."

Vick choked even worse on his appetizer. "What was that?"

Xolo hung his head. "Shit. I just assumed with you talking like that…Damnit. I'm sorry, buddy. Aubrey told me, I thought you knew."

Vick stood. "I certainly did not." He scanned the room, hoping to find her.

"Don't tell her. My wife will kill me."

"How can I keep this a secret? Jesus. Why can't she turn a shade of pink or blue so I know these things? She gives everything else away."

"You are one fertile gus. You know that? I don't suppose there's a half human - half Terian on record either. You trying to start your own race?"

Vick smacked the back Xolo's head. "One of the babies belongs to Doc Duiz. Shoots your theory to shit."

"You knew and didn't do anything?"

"If the mothers wanted to keep it a secret, who was I to intervene?"

"Um, hello. The captain."

"Yeah well, it's seems the whole crew was determined to knock someone up. I'm no better than the rest of them, apparently." He took another long gulp, emptying his glass. "How can she even know so fast? We haven't even been together for a couple weeks."

"Aubrey said they are more in tune with their bodies than humans. She would have known precisely when your swimmer hit her egg."

Vick raised an eyebrow. "Seriously?"

Xolo nodded. "I'm not going to use your lecture about millions of ways to prevent it in this day and age, Vick. I think she's good for you. I never would have thought you should give this up and settle down, but I've seen you with Aiden. You're a natural if I've ever seen one. I hope she has twins."

"Twins? Does that run in Terians?"

He shrugged, which never stopped looking funny to Vick with two sets of shoulders. "I don't know. It's in our race, obviously."

"You're more equipped for it, jackass. Every mother should be fortunate enough to have two sets of arms." Vick spotted Jody at what looked like a chocolate fountain and took off. He made his way through the crowd of Terians and his crew toward Jody. Her expression dropped when she saw the determination in his eyes. She excused herself from her mother and met him on the way.

"What's the matter? Did my father upset you?"

"Why didn't you tell me?"

"What? That I asked to leave? It's the same thing. I would have been banished for not accepting their ways. I wasn't going to fight it, so why wait for a lengthy court date and official paperwork? The result is the same."

"Not that. You're pregnant?"

She instantly turned a soft blue. He'd never seen that before. Was she embarrassed? Upset but not anger-orange? He realized he still had a lot to learn.

"I don't know how to read that shade, Jody. Are you pissed that I know?"

"I wanted to be the one to tell you, there just hasn't been a good time. Was it Xolo?"

He grasped both of her shoulders. "Don't be angry with him. I wish you told me the second you knew."

She grinned. "We were still a little busy."

"When was it?"

"On the counter. I shouldn't have allowed the second time. We would have been okay after the shower."

"If you think I'm anything but thrilled, you'd be deeply wrong."

"You have enough to worry about."

"Nothing is more important to me than you and Aiden."

"And your ship and crew. There are men hunting us, Captain. You've been shot by your own crewmember. Worrying about me and my reproductive system should not be on that list."

He pulled her tight to his chest. "You're insane. You should have told me." He released his hold on her, held her face in his hands and gave her a firm kiss. "Can we be married here?"

Her shade deepened.

"Still don't know what to make of that."

"No. We cannot be married here. I'm not a citizen anymore."

He smiled. "But you will marry me."

"If that is what you wish, then yes, I will marry you."

"What about what you wish?"

"I wish very much to kill these men who are after your son. I don't wish to be running from galaxy to galaxy, hiding from them. I wish to get away from my father before he finds out I'm pregnant. And yes, I wish to be married to you. I'm also going to be very angry with Doc Aubrey for telling her husband and him telling you."

He pulled her close again. "Don't. This is the best news I've had in a long time. If my side wasn't killing me so bad, I'd take you in the nearest bathroom."

She did her laugh that he adored so. "You're such a romantic. But that would be how we ended up in this predicament."

"Not predicament, the beginning of wonderful times. I love you. I promise you, you are all that I'll ever want."

Aiden tugged on Vick's pant leg. "Grandpa is calling."

Vick took his hand and led him to a quieter corner. Jody tugged them further down to a door with a keypad. After entering a code, she brought them into a small office. Vick raised an eyebrow.

"Don't be so surprised. I roamed this place as a kid." She picked up Aiden and sat him down on a table.

Aiden swiped his device and called up the viewing screen. Vick's father appeared.

"Hey there, pal. Nice to finally see you. You guys get to Teria okay?"

"Uh-huh. They have chocolate way better than earth's!"

"Boy, I'd sure like to try that. Did you hear I'm on my way there?"

Vick jumped in. "I did. Opex filled me in somewhat. I'd rather not discuss the details..." he motioned his eyes to Aiden.

"Understandable."

Vick bent down slightly to be more at his level. "Buddy, can I borrow that for a minute so I can talk to my dad? You should go back out to the party."

"You promise you won't hurt it?"

"I promise." He crossed his heart as an added show.

Aiden removed his Hawkeye and offered it to Vick, then reached up to Jody.

"We'll catch up to you outside," Jody said with a quick kiss.

Once they were gone, Vick continued. "Opex said you were showing up with a little help. Actually, a lot of firepower would be more like it. Is that true? Sounds a little overkill to me."

"Victor, you're not only dealing with a few men on a ship. There's far more to it than that."

"I'd thought we'd be safe here for a bit. We're halfway across the galaxy. Teria hardly even comes to anyone's mind. Why would they look here? Jody's checked the device several times. They can't be tracking us with it."

"That device of Aiden's. How did you come by it?"

"His mother left it with a Graneau with instructions. If something happened to her—" As soon as the words were out of his mouth, Vick realized what was happening. "They captured the Graneau?"

"Yes. Had I known about him, maybe I could have gotten to him first."

"My mind didn't even go there. I had no idea what was going on at the time." Vick slammed his hands hard on the table. "Dammit! We need to leave here."

"There's nowhere you can go, son. They'll always be one step behind you, but they'll eventually catch up. The team you encountered outside the nebula was only one of many. There's a whole army of Rhenharts out for this cause."

"Cause? He's a three year old boy."

"Victor, you know it's about far more than that."

Both hands ran through his hair in frustration. "Jody disabled his device, but I guess telling them that wouldn't make a fuck's bit of difference." Feeling weak again, Vick leaned again the wall and slid to the floor. "What now? You can't tell me you're going to shoot every last one of them out of the sky."

"If I have to, but there's a better way."

"The trip here almost killed him, Dad. Those bastards aren't taking my son."

"Opex and I have devised a plan."

"I'm all ears."

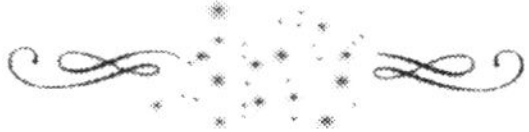

President Opex met Vick as he opened the door to the banquet room.

"Is your father still on track?"

"Yes. They'll be here first thing in the morning. By the way, remind me never to piss you off."

Opex smiled. "Make my daughter happy and you won't."

Vick crossed his arms over his chest. "You're not at all what I expected."

"Don't mistake disappointment for lack of love. I have other children to carry on my legacy, but she'll always be my daughter. There's a place for her in my heart, if not on my planet."

Vick didn't know what possessed him to want to tell Opex about the baby, but he couldn't help himself. "She's pregnant. We're thrilled, but she's scared to death to tell you."

"You do realize I could have you dismembered."

Vick felt ashen again. "And by dismembered you mean…" His eyes lowered to his crotch.

Opex nodded.

He swallowed hard. "I guess I didn't."

A faint Terian grin quirked on the president's face. "Casherri sperm indeed."

Vick let out a heavy breath of relief.

"More is at stake here than my unwed daughter's virtue."

"We're going to be married as soon as all of this blows over. I can't say why, but she loves me. She's loves Aiden too, and it's mutual. All we want is a normal life. I'll give up exploring to keep them safe."

"Don't be so quick to take that stance. My daughter is not suited to be what you'd call a housewife. If that's all she wanted, she would have stayed here."

"I'll guess we'll have to deal with that when the time comes. I can only handle one life-altering decision at a time. Let's make it out of this alive first."

Chapter Twenty-Eight

Banging on their front door woke Dusty and Katie abruptly at midnight. Katie had only gotten to sleep an hour ago. As she tied her robe together she said, "Who the heck could it be?"

"You got me." Dusty headed for the stairs in his pajama pants. "It can't be good at this hour." He peeked out the side window before unlocking the door. It was one of Dean's partners.

"Adam? Do you have the wrong house? Dean is next door."

"No, Dust. I'm looking for you and Katie. I didn't know who else to go to."

Katie stepped forward, worried. "Is something wrong?"

"A buddy of mine and his wife died a few hours ago. Bad car accident leaving a fundraiser."

Katie's hand covered her mouth. "Oh my God. I'm so sorry."

Dusty wrapped an arm around her. "I'm sorry to hear that. Do we know them?"

"Hector and Isabelle Santos. I don't know if you did. He went to law school with me and had his own firm in Edina."

"I think his name may have come up, but I can't place what for. Is there a reason you're telling us this at midnight?"

He took a minute staring hard into Dusty's eyes then into Katie's. Tears were forming.

Katie reached up and wrapped her arms around his neck and gave him a comforting hug. "Do you need to come sit down?"

He released the hug and wiped at his eyes. "He has…had two kids. A boy that's four and a two year old daughter."

Katie's voice squeaked when she spoke. "Had? Were they with him?"

He shook his head. "No, sorry. I just meant…you know. They're not his anymore. They were with a sitter. I'm sorry; I'm not doing this too well. Still in shock, you know?"

"We understand," Dusty said. "What can we do?"

"I'm the executor of his estate. He was my best friend. Hector and his wife were only children, both parents are long dead. There is no family. I'm a single dude with no prospects in sight. I'm sure when they asked me to look after the kids in the event of their death, they thought it would never happen or I'd be married by then."

Katie squeezed his hand. "That's a lot for a single guy to handle. No one will blame you. Will they have to go into foster care?"

He placed his other hand on hers. "I was kind of hoping you'd take them."

Katie's eyes brightened immediately; she turned to Dusty. He pulled her close then spoke over her head to Adam. "Of course we want to help. What do you need?"

"That answer was all I needed," he said with a broad smile as he again wiped his eyes. "They're great kids. Like I said, I'd take them if I thought I wouldn't screw them up."

Katie took his hands. "You'd do a great job, but I understand. I hate that this has happened, but I'm more than happy to take them in."

"I don't just mean help for a few days. I'd like to know they'll have a good, permanent home."

"You want us to adopt them?" Dusty said.

"That's what I was hoping. I know when you meet them you'll fall in love."

With eagerness in his eyes, Dusty looked down at Katie.

"Oh my God, Dusty." As if needing his support, she wrapped her arms tight around his waist. "As if that's even a question. Of course we…my goodness…yes. Yes, of course we'll take them." She paused. "Do the kids know about their parents yet?"

His lips pinched tight as he shook his head. "They've been asleep. I'm not sure what all they'll understand. I have no idea how to do this. Waking them with this news…" He had to take a minute to gather himself and cleared his throat. "The sitter is staying until I get there. I needed to do something by morning so Child Services didn't step in." He took a business card out of his suit jacket pocket. "The address is on the back. I was told they're up by seven. I'd appreciate any help as soon as humanly possible."

"I'll be there by six-thirty," Katie said after reading the address. It wasn't far at all.

He gave her a tight hug. "I can't say thank you enough. I'm really sorry to have bothered you at this hour. I just couldn't go another minute, keeping this to myself."

As he turned away, Dusty caught his arm. "Are you okay to drive?"

"Yeah…I'll be okay. I need to go have a bourbon or ten and crash. Thanks for helping out. I'm happy for you and the kids, but fuck. Just fuck." His eyes met Katie's. "Sorry about the French."

She hugged him again. "You're entitled. I'm really sorry about your friends. I hate to think that our joy is coming because of your pain."

He shrugged. "That's the way things work, isn't it?" He gave them a brief nod. "See you in the morning. Thanks again."

Dusty closed the door and again pulled Katie tight. "I can't believe this is happening. Can you pinch me?"

"Two kids, Dusty. Toddlers. You know what that's going to do to our schedules?"

He smiled. "Yeah. Isn't it great?" But the smile soon faded. "Well, you know. I hate this battle going on in my head. Those poor kids." He reached for Katie, who had once again begun to tear up.

"Aw, babe…" Dusty pulled her close. "I know what you're thinking. You didn't cause the accident; you didn't make these children orphans. We'll be giving them a new life because of shit circumstances, but don't you dare feel guilty over this."

"How are we even going to explain it to them?"

"I don't know, but we'll figure it out." He gave her a squeeze. "You may have to put the Captain on hold for a bit."

"No way. I'll get some reading time in where I can. Come on." She gave him a tug. "We need to get to bed if I'm going to head over there early."

Katie could not have been more wrong about finding time to read. The couple weeks that followed were an absolute whirlwind. Adam and Katie did their best to explain to the kids that Mommy and Daddy weren't going to be able to come back. They really didn't understand, as Katie has expected. Little Tony threw in a few times about "Daddy coming tomorrow then" but Olivia didn't talk much for being two. She clung to Katie and kept pointing to the door saying, "Mum?"

Their kids were thrilled to have other children around. Little Alyson was especially excited and wanted to carry Olivia everywhere. Dusty, Dean, and Adam were able to move the kids' furniture and all their belongings into Dusty and Katie's house over the next few days.

Adam informed them of a trust that was set up for the kids. "These two are better off than I am, Dust. You won't be hurting for college funds, that's for sure."

"We'd make do either way, Adam. We love them to pieces already. I don't care about their money. You're the executor, do as you were instructed, that's good enough for me."

"I knew you'd say that, but it's there nonetheless. Come by when things settle down and we'll talk. I should have the adoption papers filed in a day or so, I'll let you know when the court date is set."

"Sounds good."

Dusty's and Katie's parents came by to meet the kids right away, as did Alyson. Even Dusty's sister, Dana, made an appearance, much to Katie's surprise. The influx of people coming and going had kept them both running themselves ragged. Katie couldn't stop to even think about picking up the book when she collapsed in bed after getting the kids tucked in. It had taken two weeks for Olivia to stop waking up at two or three a.m., calling for her mother. It broke Katie's heart every time.

Tony and Alex had bonded instantly and he'd already taken to calling her Mom and Dusty Dad, following Alex's lead. Katie knew they had a long way to go, but things were already promising. She and Dusty couldn't be happier. She'd taken a leave of absence at work, knowing her clinic and patients would be in good hands with her partners.

Dusty brought Lindsay home with him from work one day. Katie insisted she stayed for dinner.

"Right, because you need one more mouth to feed around here."

"Don't be silly. We'd love to have you. You need to get to know the kids. You know you'll be Dusty's emergency back-up someday."

She'd given Katie a weak smile; Katie couldn't let it go. "Are you doing okay? You're not having any complications, are you?"

Lindsay rested her hands on her belly. Katie thought she'd really popped out in the weeks since she'd seen her. "I'm fine. I've started the adoption process. It's harder than I imagined."

Katie rested her hand on Lindsay's. "Are you getting to know the couple?"

She said, "No," with a firm shake of her head. "I can't do that. I need it to be a closed adoption. I don't want to always wonder about my...their child. I'll have to trust the agency to find a nice couple."

Katie brought Lindsay to her for a hug. "You're so brave. You are doing what's right for you, that's what's important. These people deal with children for a living. Of course they will settle for nothing less than the best home for your baby."

Just then, Deidre ran by with Alex and Tony chasing her, laughing.

"Careful, you two," Katie called out. "You're going to wear the poor girl out."

Lindsay smiled wide. "If I didn't want it closed, you'd be the best home for my baby, but you already have your hands full." She suddenly began to cry.

"Oh, honey." Katie pulled her in for another hug. "It'll be okay. We'll help get you through this."

Courtney walked in through the back patio door. Jacob took off after the boys. "Hi, Lindsay!"

Lindsay stood and received a warm hug from Courtney, and then her eyes lowered to Courtney's belly. "You've really got two in there, don't you?"

Courtney grunted. "Double trouble already indeed. My mom always said you should grow an extra set of hands with each child. Right now, I'd settle for a back-up bladder." She dropped her water bottle hard on the table. "Dammit, now I said it. I'll be right back. You two want anything while I'm passing the kitchen?"

"No, thanks," came from both of them.

Courtney came back with a bag of chips. "Lay off the salt my widening ass."

Lindsay leaned forward and grabbed a handful. "When you're right, you're right."

The three boys ran past them again, this time without the dog. A play lawn mower was involved as well as the aggravating popcorn popper toy from hell.

"I thought you hated those things, Katie?"

"It was Olivia's. We brought everything of theirs here. We were trying to make the transition as smooth as possible. The boys love sharing a room but with Olivia waking up, we've had her with us. It won't be long before she'll be in with Ali."

"Dusty won't give up his den, huh?"

"I wouldn't ask him to. We're talking about building above the garage. He can have a man cave out there when we need to split the kids up. I certainly don't need a home office. There's the whole basement to finish off as well. It kept getting put off."

Olivia walked up to Katie with her arms up. Katie pulled her to her lap and gave her a long kiss to her cheek. "The boys too much for you, sweetie?"

She leaned into Katie's chest without a sound. Lindsay patted her back.

"She's such a sweetheart. I'll take a cuddle bug any day."

They hadn't heard Ali come up from behind the couch. She stood at Lindsay's legs. "I still fit on your lap, Aunt Lindsay."

Smiling, Lindsay pulled Ali up. "You sure do, sweetheart." Lindsay held her tight as she rested her head on Ali's. "You sure do."

After the kids ran off again, Katie grasped Lindsay's hand. "You are so good with kids. I know this has to be hard on you. Are you really sure this is what you want?"

"I know it's not what I want, but it's what's best. Keeping my baby would be selfish."

"Hon," Courtney piped in. "It's your baby. No one knows better than Mom. Not every child is raised in a home with a six-figure income and two parents. I respect you wanting to do what's best, but what could be better than you?"

Lindsay forced a smile. "I understand what you're trying to say and I appreciate it. I really do. If you're trying to play devil's advocate, you're doing a great job. I can tell you're married to a lawyer."

"Now that just hurts," Courtney said, reaching for more chips.

Lindsay laughed. "I love you both, but I've made up my mind." She stood. "Thanks for the dinner offer, but I really have to get going." Katie stood and gave her a goodbye hug. "Come by anytime. You're one of the few who can stand the noise."

She smiled. "My days off are empty without it. I'll see you soon. Stay put, I'll see myself out." She waved to Courtney as she walked away.

After she left, Courtney said, "That's really odd."

"Court, just because it's not what we'd do doesn't mean it isn't what she feels is best. I won't mention it again. It's got to be hard enough on her without us harping on her decision."

"I know, but…she does daycare. She has to love kids. It just seems so unlikely for her to give her own up."

"A daycare woman who isn't ready for her own kid. Maybe it's a little like a vet who isn't ready for her own puppy." Katie crossed her arms.

Courtney laughed hard. "Yeah, like that. Oh! Like the gynecologist that doesn't want to date because he can't just look at one more—"

Katie held one hand up while the other rubbed down her face. "I remember that episode of *Friends*." She sat back down. "You can see the pain in her face. I guess I keep hoping for a miracle for her." What she really wanted to say was that she was hoping for a Frank. Her life was changed so profoundly by whatever it is that allowed Dusty to go back and fix things; she wondered why it didn't happen that way for others. Even with all she and Courtney had been through, it was one conversation she knew they could never have.

"Earth to Katie."

"I'm sorry. I just let my mind wander."

"You catching up on sleep?"

"We're almost to a normal routine. In another couple weeks, I'll look into a part-time daycare. I'll slowly get back on the schedule at work. They were at a daycare full time; I just didn't feel right sending them away all day yet. I'm sure their routine is as messed up as ours."

"You'll find your happy medium. Hey, can I leave him for an hour? I really need to get my nails done. Dean's running late."

"Of course. What's one more?" Katie laughed.

"You're a saint. You know that, right?"

Olivia wandered over again and once again asked to be picked up.

Courtney smiled. "I think she kinda likes you, hon."

Holding her tight, Katie said. "It's mutual."

Chapter Twenty-Nine

Dressed and ready to go, Vick gently kissed Jody goodbye, careful not to wake her. He wasn't the biggest fan of his father's plan, but he had no choice. He woke up Aiden and helped him get dressed. "You ready, buddy," he whispered.

"I think so," Aiden said. "Why can't Jody come with us?"

"She just can't, pal. It's better this way. Don't you want her to be safe?"

"Of course."

"Then we gotta go. Come on, Grandpa will be waiting."

His father's ship was waiting for him as promised. President Opex and Aiden Skinnard were at the boarding tube, waiting for him. There were only two guards with Opex this time.

"Thanks for coming," Vick said to his dad.

"What else could I do? You're in trouble. It's not the first time and I'm pretty sure it won't be the last." He walked over and shook Aiden's hand. "I've very pleased to meet you, Aiden. Call me grandpa."

Aiden smiled. "Okay."

President Opex spoke up. "You three better get going. I'm not sure what I fear more. All of you out there among those battleships or my daughter when she realizes you've left."

Vick said, "I have no choice."

Vick's father wrapped an arm around his shoulder and motioned him down the tube, toward the ship. Within moments, they took off.

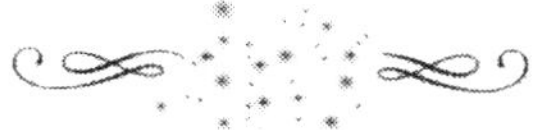

Jody reached the terminal in time to see the ship leave the hangar. She screamed at her father. "How could you let them leave?"

"I won't have your life and that of every being on this planet in danger."

"You promised he could stay!" Her hands landed on his chest. "I hate you! You've always put your position above everything else! You don't care about anyone but yourself!"

He held her wrists. "I do care, Jodessa. That's why I had to let him go. He's in his father's hands now."

She whipped herself out of his grip. "I'm taking the ship and I'm leaving."

"His ship is grounded for maintenance."

"You cannot do that!"

"Can and have. You'd best mind your manners around the Terian President, Lieutenant Opex. You're not above the law. Keep this up and you'll spend the night in a cell."

A loud explosion sent Jody into her father as the whole terminal shook. She raced to the window and saw its source. "No!" It took everything she had to remain standing. The ship that had just departed was now in a million pieces. Small pieces of debris hit the building as she watched in terror.

Spinning to her father's chest, she sobbed hard. "No! What have you done?"

He held her tight. "I'm sorry. It's what they felt was best. I couldn't force them to stay."

One of the guards went over to the screen on the wall. Even over her sobs, Jody could hear them being hailed. She turned to face the screen after wiping her eyes. It was a Rhenhart. They were even uglier than she remembered with their deep red skin, thick as armor. With their head protected by what looked like a natural helmet, it was as if this race was solely built for war. No wonder they were usually behind every war effort ever started.

She wanted to slap the grin off his face. "You're a bastard."

"I didn't fire on that ship. I needed the boy alive and that device. That missile came from your planet."

Jody bared her teeth. "This is not *my* planet!" She turned to her father, again slamming her hands onto his chest. "Who fired on Victor and Aiden?"

Grabbing her wrists again, he called the guards over. "Take her away."

"Father!" she screamed as the guards cuffed her. "You killed them? Why? You promised sanctuary! That boy was innocent!"

"Shut her up," President Opex said as he turned back to the screen. "You have no more business here. I demand you leave our orbit immediately."

"You're not going to get away with destroying what was ours."

"There was no deal to be made here. The device and the boy are gone. Go start your next war elsewhere, Rhenhart."

The Rhenhart pulled the Graneau in view of the screen. "I guess I have no use for this anymore." He ran a blade across the Graneau's throat, killing him instantly. "You're next, Opex."

Jody screamed and turned away, then brought her head high and glared at the Rhenhart. "You'll have to get in line to kill the bastard. He's mine!" She broke free of the guard's hold, but he quickly slammed her to the ground and gained control of her again.

Opex screamed at the guard. "Get her in a cell!" then turned back to the screen. "There is an entire fleet hidden behind our three moons. If you come any closer or fire one shot, you'll be destroyed."

As he spoke, a few of the fighters came into view. "Test me, Rhenhart. This is one war you won't win."

"This isn't over, Terian," he said as the screen went blank.

Jody tried breaking free once again. That earned her a blast from the guard's stun gun, knocking her out cold.

Jody didn't know how long she'd been asleep. She was surprised to find herself in the infirmary and not in a cell. Her mother entered with a wet washcloth in her hand.

"Oh good. You're awake. You had me worried, Jodessa."

She tried to sit up but her mother gently pushed her back down and began dabbing at her forehead and cheeks with the washcloth.

"It has the leaves of the mengh bush. It will help."

"I'm fine, Menawhen," is what she said, but she knew she wasn't. Her arms crossed over her stomach. She wanted to be sick. Vick and Aiden were gone. She was all alone.

Her mother placed a hand on Jody's arms. "Your father told me about your condition. Are you okay?"

"How does he know?"

"Your Captain told him."

Jody shot up in the bed. “He what? I guess that explains why he killed him.” Her hands covered her face as she shouted. “He didn’t have to kill Aiden, too!”

Her mother’s arms wrapped around her. “Jodessa stop. You don’t know what happened.”

“Yes, I do! I saw it! I hate him! I’ll always hate him! I want to leave! Now!” Again she struggled to get up, again her mother fought to hold her back.

“You’re not going anywhere without me.”

Jody’s head whipped to the door. Vick was standing there with Aiden in his arms. He let Aiden down, who ran her. Jody dropped to her knees in tears as she wrapped her arms around Aiden. She continued to cry as she swayed with him.

Vick dropped to his knees behind her and surrounded them both with his strong arms.

“You think a missile could stop me?”

She raised her head and kissed him fiercely.

“How are you here? I watched the ship blow up.”

“That’s quite a talent my grandson has, don’t you think?”

Jody stared blankly at the doorway. Vick’s father was leaning against the doorjamb. “Nice to meet you face to face at last, Jody.”

“This was your plan?” She rushed over with Aiden in her arms and hugged him tight.

“I’m sorry, but it had to be done. They were never going to stop hunting Aiden. They had to believe he was dead. I’m afraid if we told you in advance, the act wouldn’t have been so convincing.”

Leaning Aiden out just a little, she stared hard into his eyes. “Are you hurt at all? I disabled your Hawkeye. How could you do this?”

“I never needed it for small things.”

“Moving you and two grown men is small?”

“Of course,” he said as he motioned to be let down. “You said that was a piece of cake when we got back here. Can I get that piece of cake now?”

Aiden Senior laughed hard. "I'm sure President Opex will find you that piece of cake, grandson."

"Oh no he won't," he said as he walked in the room. He knelt down to Aiden. "You'll have a cake the size of a starship all to yourself." He gave Aiden a hug. "You are one special boy. I'm very pleased to have you in the family."

Opex stood, waiting for his daughter's reaction. Jody ran to him and wrapped her arms around his waist. "I'm so sorry. You truly did help and I could do—"

His hand covered her mouth, stopping her apology. "I'm sorry I had to put you through that, but there was no other way. If I could have saved the life of that poor Graneau, I would have."

Vick spoke up. "We have a Graneau on our ship, sir. She said she would have gladly given her life to save Aiden and knows that he felt the same way. For what they were making him do, he would have rather died than to continue hunting Aiden. Don't beat yourself up over it. He died a hero."

"Then he'll have a hero's celebration."

"Can you make a statue?" Aiden asked.

"Of course, son. He'll have his own park. How's that sound?"

"Great!"

Katie glanced at the clock on her e-reader. One a.m. This was going to bite her ass in the morning, but she couldn't stop, not when she'd had only had a few pages to go. She almost woke Dusty up when the ship blew up, but she knew he had to paint himself out of this somehow; she was just too into the moment to see how.

She reread the last page again then did what she was trying hard to put off. She woke up Dusty.

He groaned. "What is it, babe? Is Olivia up again?"

"No. I finished."

"You finished? My manuscript?" He turned to look at the clock. "I kinda want to hurt you right now."

"I need closure."

"And I need sleep." He adjusted his pillow and flopped his head hard on it.

"I mean, great wrap up, but really, Dusty. Something? What about Xolo's wife? Does she turn in information on him? Does Vick ever accept his father's wife? What about Deidre's message that was cut off?"

Dusty's arm went over his head. "They're called sequels. Now go to bed."

She playfully bopped him with a pillow. "An epilog?"

He pulled the pillow out of her hands and placed it over his head.

"I'll get Court to watch the kids tomorrow. We'll grab a nooner."

He whipped the pillow off. "It's been a week. We've never gone a week."

"You want to now?"

"I can't believe I'm saying this, but no. I'll take you up on your offer tomorrow." He rolled over so his back was facing her.

She leaned over him and kissed his cheek. "You owe me an epilog."

"I ain't writing it tomorrow, puddin'."

"Just promise me."

"Okay, I promise. But now I'm getting shower sex."

"Deal."

Four months had passed. Life could not have been more perfect for the Andrews family of six, two cats, and one overactive deaf Dalmatian. A knock at the door interrupted the mid-winter Sunday brunch. Dean and Courtney were over with their month old identical twins, Dean and Dustin. Courtney had fallen asleep on the couch while the babies slept in a portable playpen.

Katie was shocked to see Adam at the door. Even more so that he carrying a baby in a car seat. There was a diaper bag on his shoulders that seemed way over packed with diapers and formula for a quick stop.

She immediately waved him in. "Bring that baby in out of the cold." She gave him a kiss on the cheek once he was in and the door was closed. Dusty came over.

"Who's baby?" Dusty asked as he shook Adam's hand. Katie took the carrier from him, removed the baby wrapped in a blue blanket, and began to sway. He put the bag down, which landed with a heavy thump.

"Please tell me you haven't had another friend pass." She kissed the baby's forehead. "Not that I wouldn't want to keep this sweet thing." When she looked up and saw his expression, she felt bad for what she'd said. "You're not serious?"

"No. I'm sorry. His mother's not dead, but uh…" he looked over at all the kids at the table. "Is this a good time?"

"As good as any around here." Dusty laughed. "Come sit and have a bite. There's plenty."

"Thanks, but I can't stay." He gently brushed the baby's cheek. "Lindsay is his mom."

"This is Lindsay's baby?" Katie said. "Why do you have him?"

He pulled an envelope out of his coat pocket. "She wanted you guys to have him."

"What?" Dusty pulled the papers out of the envelope. "She gave her notice a week ago at the paper. She never said a word…" he quickly scanned the forms.

Dean walked over. "It's legit, Dust. I helped draw them up."

"And you didn't say anything?" Katie realized she was being a little loud and rocked the baby, who had stirred.

"She didn't want you to know until the time came. She was having second thoughts toward the end about giving him up, but she knew she had to do it. The thought of asking you, then taking that away wasn't an option. I have strict orders for you not to try to contact her. She said that would be unbearable."

Katie couldn't stop staring at the baby. Dusty wrapped an arm around her. "What do you say, mama?"

Adam spoke up. "It's a lot to ask. You just took in two toddlers. She knows you're running a full house, but felt you could handle it. There was no one else she would even consider. There's a waiting list of course if you say no. She said she'd understand."

Katie finally looked up. "How can we say no?" She kissed the baby again. "I can't believe this."

Something dropped in the kitchen, Dean ran off to investigate.

"So, yes?" Adam asked.

"Hell yes," Dusty said, shaking his hand. "You sure we can't contact her?"

"I'll let her know you have him, and then she's gone. Paris, I think. She needed some distance."

"I understand," Katie said, again staring at the baby. "I just can't believe this."

Adam had his hand on the doorknob. "I'll let you get back to your meal. There's a crib on the way, curtesy of the firm. Congratulations."

Katie hugged him as best she could with the baby in her arms. "Thank you."

The baby woke up and appeared to be focusing on Katie. "Oh my goodness," Katie said.

"What, babe?" Dusty asked as he lowered his gaze to the now awake baby.

"Well, I guess that settles the name debate." Although his eyes were blue, the left one was almost exactly half green.

The door opened back up. Adam said, "I forgot. She told me she loved the name Aiden, but of course it's up to you. It's her father's name."

Dusty and Katie both beamed with wide smiles.

"Tell her that's perfect, Adam. Absolutely perfect."

After the door closed, Dusty said, "I know what you're thinking. I'll change the name in the book."

"Dusty…are you sure *you* didn't come back and tell you stuff? I can't believe this."

He crossed his heart. "I swear, cupcake."

A year later, they were having Aiden's first birthday party. A knock on the door sent Katie and Dusty racing for the door. Even though he lunged over the couch, she was closer and beat him there. She eagerly signed for the package and ripped the envelope.

"It's *my* proof, Katie."

"I don't care! You never let me read the epilog!" She took off up the stairs and locked herself in the bathroom.

At the insistence of Jody's mother, a wedding ceremony was held on Teria five days after Aiden Senior's plane was destroyed. Although he could have left with any member of the regiment, he wanted to spend a few days with his son and grandson.

With Jody's help, Vick was trying to be tolerant of his presence. He wasn't actually a bad guy and was starting to soften Vick up. What he'd lacked as a father, he'd more than made up for being a grandfather.

Since Jody's father had promised a two-week leave, each crew member wanted to see it through to the end. The ship was being outfitted with new numbers and Captain Victor Skinnard was given a death certificate.

"I'd love for you to move back to earth, son. Your family needs a place to call home."

He wrapped an arm around Jody. "My ship is our home. We're not the 'settling in one place' sort of people. I'll steer us clear of imploding nebulas from now on, but I'm afraid we're not going to be neighbors."

"That's too bad, but I can't say that I'm surprised."

Lenore came up from behind them, carrying Aiden. "He'd miss me too much if he moved away, wouldn't you, Aiden?"

"You're silly, Lenore. You know you just like my help with the babies."

"This is true. Come on, they still have some wedding cake left."

After they were out of earshot, Aiden Skinnard asked, "What about that Forengi doctor? Is she going to pursue publishing her findings?"

Vick shook his head. "He blew up in an explosion. What's there to report?"

Aiden Senior smiled. "That's a good woman. What about the new baby?"

Jody smiled and held her hand on her stomach. "I'm not the only Terian who has not wished to live the ways of my people. There will be nothing special about her."

"Him," Vick said as his hand covered hers. "He's half mine, he'll be special."

She laughed and gave him a playful swat. "Oh, I have wedding gift for you."

"You didn't need to do that."

She pulled out a tiny chip and dropped it into his hand. "I was finally able to retrieve the message from Deidre. I want you and Aiden to watch it together."

"Did you watch it?"

"It's not for me, it's for you." She hooked her arm with his father's. "We'll be having a dance, come find me when you're done."

Vick gathered Aiden and found a peaceful spot of the vast yard, under a tree, to view the hologram. He placed the chip in Aiden's Hawkeye, Deidre immediately came up.

"I was beginning to forget what Mommy looked like."

"She'll always be in your heart, son. You may think it's sad, but it's sort of nature's way of helping us to move on. You'll never truly forget her."

Aden called up the keypad and pressed play.

It was eerie the way the hologram made eye contact. Once again, Vick thought she was really there. That she'd somehow time traveled to this very moment.

"Hello, my men. If you're watching this now, I don't need to recap anything about Aiden, his device, or the men after him. I chose wisely, Victor Skinnard, when I chose you to be his father."

Vick couldn't help it. "Chose me?"

As if she could hear him she said, "Yes, I chose you. I knew my son would be special and for that I needed an amazing father. You based your life on conquering places that no one has ever been to before, why should your child be any different?" She paused for a moment with a soft laugh, although a tear ran down her cheek. "I knew he needed to be part human. Most men I'd met would certainly have abused his powers for their own gain. I knew you wouldn't. I knew you'd die to protect him. I wish I could be with you both to watch him grow into an amazing young man, but I knew that was never meant to be. I've seen the future, Vick, and yours is remarkable. Both of yours." Her focus shifted, Aiden moved to stand so he could meet her eyes.

"Take care of your dad, Aiden. He's a handful. If he's lucky enough to win the affection of another woman, you can trust he's made a wonderful decision. I know you loved me and always will, but allow your heart to love her, too. I know she's going to love you. Who couldn't?" Another tear rolled down her cheek. "I hope you get to see this. For your safety, it won't play again. I love you both, but I have to go."

The hologram disappeared.

Aiden hugged Vick. "I sure hope there's a heaven."

"I do, too, buddy. I do, too."

About the Author

June, who prefers to go by Bug, was born in Philadelphia but moved to Maui, Hawaii, when she was four. She met her "Prince Charming" on Kauai and is currently living "Happily Ever After" in Minnesota.

Her son and daughter are her greatest accomplishments. She takes pride in embarrassing them every chance she gets.

Visit www.junekramin.com for more releases.

Time Travel Series:
Dustin Time
Dustin's Turn
Dustin's Novel

Romantic Suspense/Thriller:
Double Mocha, Heavy on Your Phone Number
Hunter's Find
Amanda's Return
I Got Your Back, Hailey
I've Also Got Your Front, Hailey
More Hailey Coming Soon!

Romance:
Come and Talk to Me
Money Didn't Buy Her Love
Devon's Change of Heart (Money Didn't Buy Her Love II)
I'll Try to Behave Myself

Contemporary Fiction
The Green Flash at Sunset
Baby, Just Say Yes

More to come!

Visit www.beforehappilyeverafter.com for her middle grade fantasy series written under the pseudonym of Ann T. Bugg.

Made in the USA
Middletown, DE
23 January 2017